A Darker World

A Novel

By

Lance Litherland

Grosvenor House
Publishing Limited

All rights reserved
Copyright © Lance Litherland, 2020

The right of Lance Litherland to be identified as the author of this
work has been asserted in accordance with Section 78
of the Copyright, Designs and Patents Act 1988

The book cover is copyright to Lance Litherland

This book is published by
Grosvenor House Publishing Ltd
Link House
140 The Broadway, Tolworth, Surrey, KT6 7HT.
www.grosvenorhousepublishing.co.uk

This book is sold subject to the conditions that it shall not, by way of
trade or otherwise, be lent, resold, hired out or otherwise circulated
without the author's or publisher's prior consent in any form of binding or
cover other than that in which it is published and
without a similar condition including this condition being imposed
on the subsequent purchaser.

This book is a work of fiction. Any resemblance to
people or events, past or present, is purely coincidental.

A CIP record for this book
is available from the British Library

ISBN 978-1-83975-013-7

For my wife Sharon
My family, Luke, Ryan and Sam
In memory of my parents
Pam & Maurice

Chapter 1

Friday, September 27th

The late September sun had all but vanished now. For a few minutes, the distant sky showcased an illustrious palate of multi-coloured ambers, reds, and yellows before finally sinking into the horizon.

Gill Carter glanced across at her sister Megan, slumped peacefully in the passenger seat, her hand cradling one side of her pale face, the other hidden by the steep collar and her long, straight, mousy hair.

Only the occasional light from passing cars illuminated her bright red coat and white t-shirt.

Megan was oblivious to the monotonous drone of the car's engine and the faint but persistent chatter of late-night radio. The usual late-night phone-ins of desperate individuals hellbent on airing their personal issues to Travis, the radio host. This was the ugly end of late-night radio.

Reaching forward, Gill edged the volume to a more audible level, but not enough to disturb Megan who had hardly stirred for the last hour. It had been an early start, and this was a long trip.

They shared the driving and although Gill had completed her share and despite the small of her back signalling that it was ready for time out, she did not feel compelled to wake her sister. Not just yet anyway. Besides, she was now engrossed in this charade of a radio phone-in, and half-listened in disbelief to the condescending tone of the DJ while draining the last trickles of spring water into her mouth.

"Hi, you're through to Travis" came the voice over the radio. *"What's your name and how can I solve your problem this evening?"* Gill cringed, wondering if listeners really did buy into this self-absorbed crap, hosted by a man whose ego was clearly massaged by people's misery, exploiting their failings all in the name of entertainment.

She threw another casual glance to her sister, secretly hoping she would surface soon and relieve her from the discomfort.

The firm leather seats were past supporting her and did nothing more than tease her aching back, along with her swollen ankles, a price she paid for driving in fashionable shoes.

Restless and clammy, she slid the window down a couple of inches and relished the touch of evening air bathing her face. She wiped her brow, adjusted her cream, cotton top and messed once again with the seat adjustment, hoping to alleviate some discomfort.

By now the bleak road had slipped away into darkness. Any hint of scarlet sky was now awash with metal grey and the end of another day swallowed up. Traffic thinned, the landscape changed, and the monotony of the long trip was boring down.

Between listening to trash FM and staring endlessly at the hollow landscape, Gill kept an eye on her sister, hoping the small movements would translate to full consciousness and give her the break she so desperately needed. Until then, Travis would amuse.

She was more intrigued than entertained by this trash. It wasn't the late-night boredom or the arduous journey that compelled her to focus her mind on this nonsense, no. She chose to listen to this because subconsciously she was afraid of her dark thoughts surfacing.

Gill and Megan's life has always been overshadowed by grief. Sitting, waiting, conspiring in the shadows to pounce at any time. Their Mother, June, committed suicide back in the bleak winter of Ninety-Eight when they were just fifteen years old. Megan, who was the sensitive one, wore her emotions like a brightly coloured jumper for all to see, she found it hardest to accept. Gill was the one who was there for her. Of sterner stuff, she pulled her sister through, a travesty that bonded them, and she refused to be weighed down by that fateful day.

By now her face had lost its fresh look, her artful makeup now failed to disguise a picture of tiredness and she tried hard to focus on the road ahead. The mountainous landscape pillared either side of the road, peering down like angry gods. For every mile she continued, she could sense the abandonment of security with which familiar surroundings brought. The further north she drove the more her head filled with thoughts of their father, which they had not seen for twenty years, and tried hard to resist past thoughts gate-crashing her mind.

Seeing him for the first time again after all these years was going to be difficult, even awkward. Her head was in turmoil with various expectations, she knew she had to be strong though, not only for herself but mainly for her sister.

Memories of long summer days spent on the family farm now filled her with a warm feeling of times lost. The smell of the freshly cut fields, their mum's home-cooked roasts and the overwhelming sense of freedom that only came with living in the country. But these were only tarnished by that dark day when their mother, who on a late January evening rose from her living room chair and with no obvious reason, walked outside, across the yard and entered one of the out-buildings and hung herself. No note, no reason, no explanation.

Megan found it hardest to cope with because she never really came to terms with the horror of what their mother did. So, her life was burdened with a journey of self-torture and abandonment. They somehow hoped that their father, Eric, would be able to provide the answers they both craved, but he eventually closed down soon after, unable to cope, his spirit fragmented by loss, and so he moved to the far reaches of Scotland and to the peaceful isolation it brought.

They then went to live with their Aunt, less than a month later. Megan never really understood why her sister navigated through her life without the emotional scars that she suffered, or even how she just accepted it. To Gill it was simple. Sometimes people do things in life for no apparent reason, but that was just a mask, she could accept that, it was better than the alternative, searching for answers that would never come.

Gill's attention hinged back to the radio where Travis was still demoralising poor innocent callers with his self-absorbed opinions on how they should salvage their relationships.

She was now getting bored of listening to him, so again she reached forward, glancing between the road and the radio she found a late-night station more akin to her mood. By now the road was as bleak as the night sky, devout of any shape or feature. Only the odd beam of light from passing cars broke the blackness in the distance. This was not a road well-travelled.

Out of the corner of her eye, Gill noticed Megan raise her arms above her head, spilling a yawn which sounded like it came from the bowels of hell itself. She could almost hear her bones creaking and cracking as she stretched. Megan gazed around in a moment of disorientation, then looked across at her sister.

"How long have I been asleep?" Guessing it was a while seeing the darkness outside.

"Oh, a while honey." She smiled.

"Why didn't you wake me?" she asked, her voice distorted by another sudden yawn.

"It's fine," she said ignoring her aching back. "Besides, you looked like you needed the sleep."

Gill caught sight of a half-illuminated road sign which seemed to sprout from nowhere. *The pines cafe 5 miles*.

"Don't know about you but I could use a coffee." She grinned.

"Yea that sounds good," Megan replied rooting through her bag for her phone. "I will call dad when we stop, tell him how far away we are."

She checked her phone, its phosphorous glow illuminating her face like a ghostly image and frowned. "No messages, that's strange," she said.

"You know what dad's like," said Gill. "He takes arrangements on face value." Her eyes left the road momentarily and fixed on Megan's disappointed face. "He knows we would call if there's a problem."

"What?" she snapped. "Oh come on, you say it like we saw dad yesterday, how do you know what he's like?" Pulling her hair away from her mouth and tucking the loose strands behind her ear, her hands animating her displeasure. "We haven't seen him for twenty years; I would have thought he would text to ask how far away we are."

"Hold on a sec," said Gill calmly. "He knows we're coming, please leave it at that."

Their father had contacted their aunt out of the blue, requesting contact from his daughters, he gave no reason, only that they visit soon.

Megan led an erratic lifestyle; she was restless and impetuous. She never had structure or self-belief like Gill. She was continually haunted by the past, rejecting close relationships. Her heart would not tolerate another loss of attachment. She loved her sister, she was always there for her, she would not abandon her, it was ok for her to feel *that* love, but no more.

Gill was not going to be coerced into an argument now, besides she was the one who remained level-headed.

She cast a smile across to Megan. "Look, I'm sorry, you're right, I don't know Dad anymore," she said, calmly reaching across and placing her hand on top of Megan's momentarily.

"It's ok, I'm sorry too," said Megan, staring out of the passenger window into the darkness beyond.

"It was ok to have hope you know," Said Gill softly.

"You mean foolish."

"I mean, you remembered how he was, even all those years ago, I guess it was me that forgot."

"Maybe you chose to forget."

Gill didn't answer.

"Who am I kidding," she added scrolling through the messages one more time.

"Look honey I think we're missing the point here. The whole idea of this trip is to find out why dad wants contact again after all these years, we have to give him a chance, we owe that much."

Gill watched Megan staring out window, lost in thought. She let the silence linger before she continued. "Dad had it hard as well when mum—" She paused not wanting to say the word. "When mum left us."

Megan turned; her large brown eyes narrowed. "When mum left?" she scoured. "Mum didn't leave, you make it sound like she packed her bags and walked out."

"Don't be so insensitive, you know what I meant. I don't need reminding for god sake." A small tear welled in Gill's eyes. "I found her remember, me not you."

The awful memory of that day was drawn upon again. Gill pushed back that dark memory and swallowed deeply, she removed a tissue from under her sleeve and dabbed at her eyes, careful to avoid smudging her makeup. Megan didn't say anything now, she knew she had crossed the line. She slumped back into the leather seat and threw her phone into her open, black bag.

By now there was a hint of late summer rain in the sky and Gill flicked the window back up.

"That doesn't look good," she said changing the subject.

Megan remained silent, she continued to stare out of the window, rolling small lengths of auburn hair around her fingers.

In the distance dwarfed by rolling hills, the dim glow of a roadside cafe loomed, bringing a welcome relief.

"I can almost smell the coffee from here," said Gill.

She pulled a dried leather cloth from the door pocket and created a porthole size clearing through the condensation as the summer rain had started to fall, dampening the air.

Megan spotted a dimly lit sign on the right. "One mile," she said.

"Damn this demister," muttered Gill.

As they neared, Megan became aware of a figure at the side of the road in the distance, caught in the rain-filled headlights which glistened like silver pearls in its beams.

Megan edged closer to the windscreen, pulling on her seatbelt, her eyes widened.

The figure drew nearer. A female form, sprinting through the biting rain.

"Where the hell is she running to?" asked Megan.

Gill focused through the wipers; each swipe giving a momentary frame of clear vision.

"I'm going to slow down, she might need some help," said Gill, her voice concerning in its tone.

She lifted off, slowing the car to a sensible pace, enough to decide if she should help.

"So why's she running away from the café, it's the only place of safety for miles, did we pass a stranded car?"

Gill frowned. "No, we didn't actually."

"Then why run out onto the road in this weather."

"I'll slow up, just to see, but I'm not stopping, not on this deserted road."

Megan tried hard to find reason in the woman's actions, to choose to run away from the only source of civilisation, shelter, and security for miles. It didn't make sense to her.

The car slowed, an air of scepticism crept in, and Megan shifted nervously in her seat.

As Gill passed, barely above a crawl, Megan became bewildered by the actions of the woman, her face carved out a curious gaze, her chocolate eyes followed her like a camera tracking a fast-moving animal through the bush, resting on her terrorised face, now only a couple of feet from the passenger window, half tears half-blood, smeared across her cheeks with a large red stain across her coat like someone had flicked a paintbrush next to her. A desperate look of fear exaggerated by her staring panic as the woman stared back through their window.

Megan shrieked, engulfed by the sudden and unexpected sight.

Shocked by her sudden shrill, Gill squeezed hard on the steering wheel and accelerated away, the tyres battling for grip on the slippery surface.

For a moment Megan remained quiet, but her breathing wasn't.

"What just happened?" asked Gill, her eyes switching nervously from the road to the rear-view mirror, hoping to catch a glimpse of the woman, but only darkness stared back.

"She looked like she'd been in an accident, we need to go back," said Megan quickly.

"You startled me," sighed Gill. "She's obviously in trouble," she replied, her eyes fixed on the rear-view mirror.

"Ok, we'll pull over, get a coffee and find out if anyone there knows anything," replied Megan.

Gill didn't like to leave anyone in need of help, although she had come to realise that there is a fine line between helping and getting involved with trouble, she didn't like this.

"Well, ok, I could certainly use the break, and a coffee," said Gill, appeasing her sister.

"Ok, but I still don't understand if she was in trouble why she didn't go to the café."

Megan turned around, staring out of the back window, she knew she wouldn't be able to see her, but it somehow made her feel she cared enough to try.

"Maybe she came from the café," suggested Gill.

She turned into the café, the loose shingled entrance was boarded by a high, thick-set hedge on one side and a five-foot plastic statue of a jolly-looking chef with the words *welcome* and a big smile on the other. The large open gravel car park was plagued by large potholes, beyond, a border of fir trees and wasteland. This was a solitary place.

The car park was not a busy one, a large arctic lorry, a black 4x4 and an old red saloon car with a roof box and trailer were the only vehicles present.

Gill let out a large sigh, happy for the break but plagued by the thoughts of the woman.

She grabbed her cream, woollen jacket and gazed in the mirror, making a half-hearted attempt to play with her short, dyed blonde hair and apply more burnt orange lipstick which matched her coloured beads and pencil skirt.

Exiting swiftly, Megan barely had time to put on her coat before reaching the double glass doors, lit by a single hanging light and surrounded by marauding moths and flying insects.

Chapter 2

The Pines cafe was typical of most roadside café's, unappealing and lacking in finesse. Set down off the road it was not plagued by a lot of custom, just the brigade of hungry truckers and occasional passer-byes or lost and tired travellers. The single-story building with a high-pitched roof sat back from the road. The dark stained wood cladding had not aged well over the years. The three large Georgian style windows, which looked out onto the car park, were framed with bamboo blinds. A square, rusty metal-framed sign hung low from the front and the tired lettering barely legible. Inside, the array of brightly coloured menu boards and flashing fruit machine lights drew the attention from the poor exterior. Red leatherette seats in cosy wooden booths adorned the inside, contrasted by the black and white chessboard floor. Aluminium counters lay bare to the absence of care and pride and the dried and withered plants were a long-forgotten attempt to personalise the inside. But the constant smell of boiled coffee and fried food was an all familiar scent. Despite the absence of lustre, it was always a welcome sight.

They entered the café, Megan smiled and took a deep breath through her nose "Mmm, smells good."

She folded her red corded coat over her arm and pointed to a cosy booth by the window. "This will do," she said parking herself down. Gill followed rubbing the small of her back on the way, hoping the pain would seamlessly disappear.

Gills lifestyle was very much different from her sisters, she was focused and ambitious. She paid her bills and allowed herself a good lifestyle. This was not a place she would normally frequent, but knowing that choice was not a luxury up here in the middle of nowhere, it would suffice. Plus, she needed the break now and the long journey had made the coffee that much more desirable.

Megan glanced casually around the room. It was quiet. In the corner opposite sat a family with their young son enjoying the house milkshake with all the trimmings. She looked at the boy sucking the last drop of shake through the candy-twisted straw, his cheeks drawn with the all familiar sound of an empty cup. On the table in the corner sat a large, burly man with a checked shirt and a red baseball cap and the word *Rookie* sewn on the front, stooped across the table, slurping coffee and flicking through the local paper. But she was more drawn to the two middle-aged men in the booth down from them, dressed in neatly tailored suits, polished shoes and crisp white shirts, it was clear they were businessmen, but somehow, they seemed out of place. Their hardened faces patterned with various size scars and chunky gold jewellery appeared rather odd in contrast to their attire. With his phone in one hand and manipulating triangular shapes with a napkin in the other, the larger man seemed somehow anxious.

Megan's brief people-watching moment was interrupted by a waitress who seemed to come from nowhere and loomed over their table. She was mid-fifties, large but not to excess, dyed, red hair tied back, white stained piny with the name *Mary* pinned to the right. Her bright red lips and jovial manner turned a smile as she pulled a note pad and pen from her top pocket.

"Hi what can I get you two?" she asked in a broad Scottish accent, readying the pen on her pad.

"Oh, just two coffees please," said Gill pulling her purse from her bag. Mary went through the usual spiel of house specials and offers but they both graciously declined, having stopped earlier for food.

Gill pulled down on the thin wooden blinds and gazed out towards the car park, she couldn't help thinking about the woman on the road.

"I feel bad for that woman back there, we might have been able to help her," said Gill turning away from the window.

She looked down at the table and played nervously with the sugar pot, her mind wandering momentarily.

"I just felt scared and guess, just shocked when I saw her face. Did it not seem odd to you she was running away from here?"

"We don't know that for sure," replied Gill looking at her phone briefly. "It's later than I thought," she replied, not really wanting to think too much about it.

"I'll ask that waitress if she was here," said Megan, looking across to the counter.

Megan was thoughtful, she had a good heart. This was supposed to be a trip to see their father, but Megan started to feel they might end up being consumed by this mystery woman. They had lost enough time as it was. That was her fault though, as she was not even ready when her sister came to pick her up earlier in the morning.

Megan differed from her sister; she was not the methodical organised person her sister was. She stumbled through her life from one failure to another. She knew deep inside she was running away from the loss of their mother. She always felt a pinch of guilt that Gill was the one who always pulled her through, especially when she quit her job as a photographer's assistant after three months. Megan would casually say her life was like a speeding train, occasionally it would de-rail and Gill would always be there to put her back on track. She had her own flat, it was basic, it represented her life. Unorganised with little impression of a settled mind. Megan always joked it was minimalistic, but it was hers. Gill only ever described her flat as cosmopolitan, polite for messy. When Gill did come over for the odd occasion it was usually because her beautician Harvey De Mare was on that side of town. Harvey was, for want of a better word, delicate, and of course gay. He was always sickly sweet to Gill and complimentary. She liked that.

The cafe had that distinct late-night atmosphere of lowered voices and polite clattering of china, only the routine jingle of the fruit machine refused to succumb to the silence.

Mary returned with their coffees, placed them down carefully and left with a courtesy smile. As she turned to walk away, Megan gave in to her curiosity.

"Excuse me," she hollered.

Mary turned back.

She paused for a moment, still playing with the sugar pot, unsure exactly what she was going to ask.

"Did you happen to notice a woman in here earlier, about late thirties?" She looked at Gill briefly for confirmation. "She was wearing a cream or white coat and black trousers I think."

Before the waitress responded, Megan caught sight of the two businessmen out the corner of her eye. The larger one faced her, made eye contact, then returned his attention to the other and said something, but not English, maybe Polish, she thought, but couldn't be sure. She watched him curiously turning his phone around in his hand. He was unshaven with short-cropped black hair and rugged features; his tightly fitted suit contoured his muscular torso to the point of being comical. But she somehow knew there was nothing comical about his demeanour. She caught sight of his single diamond stud and an unusual tattoo of a fish behind his left ear. She was unable to observe the second man, of slight build, he was obscured by the booth's framework.

Megan had an eye for detail, she would always say this was her one true gift, that's why she left her job with the photographer. He never saw the talent she had despite her failed attempts to intervene with her opinion on some shoots. So, she left. She was a clever woman, not in the way her sister was, she didn't have the patience or intellectual prowess needed to manage corporate hospitality, she had social intelligence, she could enter a room full of people and know what was going on, she was always one step ahead when it came to figuring people out. She could instantly dissect, connect and understand what people were feeling within a few minutes. She just knew people.

Mary leaned down to their table, Gill took a sip of her coffee before giving the waitress her full attention, she had waited a while for this coffee.

"Yes, there was a woman in here with that description" She glanced around the room before returning her attention.

"She was in here about half-hour ago, she was very, how would I say, edgy. Why, are you looking for someone?" she asked.

"Kind of, was she with anyone else?"

"To start with no. She ordered a coffee and I noticed she was very nervous about something, she clearly had something on her mind because I remember asking her three times if she wanted cream or milk, poor child. when I returned to her table with a coffee there was a man sat with her, I'm sure he wasn't there when she came in."

"Her husband?" interrupted Gill.

"I don't think so. She looked uncomfortable with him, you know when you look at couples and you think, well those two don't look like a match, well that's what I thought."

"What did he look like, what was he wearing?" asked Megan.

Mary stood for a second, thinking.

"He was already sat down when I brought her coffee, but he had a dark maybe black jacket on." Mary wiped her hands on her pinny, more habit than necessity. "She did leave with him, but something was odd."

"What do you mean odd?"

"Well, it seemed like." Mary paused for thought. "Like she didn't really want to leave with him."

Mary's attention was needed elsewhere, there weren't many people in there but the family in the corner had just grabbed her attention.

"Sorry got to go," she said, turning away from their table.

"That sounds suspicious don't you think?" asked Gill.

"I don't like the sound of it, makes me feel a little uncomfortable if I'm honest." She kept the volume of her voice low, still aware of the two suits taking more than a glancing interest in her conversation with the waitress. She had a bad feeling.

"Where is her car then?" asked Megan quietly, already matching the two cars and lorry to the people in the cafe.

"Where's the bloke she left with then?" She sugared her coffee and stirred.

"Need to go back and find her, she's in trouble and we just left her there at the side of the road like an injured animal," she exclaimed, tapping the table nervously with her fingers.

"I don't know," replied Gill, sitting back in her seat. "One minute you want to drive off and the next you want to go back, have you forgotten why we're on this trip? It's late and I'm tired, we had our chance to stop." She sank the rest of her coffee and stood.

"I didn't ask you to drive off."

"I'm going to the bathroom," replied Gill.

Megan grabbed her hand as she stood.

"Tell me you're not just a little bit curious about all this."

Gill knew her sister was right, but she didn't want to get involved anymore. She grabbed her bag, left the table and made her way to the toilet, across the cafe through the double doors and down a narrow corridor on the right.

As she entered the washroom, her breath was stolen in a single moment. For a split second, her brain refused to register what she was seeing. On the floor in front of her was the body of a man, lying on his front, black leather jacket and dark jeans. The white tiles highlighting the deep red pool of blood that surrounded him. She hid her face in her hands. Every part of her body said scream. But she didn't. Her racing heart fired adrenalin and her mouth turned dry. She quickly turned to the three cubicles, all empty, she couldn't think, her mind rallied for a rational thought that never came. It was then she made the connection between the woman covered in blood and the corpse in front of her. She left the washroom quickly, her trembling legs struggling to carry her. She burst through the doors and out into the dark of night, bracing herself against the wall to gather her thoughts. She took several deep breaths before pulling her phone from her bag to call the police, her trembling fingers, stuttering over the keys.

Numb with shock, she returned quickly to the cafe.

Megan noticed her sister approaching, her pace was unusually brisk and there was no hiding the fact that something was dreadfully wrong. Instinctively she started to shift across the seat ready to stand. Grabbing her bag and coat she had a feeling they would be leaving quickly by the look on her sister's face. Gill didn't get a chance to say anything before Megan spoke.

"Gill what's wrong, why you all wet, you ok?" as she reached out to hold her arm, she felt the trembling.

"We need to go, I need to get out of here, please Megan," she begged.

"Hold on your not making any sense what's happened?" asked Megan rising from her seat.

Megan again, caught sight of the two guys in the suits suddenly taking more interest in them than she felt comfortable with. The cafe area was not overly large and Gills entrance was not easy to ignore.

Her breathing was clearly not in sync with her words as she struggled to articulate her ordeal.

Megan's animated expression was noticed by the two men in dark suits, made more obvious now they were standing.

A sudden and clear conversation was exchanged and its harsh tongue now clearly in Russian.

Megan sensed a connection. The woman running from here, the man lying in the toilets and the anxious manner of the men opposite gave her a very sickly feeling.

"Let's leave, now," said Megan, handing Gill her coat.

"But the police, I called them, we need to wait," said Gill, still shaking.

"I need to let the waitress know there's a body in the toilet and the police are on route, but then we're going, ok?"

Gill turned to Megan with a sorrowed expression. "That woman we passed."

"Yes, I know, we'll talk about it later."

Gill nodded, her eyes welling, she sat back down, staring vacantly into hexagon-shaped sugar pot.

Megan dashed to the counter, the man in the rookie cap attempted to make conversation but she ignored him.

She Peered back, watching the deflated figure of her sister, then to the two men, buttoning up their jackets and preparing to leave, mindful of the attention she was receiving from them now.

The fragrant smell of coffee and cooked food quickly turned to the ugly taste of fear and dread.

Megan briefed Mary on the incident, she too, clearly shocked and exchanged a brief conversation with her.

She returned to Gill quickly, snaking around the empty tables, aware of the menacing looks she was still receiving.

"Ok let's go, the police will have to talk to Mary," stated Megan with urgency.

"Mary just told me the guy who sat next to that woman came in with the two men in the suits," said Megan pacing toward the entrance with her sister.

"We should wait in the car?" said Gill tearily.

"We're not waiting, trust me."

Megan took her sister's hand and marched toward the doors.

As she turned for one last time, she saw them both rise, their pace matching theirs, his fierce gaze fixed on hers, sparking her to run.

They both exited the double doors, Gill glanced down the narrow white corridor toward the toilets as they headed out. Mary and another member of staff were outside the toilet and had placed a tall yellow cone outside and hung a sign saying '*closed*'. She noticed the spotty-faced young lad with Mary. He could not resist opening the door just a little to quench his morbid curiosity. Most people never see a dead body in their life, but she had now found two.

They dashed through the cold rain toward the car.

Megan looked back.

The two suited men were in the corridor, one heading toward the toilet, pushing the young lad to one side.

"Keys, your keys, quickly, we need to go *now*," she said, watching Gill search frantically through her bag.

Gill retrieved the keys and pressed the fob. The central locking popping with a flash of hazard lights.

Gill fumbled the key into the ignition and the BMW burst into life, the headlights spotlighting both men approaching at pace, the larger man drawing a gun from inside his jacket.

"Jesus Christ Gill drive!" shouted Megan, watching in horror as the man aimed toward them. Gill slammed the car into gear, spitting stones everywhere. As she swung around clipping the large plastic statue of the chef and headed for the road, they both screamed in unison as a loud bang rang off and the rear screen exploded behind them.

Chapter 3

Friday 27th 9:03 am

The morning sun was warm by now, enough to slowly burn the early dew from the tended lawns and warm the air.

Jane pulled her car into a space and exited swiftly. She was late this morning; she was late a lot of mornings. Juggling two kids for school didn't help. Her husband was away with work, so she was left to do domestic battle alone.

She locked the car and hurried across the car park and up the steps to the hospital entrance, simultaneously pinning her identity badge on as she entered.

"Morning Grace," she said as she hurried past reception, too quickly to wait for a courtesy reply. She entered the lift and summoned the fourth floor, *'Trauma ward'*.

Before the doors had closed, a large pair of hands grasping a tatty blue folder protruded through and they opened again.

"Ah, morning Jane," said the Doctor with a large grin.

"Morning Doctor Johansen," she replied.

Although they were close colleagues and good friends, she still maintained a level of respect to call him doctor rather than Sven. He was a tall man with slick grey hair and a long chin, his thick, black-framed glasses lay to the end of his nose and his newly starched white coat accentuated his stature as he peered over the top of them.

Blackwater was not a huge town, in comparison to city standards. There was one road in and one road out, not counting the two tiny roads that wound their way out towards the distant mountains.

The six-story hospital was not a particularly modern building, the Victorian-style brickwork and art-deco styling gave hint to the age of the building but inside it was as modern as any hospital with the latest in cutting edge technology and medical machinery. Dr Johansen was a humble doctor whose reputation in Sweden had afforded him the luxury of working almost anywhere, but a modest man he chose Blackwater of all places. He enjoyed the desolate silence of the wilderness and the appeal of the snow-peaked mountains in the winter. Only five miles separated Blackwater from the frontiers of tranquil harmony where nature was king, and humans had no place to interfere.

Along with nurse Stevens, Dr Johansen had a team of specialist dedicated to treating head and brain injuries at the hospital.

"How's Dale these days? still grinding the wheel of fortune in the world of architecture?" Smiled the doctor, his bushy eyebrows rising to meet his fringe. Jane returned a smile and responded to the small talk that was customary in these circumstances.

"Oh, he's working hard on a new project now, he's away a lot at the moment."

A sudden jolt announced their arrival.

"Have a good day Jane," said the doctor allowing her to exit first.

The fourth floor was not a large ward, it ran the length of the hospital with one intersection halfway down, this led to the lifts and stairwell. The theatre was at one end with eight recovery rooms on either side. At the other end were twelve beds altogether in separate rooms and a nurse's station with a small waiting area next door.

Jane signed herself in at the nurse's station and checked her work rota for the day, her eyes following the various scribblings on the whiteboard. She tried hard to look enthusiastic, but truth be known she was tired of this place, having been here for the last five years she longed to be part of a bigger team in a large hospital, a move to the city. Her husband had roots here and an established, successful business which she supported but secretly her heart was not here.

Martha the ward sister, sensed her look of empty enthusiasm and suggested she grab a coffee before she starts. She was thoughtful like that.

"Thanks, I will," she replied as she turned to the coffee machine in the corner. She removed some coins from her purse and took a moment to reminisce over the pictures of her two children, Molly and Jacob who were now seven and nine. She smiled to herself and accepted how lucky she was. Her job was fraught with the day to day tragedies and lives destroyed by the hand of fate that decided when and where it would strike. Tearing families to pieces, stripping away hope and teasing the human spirit for the unlucky few. Cursed with sometimes life-changing accidents many are left with the remains of a once enriched life. She liked her job, she was propelled by the need to help others and to make a difference, even just a small one.

For a moment Jane felt rich, rich with love and in health. She dropped in the coins and took her coffee.

As she took her first sip she looked to Martha across the station, a towering mass of multicoloured files adorned the top, with multiple wire baskets of new and discarded case notes. Her station was the centre point of activity, an information centre permanently circled by doctors and nurses.

Martha was very good at her job, a multitasking and formidable person, she could navigate, consume and consistently manage patient and staff information from memory. Everyone knew that without Martha the king of chaos would ensue.

Amongst the orchestra of sounds, Jane failed to notice Martha's phone ring. She walked past her station with coffee in hand, lifting her cup to Martha and miming a thank you in her direction. Martha suddenly raised her hand to Jane, signalling her to halt. She stood biting at one of her nails with a quizzed look on her face, watching as Martha replaced the handset.

"There's a gentleman downstairs who wishes to speak to you about something," said Martha, her face as puzzled as hers.

"Did he give a name?" she asked.

"No," replied Martha, lowering her purple rimmed glasses to the end of her nose. "It sounded important and asked for you," she replied pulling one of the files from the pile. "Tom Granger," she said thrusting the file into her hand. "He's your patient when you return."

Jane sensed a sternness in Martha's voice. Maybe because she was late and had already been called away before she had even attended her first duties.

She took the file from Martha and gave her an apologetic nod. She put down her coffee, made her way to the lift and tried to imagine who could be asking for her. Entering the lift, she glanced herself in the mirrored walls and groomed her long, blonde hair which ran straight down without a hint of a curve, re-tying the band and pulling on the hem of her skirt to straighten out her uniform before pressing 'G' for ground. She then repositioned her badge which she had pinned in the morning rush.

She exited the lift and into the open reception, which was almost cathedral-like, the morning sun had spilt in like an avenging tide, washing the walls and tabletops with a fury of light. Elongated shadows stretched across the floor, touching each other in their wake and the air was warm and comforting.

She looked around the foyer scanning the few people in reception, deciding if she recognised any of them. A large man, well dressed in a black suit and red shirt approached her, taking her almost by surprise.

"Is there anywhere we can talk in private?" came a stern voice. There was no handshake or greeting.

"Yes, follow me," she said hesitantly.

She crossed the foyer, behind the reception desk and across to a light-coloured door marked *family room*. She knew this as the darkroom. Not because it had little light but because this was where families and relatives were taken to, very often to receive bad news about a loved one.

She headed towards the room, enjoying the brief warmth the sun provided in her crossing. She imagined various reasons why this official-looking gentleman wanted to speak with her. Maybe she thought, it was someone from the school, maybe Molly or Jacob have had an accident, maybe they are ill. Her rational mind quickly dismissed that; besides, the school would just phone her at work, not ask her to meet someone downstairs.

She opened the door, sensing the man behind her. The room was no bigger than a small bedroom, a blue sofa at one end and two high backed armchairs at the other. On the wall in the middle was a tray with various leaflets about death, counselling and helplines.

"Please have a seat," she said closing the door behind them and offering a hand toward one of the chairs.

The man declined with a simple shake of his head.

She remained standing. His presence made her nervous.

"Let me explain what is going to happen," he started. "Two of my comrades are on their way with a teenage boy who has sustained a head injury, you will inform only me about his condition and progress, there will be no exchange of information with the police or anyone else. Only treatment. This is very imperative."

The man was well-spoken with a Russian accent. He was well-tailored and spotlessly groomed; his crystal blue eyes did not belie his authoritarian presence. Her gaze cast casually over the man's smooth skin and lay focused on a small tattoo behind his left ear. A tattoo of a small goat. His manner was stern and clear. His hands lay behind his back and his six-foot-plus stature towered over her mere frame. She felt slightly intimidated, even a little scared and apprehensive. Her head was spinning with a thousand questions, she shuffled about nervously but decided his manner was not acceptable. Politely but assertively she responded.

"I'm not sure if you know how this works but I will explain Mr?" She tilted her head slightly and paused for his response.

"Just call me Max, that is all you need to know," he replied in a deep and firm voice.

"Ok Max, first we will require the patients' full name, address and date of birth. We will need to speak with the parents and of course, if you can give us a picture of what happened, that might help the doctors determine what course of action is required.

She unfolded her arms and placed them in front of her, sensing she no longer needed to be assertive. Max maintained eye contact and his posture unchanged. Jane waited again for his response.

"What would be the usual procedure in this case? The boy has sustained a gunshot wound to the head; he is breathing but unconscious."

Jane was slightly shocked at his statement, giving way to more questions of her own. *Why was no ambulance called? Why no information? Why ask for me?* She thought this very cloak and dagger but remained professional and responded accordingly, hoping this was going somewhere.

"Ok, first off the police are notified automatically when a gunshot is involved, the boy will be examined and given a CT scan to determine if there are signs of haemorrhaging or hematoma, which is a possible blood clot, a craniotomy could be required but only if the surgeon deems this viable, depending on the depth and location of the bullet, he will then—"

Jane was interrupted before she had finished with another confusing question.

"Would the boys head be shaved prior to surgery?"

Jane frowned and folded her arms again, recoiling backwards slightly by the strange question. *Why was he saying the boy? Why not his name?* she thought. She had become aware that an injury involving a gunshot is always suspicious and invariably brings with it unsavoury people. She glanced at the clock on the wall, she had been in the room now for five minutes and not really understood why he had asked for her when a doctor would have been able to clarify all this in more detail.

The warm sun peered in through the opaque glass of the door, the pace of the hospital had picked up and the foyer amass with busy people, the strong scent of lemon fresh waved and snaked its way through the corridors, a familiar scent left by early morning cleaners.

Jane would answer this one last but strange question and make her excuses to return to the ward.

"Yes, the head would be shaved, this is standard procedure prior to surgery, why do you ask?" she replied curiously.

"The shaving of the head or the involvement of the police will not take place, do I make myself clear? You will be required to do what is necessary to ensure the boy's recovery but no police. I hope for all of your sake's these simple but necessary requests will be followed," he stated coldly.

"So how exactly do you propose we operate to save this boy's life if I'm not to prepare him for surgery?"

"If surgery is required, then you will just make him comfortable, that's all. I'm sure an intelligent woman like yourself can understand that."

She shook her head and felt a slither of anger rising towards his arrogance. *How dare he dictate how we run a hospital, as to what we do and don't do,* she thought. She guessed this man and maybe his colleagues were involved in a less than legal activity, but it was her job and she was going to follow protocol.

"Ok, Max, with all due respect, there is no way we or any other hospital will be able to treat this boy without doing any of the things you mentioned, they are protocol and law I'm afraid. We are not interested in why this boy got shot or how you or your colleagues are involved, that is a matter for the police. We treat every patient without presumption or discrimination, and I will do everything I can to save this boy's life," she said assertively.

Jane stood her ground. He had wasted enough of her time with ridiculous questions, maybe in his country they get away with this stuff but not here.

"Do you like picnics?" he asked, with a stone-cold look.

"Sorry?" she said, frowning and looking up at the clock, wondering how much more of her time this jerk would waste.

"You see I am a man of detail and of planning. If I were to go on a picnic, I would make sure the wine I chose would complement the venue and of course the exact right temperature, along with lead crystal glasses of the right size, weight and shape for the appropriate wine. The caviar would need to be beluga, chilled, sourced from exactly the right age of fish and the cheese, yes, the cheese. That too would most certainly have to compliment the wine and so too would the fruit, fresh you understand."

Jane half-listened in a daze, wondering where this was going and what exactly was his point to this.

He continued.

"In order for all these to be enjoyed, the location, weather and humidity would either enhance or deny the moment of enjoyment. So, you see the detail and preparation are of importance, but, if say one piece of the fruit is bruised or the wine not of an acceptable temperature, then that would spoil everything and so it would have to be removed. Do you understand, nurse Jane Stevens?"

She felt more than slightly awkward and confused about his intentions or the point of his conversation. She was, however, a little curious as to how he knew her first name. Her badge simply had her last name. '*Nurse Stevens*'.

It was only then that all of this would become clear. The man still looking into her eyes produced a large manila envelope from behind his back and handed it to her. As she opened the flap and pulled out its contents, a frightening revelation began to take shape. Now she had the contents in her hand he uttered one chilling sentence. Nothing more, nothing less.

"I hope there is nothing that needs to be removed from this, shall we say picnic."

She stood motionless. She could not believe what she was looking at. In her hand were two A4 size black and white photographs. One of her two children coming out of school and one of her husband leaving her house.

Max gave her a moment to take in the enormity of what he had handed her. Then with one hand, opened his jacket, almost seductively, showing the satin cold steel grip of his Glock pistol.

He said nothing.

Time stood still for her, the awareness of irritating questions, the assertive stance and the warmth of the mid-morning sun, all gone. She now understood the analogy of the picnic. She didn't know how long she had been staring at the pictures, she even considered that this was a practical joke; although painfully sick. Her brain could accept this over the stark reality of what was really taking place.

She looked up from the pictures to his cold motionless expression. "I don't understand, why me?"

"Simple," he said with the absence of any compassion. "Your role is to collate, report and prepare the patient for surgery, all of which would invariably conflict with my request. I cannot allow this to happen."

She sat, with her hand over her mouth, conscious she was containing her overwhelming urge to be sick. Max took a black phone from his inside jacket pocket and handed it to her.

"The phone is programmed with one number. Mine. You will always keep the phone with you and notify me of any changes regarding the care and progress of the boy. You will answer the phone after three rings, failure to call or answer will, of course, have consequences. You have twenty-four hours to do what you need to do with the boy." He broke his pose and opened the door. Turning back, he gave her one last tormenting look.

"You will tell no one of this conversation."

The door closed.

The silence was worse.

This morning she cursed the coffee-stained rings left on the table and the fact she wasted ten minutes prying a piece of burnt toast out of the toaster with a knife. But these small but annoying problems she would relish now, even wrap them up in a big bow and worship them compared to this nightmare.

She picked herself up, composed herself and dug deep inside. This is real. These were obviously dangerous people who would go to any length to protect whatever it is they are into. She knew there was no way she would put her family in danger, she was angry now, even dangerously defiant at being put into this situation. She was also intelligent enough to realise she could not carry out his wishes. There are too many people to persuade, too much paperwork to make disappear and too much protocol to deceive for her to get away with this. She needed to figure out how she was going to play this. She could take her family and run but would Dale, her husband, believe her? Plus, he would call the police. She couldn't have that. Besides, she didn't hold the photos now. No that was not an option. The boy, the boy who didn't even have a name must be important enough for them to bring to the hospital. Maybe their religion prohibited cutting hair. But he would say that surely. Her mind raced with numerous questions.

The only sound she heard now was the wall clock. Not the bustle of people or the continuous noise of phones and not even the screaming of small children plagued by their misery and pain. *Tick tick* went the clock. She left the room and shuffled toward the lifts. She stood facing the doors, unaware she hadn't pressed the call button.

"Think this will help," came a voice next to her. A tall thin elderly man with tan trousers and a paisley green shirt reached for the button, his thick white hair lay soft on top like a snowdrift on a wall. His kind face was a million miles from her world right now. He sent a charming smile her way, sensing she was upset. The lift arrived, and the doors opened.

"After you," said the man pausing for her to enter first. She managed a strained half-smile.

"I'm Alex Fuller, Dr Alex Fuller," he said holding out a hand. If she answered him, if she opened her mouth for one moment, she would breakdown. He didn't wait for a reply, he gently removed his glasses and placed them in his top pocket, placing a gentle hand on her shoulder. "You seem troubled my dear." Jane's ability to return a convincing gesture of kindness was empty. Just ten minutes ago her world that she believed was safe, maybe even repetitive but secure was torn from her. In front of her now was a hand of kindness, a face whose eyes did not hold a deep lifeless pool of misery. This was a kind man, and she managed a reply.

"I've just had some bad news, that's all," she said managing a smile which lacked sincerity.

Somehow the low mechanical groan of the lift, the shiny tin, and the familiar scent of antibactcrial smells was subconsciously comforting. Perhaps it was the security of the enclosed metal space or the kind gesture of the elderly doctor, but she began to feel she might be able to keep a straight head, enough to figure out what she was going to do.

"You know the release of Serotonin has been proven when a problem is shared," he said with a smile, trying to make her feel better.

"Thanks, but I don't think you would want to share my problem," she replied with a momentary glance.

As the doors opened, she stood for a second. Dr Fuller left the lift and disappeared down the corridor.

Martha was still fixed to her desk, surrounded by staff all competing for information and direction. How was she going to handle this? Dr Johansen is not a man you burden with a story like this, he could not be manipulated to play along with the twisted task she was supposed to take on. If she didn't call the police, her colleagues would. Request number two would be broken straight away, maybe it already has. The boy had probably arrived already.

She fixed her gaze toward the end of the corridor and the two recovery and emergency rooms. She sat for a moment on one of the chairs in the corridor to compose herself, just long enough to figure a way out of this. Time had marched faster than she had been aware. Maybe twenty minutes, maybe an hour, she had no clue, but a voice broke her semi-conscious thought.

"Nurse Stevens," came a voice behind her.

"Dr Johansen," she replied standing up.

"We've just admitted a young boy," he started with no small talk. "Unfortunately, we don't have any information on him, other than he has a gunshot wound to the head." He looked down over his awkward glasses. "He apparently was just left in the foyer," he said handing a green file to her. She took the file and so desperately wanted to blurt it all out, tell him about her meeting downstairs. But she couldn't.

"Age approximately early teens, don't have a name, no ID or personal belongings." He grabbed the file back from her momentarily and thumbed through the white pages. He's gone for a CT scan so we can evaluate the level of penetration and damage. It looks like the bullet might have penetrated the superior temporal line and is possibly lodged somewhere in the cerebral cortex." He closed the file and handed it back to her.

"We are unsure of the extent of brain damage at this stage. It looks as though the bullet split, it's difficult to distinguish but it looks quite small for a bullet wound. He was brought in, in a comatose state, we, of course, will need to test for brainstem neurological function, we should know more after further scans, which I would like you to organise please, Jane."

She didn't say anything. She remained vacant.

"Can you ask Martha to inform the police, in case we are dealing with a bullet wound, Martha is getting hold of hospital security, we will need to let the police have the CCTV footage from downstairs, so they can trace who left him, we need to identify this boy."

What if the security tape showed her talking to Max? How would she explain that?

For the second time today she was speechless, the frenzied pace of staff, the piercing hospital lights, and the metallic noise of trolleys and machinery could not bring her back from the world she now found herself in. She stared at the folder she had in her hand. Dr Johannsen's instructions were short and without fuss, he was a busy man and a far cry from the jovial manner displayed earlier in the lift.

She couldn't experience a more diverse turn of emotions, how can one hour be so different from the next? The decision was made for her, the instructions were broken. She thought about her two children, their innocence in this nightmare situation and her husband Dale. Now their fate was in her hands.

Chapter 4

Friday 27th 11:05pm

The Pines cafe was now plagued with activity. The piercing blue lights from the police car cast its electric hue over every contour of the building. The fluorescent jackets of the two policemen standing by the cafe door reflected the light back to the cars.

Detective Chief Inspector John McBride rolled out of his car and pulled a pair of latex gloves from his jacket pocket. He was a short, stocky man with a receding grey hairline more advanced than his years. His torso echoed a man whose diet was anything but healthy and a faded tan, the last reminder of a recent holiday. He stood for a moment to take in the drama. The evening weather did nothing to lighten his spirits. The month of September struggled to hold on to the remnants of summer, especially up here near the edge of the mountains. McBride strolled slowly toward the entrance, lifting the fluttering police tape near the doorway and flashed his ID card. The two officers nodded and simultaneously moved aside. As he entered the café, he was greeted by Sergeant Matt Cribb who was first on the scene. McBride made his introduction and opened the conversation.

"What's the story here then?" he asked placing a piece of gum in his mouth. A man of ritual, this trait was very much part of his routine, assisting his mind to make sense of the situation.

"We received a call from a woman around forty minutes ago," he said flicking through his notes. "A Gill Carter phoned the police at Ten twenty-two this evening, she was asked to wait until we arrived, but according to Mary Tripp, the cafe owner, she left with another woman. But get this, the woman who was with Gill Carter was asking questions about another woman we suspect was involved. She was in just prior to this Gill Carter arriving. Mary Tripp recognised our John Doe leaving with our suspect."

"Seems he didn't get very far then," humoured McBride.

"Any ID on the vehicle she left in?" he asked.

"Unfortunately, not," replied Cribb.

McBride's attention was grabbed by several flashes coming from the corridor toward the toilets. The whitewashed brick corridor was stained with smeared blood. He spotted the scenes of crime investigators in white overall suits, one standing in the doorway of the toilet and the other halfway down the corridor photographing the dark blue carpet. He allowed a smile to creep in, reminiscing about a low budget black and white sci-fi film from his teenage years, featuring Martians in white suits, no matter how many times he saw them it still triggered this childhood memory.

"How long have SOCO been here?" he asked

"About fifteen minutes."

"What about witnesses in the cafe? have they been questioned yet?" he asked looking toward the cafe area. The fragrant smell of hot coffee waved its way to the entrance and McBride could have quite easily slipped through to the counter and sink a mug. Caffeine was very much a key ingredient, especially at this hour. But he knew it was going to be a while before he could indulge.

"Sergeant O'Connor is in there now taking statements, I managed to secure the area, but the rain isn't helping with any evidence in the car park," replied Cribb.

"Here better put these on," he said presenting a pair of plastic shoe protectors. "The coroner is with the body now."

"Thanks," McBride replied, placing the plastic liners over his tan shoes. He proceeded carefully towards the lady's toilet where the body lay. He moved carefully around one SOCO who was placing a numbered yellow evidence tag by a small blood spatter just outside the toilet doorway. McBride entered, cautious not to hinder any evidence around the scene. He crouched, joining the coroner beside the body, his old knees creaking in the process. The second SOCO was collating the scene with several short flashes, photographing the walls, cubicle doors and body. The Aroma of stale urine had been replaced with the scent of blood. This scene was now a million miles from the sun-kissed beaches of Mexico he was on the week before.

"Ok, what can you tell me?" asked McBride, staring at the silver scissors protruding from the side of the throat.

"Well he's mid to late thirties, cause of death is more than likely to be from the four-inch nail scissors in the sternomastoid, piercing the carotid artery but can't give you a definite reply until a full post-mortem has been done, there are no defensive wounds on his hands or arms, my guess is he either knew his attacker or was taken by surprise," stated the coroner.

McBride looked closely at the large dark pool of blood which framed the body, some of the blood had found the gullies between the glazed white tiles, streaming away in straight lines.

"Time of death?"

"I would say no more than two hours as the body is still in Algor mortis, body temp has dropped quite a few degrees, bearing in mind its cooler in here than the cafe area."

"Any ID or wallet?"

"Not that I can see, he has a small tattoo behind his left ear of a lion if that helps. Haven't turned the body over yet to check the pockets, you can do that if you like and you might want to look at the end of his fingers."

The coroner gently pulled up the right hand of the body and twisted it slightly, turning up the palms for McBride to see.

"I've only ever seen this once before," said the coroner.

McBride stretched his head closer to the hand, in particular the fingertips.

"No fingerprints," he said returning the glance.

"I've seen this before," he replied. "They've been removed by acid deliberately to avoid identity," he stated. "These are professionals."

"Guess this opens a can of worms for you," smiled the Coroner.

"I doubt there's a loving family somewhere that's going to miss him," replied McBride closing his attention on the blood-smeared door frame.

"Like I said, I will be able to tell you more after I've done a full Post-mortem," he replied closing his bag.

McBride leaned over the body again and pulled up the corner of the black jacket revealing the inside pocket. He felt a hard metal shape, instantly recognising it as a handgun. With his other hand, he took a plastic evidence bag from his pocket and placed the gun inside. This changed things too. Exhaling loudly, his mind wandered back to the beach in Mexico, a long way from this cold, stark and pungent toilet, but his getaway was short-lived. He looked again at the coroner who had now stood.

"This investigation is not going to be straight forward."

He examined the gun he recovered, unaware of the last few camera flashes bouncing off the white tiles. He held the gun out in front of him, briefly stopping to chew on his gum. He studied it as if willing it to tell a story, he knew this was a Makarov, a favoured gun by the Russian criminal underworld. He also knew this meant that John Doe was part of something bigger. His thoughts teased him somewhat, organised crime was not something he would expect up here in the furthest reaches of northern Scotland.

McBride was suddenly distracted by a voice behind him.

"Sir," came a shout from Sergeant O'Connor his colleague, a well-built man with a worn looking face, an example of a man paved by cigarettes and booze.

McBride responded with a glance, slightly annoyed by the invasion.

"I've interviewed the few people we have and there seems to be an interesting picture emerging here."

"Ok, enlighten me," he asked.

"Well, it seems there were three men in here who all came in together and this John Doe was one of them." He scratched his head briefly. "It's looking like your victim, and I quote from Mary Tripp, left the cafe with a woman who seemed quite uneasy about leaving with him, possibly under duress," he added. "There is one other interesting thing, this Mary Tripp reckons they had an accent, she thought maybe Russian, continued O'Connor staring at the Makarov that McBride was still holding in the evidence bag.

"That's a Russian fire-arm, got a feeling this is going to involve Interpol," said O'Connor.

"Yeah another marriage breaker of a case, thought I'd left all those behind with the big city lights," replied McBride still staring at the gun.

"Least you still got a marriage, mines been on the rocks more times than a smugglers boat," grinned O'Connor.

"Didn't anyone tell you; you're married to the job?"

"Yeah true, it screws me more than the wife does," mocked O'Connor.

McBride's mood remained unchanged. The seriousness of the night's events concerned him. He smoothed his thinning hair; this was going to be a complex case and he knew at some point Interpol were going to be involved. This he hated.

McBride put his hands on his knees and gently pulled himself to his feet, groaning all the way up. His agility had deserted him a long time ago. He pulled another strip of gum from his jacket, added it to the one he was already chewing and stepped outside.

The ambient temperature had dropped significantly. Enough for McBride to blow into his hands. The wind had picked up the pace and danced the nearby trees.

"What's your take on this then?" O'Connor asked.

"Honestly? I'm puzzled. It's not the what that concerns me, or the why, it's the where. Up here, away from civilisation, it doesn't fit. These are seriously connected people, part of a large plan, but how does that woman who by all accounts doesn't fit the picture get involved? We know she didn't really want to leave with him, maybe her only escape was to plunge the scissors into him. He must have followed her into the toilets, giving her time to pull them out before he entered."

"But why?" asked O'Connor.

"That, my friend, is the question."

"Self-defence?" O'Connor suggested.

"Could be, but unlikely she would be able to resist his strength and have time to pull the scissors from her bag." McBride rubbed his chin like the rough stubble was soothing.

"I spoke to the lorry driver, Frank Gibbs, who swears he heard what sounded like a gunshot shortly after those two women left, it would seem the other two men in suits followed after the women, one being Gill Carter. This was also confirmed by Mary Tripp."

"If that's true, it was not our John Doe who fired a gun. His weapon has not been discharged recently, so we can also assume the other two men were carrying as well."

"Any CCTV cameras?" asked McBride looking up toward the doorway.

"You're kidding, out here?" smiled O'Connor. "We're not that lucky."

"Ok we need to find this Gill Carter, and the woman with her, get on to control, I need the number she used to phone it in, maybe she will talk to us even if she didn't want to hang around, they seem to be key in all of this," said McBride confidently.

McBride returned inside to the body, mainly for some warmth, but also to study the scene once more. He stared at the small tattoo of a lion behind the left ear, he had seen something like this before on a police photo, but not of a lion. His memory was refusing to play ball at this moment.

"Whatever happened here, this scumbag lying on the toilet floor probably deserved it. My hunch is our suspect is more of a victim who managed to escape," said McBride.

"Question is what did they want with this woman," asked O'Connor staring at the body. "Maybe we'll get an ID from the prints on the door frame or scissors," he continued.

"Assuming she's in the system," replied McBride.

McBride turned from his colleague, giving the impression he had just had a sudden idea and moved swiftly out along the corridor toward the door. He reached inside his jacket, pulled out his phone and dialled. He stood with the phone to his ear, the other hand massaging the small amount of change in his pocket.

Chapter 5

Friday 27th 10:28pm

The BMW snaked erratically. Its wheels scrambling for grip on the loose shingled surface as it charged out of the car park and the engine singing loudly under Gills heavy right foot.

Inside the air was electric, shards of crumbled glass lay scattered like tiny diamonds.

Turning right they headed north again, the inclement weather making visibility a luxury as the cold air was sucked in through the gaping hole where the rear window once was. Gill's hands were visibly shaking on the wheel and tears streaming down her face. As the initial shock subsided, she became aware of a dull and excruciating pain in her left shoulder, each movement of the wheel only serving to aggravate her discomfort.

Megan was crouched, her head buried below the dashboard, hiding, her ears still recoiling from the sound of the exploding glass behind her. She lifted her head, her brown eyes were now pools of bloodshot pink, and her skin ashen. She looked across at her sister and to the blood, now seeping its way through the top of her coat. She glanced down at the shards of glass sprinkled over her red coat and jeans. She was lucky. She had escaped injury.

"Gill you're hurt," shouted Megan, looking to the pain surfacing on her sister's face.

She ignored her; too intent on making distance her objective to realise the extent of her injury. Consumed by shock, her subconscious mind transported her back home in Beacon Hill.

Beacon Hill was not actually on a hill. It was as flat and level as any of the roads around there. Neat cut hedges and tendered gardens. It was a typical residential road, the epitome of working-class, a kaleidoscope of summer colours adorned every front garden and number seven was no exception. Gill lived there for the last twelve years, the last two and a half on her own, ever since her husband Lenny left her. She was career-minded. Lenny wasn't. She never wanted kids, but she was always aware he did. They never spoke about it. Then during one of her works parties, Lenny found himself drinking too much and all his resentment finally surfaced. She remembered, standing in a grand hall filled with architectural beauty, high profile clients, soothed by classical music. It wasn't even an argument, she credited him for that, not shouting at her like some drunken halfwit who had just wandered in from the pub and embarrassed her in front of her work colleagues. He just looked at her and told her he needed more from life. Gill got over it. Eventually. She even half expected it.

Burying her pain just like she did with the suicide of her mother. Although she only convinced herself of this to make sense of her world and she didn't want to end up like her sister, controlled by grief.

Gill managed to keep the house, she was happy there, settled and content for the moment.

It hadn't always been that way for her, or her twin sister Megan who lived on the other side of town. They were not the usual stereotypical twins, they didn't share dress sense, interests or even opinions on most things. That's not to say they were not close and today was very much about being united.

Bang. The sound of reality came crashing back. No longer would her memories hide her pain. She didn't know how long she had been in this dream state or how she hadn't crashed.

As the cold air whipped violently around the interior, Gills senses returned with vengeance and she was now fully conscious of her pain.

Megan turned and peered back through the shattered rear glass. A sobering thought entered her head. *What if they followed? How long would it take for them to catch up?*

"Pull over," she said panicking, still gazing out the black hole and anticipating a following light.

Gill didn't argue, she just pulled the car up to a stop.

"Climb over I'm driving now," she exclaimed. Gill fell into the passenger seat, grasping her arm and wincing.

"What are we going to do Megan? What just happened?" shrieked Gill.

"We need to get off this road, then I need to look at your arm."

Megan cupped her sisters face in her hands, her cold pale face reflecting her own "It's going to be ok," she said.

Megan slammed the car in reverse and weaved her way backwards eyeing a small single narrow track between a boundary of fir trees. She then pulled into the track about thirty yards and cut the engine and lights.

Gill was silently surprised by her sisters cool and rational thinking in all the mayhem. She was not used to her taking control. For years it was her that took care of Megan. Kept her straight, guided her, and even supported her when she left her job.

Megan tentatively peeled back Gills cream coat now stained with blood.

She paused for a moment, reluctant to turn on the interior light.

Paranoia followed.

A part of Megan was secretly excited by this, the twist of danger, the reality of something so real and unpredictable, it fired her up. She never excelled at anything, apart from her social perception and her analytical people skills, but unfortunately, it wasn't a tangible skill and pointless on a CV. She felt strong and surprised by her own rational thinking.

"Tell me this is not happening. Why us?" asked Gill confusingly.

"I'm sorry, it's my fault, I should have just minded my own business."

Gill reached for her hand. "It's not your fault, you want to help people, that's admirable. We just picked the wrong person," she replied.

"I can't stop thinking about that poor woman, what if she was on the run from them, we just left her, at the side of the road," said Gill, wincing as Megan removed her coat from her shoulder.

"She killed that man, didn't she?"

"I really think she killed him to get away," said Megan.

"Maybe we should've waited for the police to turn up."

"If we had, we'd be dead now," replied Megan, checking her wound.

"Not if we stayed in the café."

"You've been shot, the bullet that smashed the window must have hit you. I need to get you to a hospital, it looks bad."

"Let's go back to the café, the police will be there soon, they can help us, we can explain what happened," suggested Gill, still wincing from the excruciating pain.

"Ok, give it ten minutes, then we'll go back."

Megan paused.

She froze, staring out through the gaping hole in the back. The faint sound of a car grew louder with every passing second. A beam of light penetrated the trees and her heart raced.

She surmised the road was a quiet one, especially this time of night, so what were the chances of another car driving by mere minutes after them?

"It could be them," she whispered.

"Shit this is bad, what if it is them? What do we do?" asked Gill, panicking.

"I think we need to run into woods, at least we can't be trapped."

Megan grabbed the door handle and looked towards the trees to the side.

"You ok to run?"

Gill nodded; her eyes full of fear.

Megan opened the door and ran to the cover of nearby trees, followed by Gill, and waited.

They watched the lights pass but seemingly slowing down.

The car stopped, just past the entrance to the track. Megan hadn't realised they had left the doors open. The interior light was not a bright one but against the darkness, it was enough to be noticed from the road.

"Shit, wait here," said Megan as she sprinted across the wet grass. She shut the doors just as the car reversed parallel with the entrance to the track. *Was it too late though?* She thought. Now she was scared. This was not a game. There were to be no losers, just live or die. Could she possibly talk her way out of this, tell them the truth, the woman on the road? *Don't be silly,* she told herself. Now she was doubting her decision to stop. Was she foolish? maybe they should have just carried on north. It was too late now. She felt the cold, the bitter rain brought goosebumps to her skin. She sat on the ground, hiding with her back to the bumper of the car.

Gill was struck by the silence. Other than the sound of the rain finding its way through the canopy of foliage and the sound of her own heart pumping, it was dead quiet. The last time she scrambled around in the woods was when she and her sister were kids. Their parents' house backed onto to a small square cornfield, beyond this was a small wood. Often, they would play hide and seek for hours. Summer was an adventure, the excitement of their imagination conjured up their many games of fantasy, the innocence of kids in play, swashbuckling yarns with a boy called Ben who lived next door. She remembers how their father used to sound his horn on the Land Rover, once to let them know tea was ready and twice for playtimes over its time to come home. There was a small part of her that would relish the sound of that horn now, just for a second it would remind her of how safe she would be. If only their father knew the situation they were in, she desperately wanted this journey to end.

Tentatively she emerged from the cover of the undergrowth, she felt the waterlogged floor seeping through her heeled shoes. A loud cracking sound came from under her foot. The more careful she tried to move the more aware of the noises she became. A small woodland animal scurried across her path and disappeared into the undergrowth, keeping her senses on high alert.

Megan dashed back to her sister and knelt, the wet grass seeping through her jeans and the droplets of rain falling onto her hair.

Gill groaned. The pain was now taking hold, and her ample frame shook.

Megan was still acutely aware of the car parked at the edge of the track less than thirty yards away. The monotonous throbbing of its engine playing in the background was almost taunting. The distant sound of an owl echoed behind them, the wood was alive, a hive of nocturnal activity and Megan was growing impatient now.

Then, just as she was figuring a way out, the sound of doors slamming echoed through the forest and the realisation of the impending danger became real. Gill's breathing became fast and she tightened her grip on Megan's waist, pulling her close for warmth.

Megan wiped her face, peering along the track which disappeared into the void, her eyes strained, trying to make use of the little light. There was no moonlight, just dark rolling clouds. Megan grabbed Gills icy hand, ready to run, but paused. Above the sound of nature, two voices echoed a short distance away, becoming louder, familiar voices, like the ones in the café, and again in Russian.

Their hearts raced.

"We need to move from here before we're spotted, come with me," said Megan, barely above a whisper.

Megan took her moment, and with Gill in tow, set off up the narrow track, her hand tightly wrapped in hers. The deep, soft, rutted track was no match for stylish shoes, and Gill's ankles were not prepared for this terrain. She was not like Megan who dressed for comfort in jeans, tee-shirt and trainers. Skirts and heels were who she was, she took pride in herself, lavished her money on nice things. But now she didn't know which hurt the most, her ankles or her shoulder. She followed her sisters lead, heading further up the track and deeper into the forest, stumbling under the uneven surface. The dense copse overhung the track with sporadic fingers of foliage catching their faces as they ran, panting heavily but not stopping.

Advancing closer, beams of light sliced through the darkness like lightsabres.

Both were now a fair way up the track, and the forest thinned, revealing a wide-open space with a carpet of course heather and grasses. Out of breath, their lungs burning, they stopped, glancing back up to the forest they came from.

Megan had her arm around Gill, pulling her in close, aware of her sister's discomfort, contorted from the pain of the gunshot wound. Megan felt the wetness on her hand, knowing this was her sister's blood, there was no colour in the dark, but it was sticky and warm. Releasing her grip, Gill slumped to the ground, trembling, she didn't care how wet and cold the ground was, or how uncomfortable. She was frightened and tired.

Megan stood, gazing back toward the track she caught a glimpse of torchlight sweeping through the branches, occasionally its penetrating beam would catch their faces, but she knew it was too far away for them to see them.

She suddenly realised their phones were in the car, along with the rest of their belongings, including both overnight bags. She thought about their father for a moment, how he would be expecting them soon, maybe he would try and call, if only she could wind the clock back just a couple hours. She cursed inside, how had she been so stupid getting involved with this woman's business. She was angry with herself, but strangely she also felt some compassion for her, who might, she thought, be in the same boat as them. On the run, scared, threatened, maybe she killed that man in panic and pure desperation. She wondered for a moment where she might be now, alone in the dark on the side of the road still eager for someone to help, maybe another late-night passerby picked her up. She hoped she was safe.

Bereft of thought now, she quickly snapped back to their own, and very real situation. There was no room for self-pity, she had to get help from somewhere, trying to think straight was near on impossible and the inevitable was looming, the voices came closer and the torchlight brighter.

"Gill get up, we need to move," she said, offering her hand.

"I feel tired, my shoulders hurting and I'm cold," groaned Gill.

The rain was now perilous in its descent, the cold wind occasionally blowing, their fingers aching in the coldness. Her coat gave little protection and soon the dampness was felt through her t-shirt, along with her white trainers, now soaked with the coffee coloured water which filled the ruts.

Gill was in shock, and Megan had to keep her warm.

"I need to get you help; we have to keep moving."

Megan pulled on her, raising her to her feet again. It was then out of the blue she remembered a scene from a movie.

"Take your shoes off," instructed Megan

"What? What for?" asked Gill.

"Give them to me, quickly," said Megan.

Gill removed her shoes and handed them to her.

Megan took the shoes and placed them on the ground, she positioned them with the heels angled into the softened soil, placing one hand on her sister for balance, she raised her right leg and brought it down hard angling her weight toward the heel end of the shoes. There was a small cracking noise and Gill looked in horror as Megan did the same again with the other shoe.

Gill looked in disbelief.

"I'll buy you some more, you can run better in flat shoes, less likely to break your ankle and get caught, now we need to move."

She took her hand and led them off the track, up a small grassy incline and through a curtain of overhanging fir trees, which provided them with some cover for now.

"Where are we going?" asked Gill.

"We need to get back to the car, to our stuff."

"Aren't we supposed to be running away from them?" exclaimed Gill.

"I know, but we're doubling back through the forest, we're going to make a dash for the car, trust me," replied Megan.

She considered the distance and terrain between them and their car. There were a good twenty yards of open space before they hit the dense forest, she also considered how far away the car was. Her plan was to make their way back through the forest parallel to the track.

"You ready?" Megan asked.

"I guess so," she replied, still unsure of the plan.

Megan took one last look toward the track; she could still see the torchlight flickering through the trees.

Without further hesitation, she took off with Gill, out from the cover of the fir trees and across the open ground toward the forest. The steady hiss of rain played its part in covering the thud of their footsteps. Gill held onto her sister's hand as if it were a lifeline, her ankle pained with every step on the uneven ground, and the long grass tugged their feet, almost tripping them in places. Megan panted hard, filling her tiny lungs with air, she didn't look across at the track, scared she might be caught by the beam of light, if she couldn't see them then maybe they couldn't see her, but she was aware of a distant flicker out of the corner of her eye. The darkness of the trees loomed close, its maze of branches like arms of comfort as they entered the undergrowth.

Gill leant against a tree, panting heavily, her lungs begging for air. Megan looked across toward the track, the light was now moving further on, up towards their previous hiding. She heard the faint voices just above the sound of her wheezing chest.

"Sorry, but we need to keep moving," said Megan, catching her breath.

"What if they have our stuff, our phones, how the hell are we going to contact dad?" asked Gill, shivering.

"I don't know, we'll cross that bridge then, I guess," replied Megan blowing into her cupped hands to warm them. Her feet were now waterlogged, her white canvas trainers had lost the battle with the long-wet grass, but she tried to ignore the penetrating cold at the end of her toes.

Megan moved on up the track, she could just make out the distant shape of a car, nestled between the line of trees.

Again, she moved steadily, weaving around the trees toward the edge of the track. The woodland floor was a carpet of sounds, twigs snapped, and water-filled ruts belched under a heavy foot. They crouched, their legs aching. On the boundary of trees, Gills car was now within reach.

They waited. silently. patiently. Gill tasted the cool refreshing rainwater as it trickled down her face and nestled on her lips, she was thirsty now. She gazed through the tight weave of branches, still tracking the torchlight in the distance.

"Wait here, I'm going to check the car, see if our stuff is there, I just hope they haven't taken it." She took a deep breath. "If something happens, run back to the road, back to the café, promise me, the police should be there by now, just explain everything," said Megan.

"But we could both go now, back to the cafe," suggested Gill, with hope in her voice.

"We will, but we need our stuff first, I need to know if it's still there."

She realised she hadn't thought this through. She was nervous, this bold decision did not come from courage, but through desperation. She put her own fears to one side for the sake of her sister.

Chapter 6

Friday 27th 9:52am

Jane didn't know how long she had been standing in the same spot, unaware, disconnected, at the centre of her own universe where everything orbited around her. She snapped out of it, startled by a voice, a deep voice, and one that clearly lacked patience.

"Nurse Stevens," came the voice, probably for the third time at least, judging by the tone.

"Sorry, what?" she responded, looking up to see Dr Fuller.

"I don't know what news you've had but something tells me you shouldn't be here." She remembered her brief conversation with him in the lift, his kind words of concern, she felt almost an obligation to give him the truth but knew it would unfairly involve him.

"I just need a bit of time to figure something out," she replied, staring at the abstract patterns on his shirt.

His long gangly fingers lay softly again on her shoulder and she felt his compassion run through her.

"A problem shared my dear, remember," he replied.

"I haven't seen you here before, are you a visiting consultant?" she asked, trying to forget her dilemma for a moment.

"Retired, I'm here to catch up with a few people."

"Dr Johanson?"

"Oh, yes, him, you haven't seen him have you?" He smiled. He was always smiling she thought, his fingers were still perched on her shoulder, but she didn't mind.

"Yes, I was just talking to him a moment ago, he went through there," she replied pointing towards the two blue doors halfway down the corridor.

She fingered nervously with the file, flicking its pages repetitively, her brief conversation had distracted her from thinking about her next move. Dr Fuller then removed his hand from her shoulder and left.

Jane followed him with a look of curiosity as he disappeared through the double doors, unaware she was standing in the middle of the corridor. A young porter squeezed by with a laundry trolley full of white sheets and bedding, his pace was slow and unenthusiastic, the tinny sound of a beat emitted from his earphones as he immersed himself in whatever funky beat he was playing on his iPod. She kind of envied his job now, no pressure, little responsibility, but above all the lack of need by mindless thugs to use his position for their own manipulation.

She jumped for a moment, it was a phone ringing, suddenly realising it was the one in her pocket, she had forgotten about the phone Max handed her downstairs. She reached into her pocket and pulled it out, her heart skipped and she felt a tingling in her stomach as she stared at the screen. Just the words *'private'* glared back at her, then she remembered his words about answering it within three rings. She didn't know how many times it had rung but she answered it anyway and hoped for the best.

"Hello," she answered, her voice quivering.

"I distinctly told you to answer within three rings. I counted five," he replied, his tone remaining unchanged from the one he used earlier. Cold and haunting.

"I'm sorry," she blurted. "I was carrying some files and had to put them down to get the phone out." She lied, of course, the only thing she could think of, but now she waited. There was an agonising pause.

"I will allow this to be your last and only mistake. Now, do you have any information on the boy?" he asked.

She let out a small sigh and realised she would have to have her wits about her from now on. Not wanting to be heard she turned and walked towards the cleaning room. She took a second to look around before entering the small walk-in cupboard room. Silvery aluminium racks lined the back wall with a variety of plastic containers, boxes of gloves, and an assortment of other hospital cleaning items.

She continued with the conversation.

"I'm still waiting for the results of the CT scan; we will know more when we get those." She took an opportunity to try and acquire some more information.

"It's very likely the boy will need an operation, how am I supposed to carry this out without breaking your rules? If I don't prepare him for surgery someone else will. Dr Johansen is not going to listen to me, he already told me to involve the police, which I haven't but it won't take long for him to figure that out. They're going to get the security tapes which will show us talking and your colleagues bringing the boy in," she rambled.

Slowly she felt her words breaking down, sticking in her throat, her eyes filled with heavy tears and she no longer had the strength or will to stand. She slumped onto the vinyl floor, burying her head in the wing of her arm, a tiny stream of tears made its way down her face and dripped onto her blue uniform. Exhausted by worry, nerves strained, her body tensed as she felt resentment rising with every breath. Consuming, taking control and throwing all reason and clarity out of the window.

"Damn you for screwing with my life, who the fuck do you think you are? Get someone else to do your dirty work, leave me and my family alone," she ranted.

Before Max could reply she cut him dead and dropped the phone to the floor beside her. She buried her wet face in the palm of her hands and sobbed until no more tears would come. She reached up to the shelf in front of her and grabbed some paper towels, wiping her face which was swollen and clammy, stinging from the salty tears. She sat listening to the clatter of people walking past the door, going about their business, unaware and carefree. She stared at the yellow label on the bottle in front, fixing her gaze, but this was short-lived by another piercing ring. She picked up the phone and answered, the realisation of her actions was now speeding towards her, how could she be so stupid. She thought about the photos, she felt sick again, then came the haunting voice.

"Was that necessary?" he asked, his tone was still chillingly calm despite her rant. "Let me make something clear to you," he continued "If any of these rules are broken the only thing you will have left of your family will be photos and memories. I don't think you quite grasp the situation you are in, but I can see you are a spirited woman, I almost admire your courage and tenacity, but I have to say I also take some pity in your naivety."

She remained silent, staring down at the floor, rolling her wedding ring round her finger. She had no choice. For the second time today, she was off the hook, relieved, but she couldn't keep playing with her family's life. He wasn't going to punish her for that, but next time maybe he would. For the sake of her family, she would have to swallow humble pie.

"I won't do that again, I promise," she replied, her voice now had the tone of surrender, and he knew it.

"No, you won't, but to make things simple and to help you understand I'm going to explain a few points. First, you are just one piece of the picnic. All you must do is worry about your part, don't call the police, lose the file, bury it, whatever you must do so there is no paperwork at the end. Do I make myself clear?"

"Yes, but with all due respect, I need to point out that if the CT scan picks up a hematoma then we would certainly have to perform a craniotomy. This is where a piece of the skull is removed to relieve the pressure on the brain due to swelling, if this was not allowed then he would most certainly die," she pointed out.

Jane did her best to make sure he knew the extent of her situation, she knew he was an intelligent man, trying to get her side of a delicate situation across was imperative for her. She decided to take the opportunity to quench her curiosity. She could understand him not wanting the police involved, she got that, even losing the file, but why the concern over preparing him for surgery? "Why don't you want us to prepare him for surgery? I don't understand," she asked hesitantly.

"That information I cannot share. But if there is a Hema -, whatever the medical term, you will not perform this. If the boy dies as a result, then so be it, we will make arrangements to collect the body, you will not perform a post-mortem or allow the body to be taken anywhere."

"How can you be so cold? This is a boy's life you're playing with," she replied angrily.

"Just remember your instructions." He ended the call.

A sudden chill crept over her, taken back by the coldness of this man. How can any human being be so callous towards a child? Jane remained seated for a moment, her heart pounding, trying to gather her thoughts which circled her head like a stampede of wild horses. She glanced at the watch on her uniform. 10.43am. She slowly rose to her feet and replaced the phone into her side pocket. Once more she dabbed her eyes and straightened her uniform, taking a deep breath, she exited the cupboard and entered the busy highway of people, recoiling briefly from bright lights of the corridor. In all the madness she had misplaced the boy's file.

She hurried down the corridor toward where she had last spoken to Dr Fuller. As she eyed the water dispenser on her left and the blue file perched on top, she allowed herself another feeling of relief. It still did nothing to play down any part of her nightmare, but it was a relief non-the less. She placed the file under her arm and started toward the washroom. As she approached, amid the wave of human traffic, she saw Dr Johansen talking to Carl, the head of hospital security.

She slowed, pausing at the door, watching as the doctor stood, arms folded, his face signalling his confusion about something. She realised the possibility that the CCTV had seen her talking to Max was out. It wouldn't be long before they would come looking for her, asking questions. She needed to talk with Carl, they were friends, often crossing paths in the canteen and exchanging small talk over stale hospital sandwiches. He was a well-proportioned man with recessed eyes, good posture and a military-style haircut. He was very much a loner, apart from a brother in the states he had no family, having spent most of his life in the military, he never elaborated, and she never pushed. Like most ex-forces he struggled with civvy street and stereotypically he ended up in security. But he hated it. He often talked about going to the states to work for his brother. She was aware he had a crush on her, his juvenile flirting and ego flexing antics told her this, but Carl was harmless, he knew her loyalty and happiness with her husband Dale was not to be broken. She liked him all the same, and he was never judgmental. Despite their friendship and although he would take no pleasure in it, she feared he would be required to produce the CCTV footage, leaving her with some awkward questions to answer.

Chapter 7

Friday 27th 23:50

McBride stole a moment to bathe his lungs in the fresh evening air, exchanging its fresh scent from the smell of stained blood. Reflecting on the scene, he stood upright and still. His brown piggy eyes not looking or focusing on anything. His calculating mind was not distracted by the departing of forensics or the witnesses scurrying to their cars, eager to evade the evening with tales of excitement.

"Think we have everything we need for now; all the areas have been processed, just a case of putting the pieces together," said O'Connor walking up beside McBride and stealing the same welcoming air.

"Just came off the phone with control, the number Gill Carter called on is registered to an address in Devon, question is, what's she doing up here, miles from home?" said McBride, still staring out into the abyss.

"You tried calling the number?" asked O'Connor.

"Yeah, several times, it rings but no answer, left a message to contact us. She's our key witness, told her there was nothing to worry about, don't want to scare her. She could really help us, in fact, get the local police to check out her address, talk to neighbours, employer, find out what sort of person she is, why's she up here. If she's got nothing to do with this then she'll contact us, she could be the only link to finding our suspect."

"I'll get them to go around tomorrow," replied O'Connor.

McBride's gaze was now fixed on the disappearing taillights of the forensics van. "It still leaves us with our victim in the toilet. What was he doing up here with the other two suited henchmen? Find the woman, and maybe we might catch us some big fish as well," he said. "Come with me a moment," asked McBride.

"Why, where are we going?"

"We need to talk to this Mary Tripp again."

"She's already been questioned," replied O'Connor.

"Yes by Cribb, not the most experienced, plus one thing I've learned in this job is, what is sometimes written in a statement is not always translated as it was said and not all the details noted, you can learn a great deal from watching people say things." McBride removed his hands from his pockets and strolled into the dining area with O'Connor in tow, the aftermath of activity had now transcended into an anti-climax, only the soft ambient lighting remained. The assortment of beverage machinery churned to a halt and only the faint after-smell of food still noticeable.

"Any chance of a couple of coffees please Mary?" asked McBride parking himself down in one of the booths. "Milk and plenty of sugar ta."

McBride unbuttoned his grey tweed jacket and groomed back his thin hair. O'Connor shifted inside. His thick fluorescent jacket made him look more like an American footballer.

"Yes sure," she replied, wiping down the last countertop.

After a couple of minutes, Mary delivered their coffees and hovered for a few moments at their table.

"Terrible business this, you'd think a quiet place like this would be safe from trouble. Six years I've been here, was it a murder then?" she asked curiously and threw the blue checked tea towel over her shoulder; her hands lay firm on her ample hips and her soft eyes widened in anticipation of a reply.

"Sorry, we're not allowed to discuss the case with you," replied O'Connor, stirring the rich froth into his coffee.

"Oh, ok, I understand," she replied disappointedly.

"I would like to ask you a few more questions if that's ok with you," asked McBride.

"Ok, but I told one of your officers earlier everything I remember."

"Sure, but I just need some more details that were maybe overlooked, it's ok, nothing to worry about, just want to clear up a few points," said McBride acknowledging her slight restlessness. He pulled out a large leather-bound notebook and placed it on the table in front of him, his stubby hands held firm a silver pen which he clicked open.

"Ok, Mary, the two women who sat over there." McBride turned and used his silver pen to point to where they were sitting." Did they enquire about the other woman by name or just by description?"

"Only by description," she replied.

"Did they describe what she was wearing, how she looked, how did they ask about her?"

O'Connor sipped his coffee slowly, savouring its taste. Mary stared up toward the ceiling, twisting her silver necklace around her neck, shooting jewels of reflective light around the room like a disco ball.

"They asked if I'd seen a woman in here, late thirties, dressed in black trousers and I think a light coat, cream coat, sorry I can't remember exactly."

"So, they described what she was wearing but did they say my friend, sister, auntie, did they give the impression they knew her or was meeting her here?"

"No, just a woman, they both seemed like they were concerned about her, almost eager to see her I would say."

"Ok, the woman you described as about your height, long blond hair, etc, but can you describe her manner, how she seemed, acted, spoke, any accent, peculiar mannerisms? Sorry I know this is difficult but anything you can tell us is helpful," he assured her.

O'Connor impatiently sunk the last drop of his coffee and sat back.

"She was definitely nervous, she kept looking around, when she paid for her coffee, she dropped her change, she looked like she had a huge weight on her mind poor girl."

"The man who left with her, tell me how he was, his behaviour, how did he interact with her and the other two men who were sat there, anything odd or suspicious?"

McBride turned his notebook, exposing a clean sheet, despite his earlier craving for caffeine, he was too preoccupied for now.

Mary exhaled from her ruby red lips and scratched at a small spot on her forehead.

"The three men came in together. The man who was found, he's the one that ordered the drinks. He had a Russian accent, could be polish, there's a lot of them here now. Didn't hear the others speak, one was on his phone, but they were speaking in Russian, whatever it was, when I came over. The woman came in and sat near the back, I had to go behind the counter but when I returned with her coffee, he was sat with her."

"Did he sit next to her or opposite?" interrupted McBride.

"No, he sat next to her, almost leaning into her."

"How did they leave together; did you see them leave?"

"Almost straight away, he had his arm around her, but she looked really uncomfortable, almost frightened," she replied.

"Couple more questions, apart from what the two men were wearing, did you notice anything else, scars, marks, tattoos?"

"Yes actually, I noticed a tattoo, on the large man, a tattoo below his left ear, but can't remember what I'm afraid."

McBride raised his thick eyebrows and glanced across at O'Connor.

"Ok, one final question, did anyone arrive before the woman left and the two women arriving? This is very important."

Mary took a deep breath. She wiped her hands on her apron nervously, several times.

"I think Frank Gibbs, the lorry driver, he's a regular you know, he always pops in if he's heading up this way, talk to him," replied Mary.

"Ok, we will. Thank you for your time, we won't keep you any longer."

Mary returned to the counter and continued to finish closing down. McBride struggled to hold back a yawn before checking his watch and sinking his lips into his long-awaited coffee.

O'Connor reached inside his jacket and pulled out his witness notes, licking the end of his finger he flicked through its pages stopping at one in particular. He folded it over and slid it across the table to McBride.

"Look at the notes I took from Frank Gibbs."

McBride picked up the glint of seriousness in O'Connor, surveyed the notes and looked confused.

"Was he sure about that?" asked McBride. He sat almost motionless, his coffee cup held in mid-air, almost as if his brain could not cope with movement and thinking at the same time.

"I didn't put two and two together until you asked Mary that last question," said O'Connor.

"So, there were only two vehicles in the car park when Frank Gibbs arrived, a black 4x4 Range Rover and a red Vauxhall with trailer, yeah?"

"Yes, we know the Vauxhall belongs to the Taylor family and we now know the three male suspects arrived in the black 4x4," Replied O'Connor.

"So, our suspect didn't arrive by car, or leave by car?" asked McBride, placing his empty cup down. "Question is, why would a lone female be out here in the middle of nowhere without a car?" He pushed the cup to one side and wiped his mouth on the napkin. "Shit that doesn't make sense, it's got to be a good twenty miles to the nearest town."

"There's a lot here that doesn't make sense yet, we need to talk to this Gill Carter," said O'Connor.

McBride smoothed his stubbled chin, returned his notepad to his jacket and stood from the table. "With a bit of luck, she will call us, let's wait and see what forensics turn up with. Fingers crossed we get a hit on the prints.

McBride buttoned his jacket and patted O'Connor on the back. "I think we have enough to be going on with, let's wrap this up for tonight."

Chapter 8

Friday 27th 9:58am

Jane left the washroom and headed down the corridor where Dr Johansen was engaged in conversation with Carl. Her short steps served as an opportunity to focus on what she would say, but still, there was hesitancy. Before she had a chance to make eye contact and commit herself to the conversation, Dr Johannsen's gruff voice took over.

"Ah, Nurse Stevens, I've got some bad news." The Doctor removed his glasses slowly, holding them in his right hand. "Unfortunately, we've lost the boy, he didn't really stand a chance, the CT scan showed a massive intracranial hematoma," explained Dr Johansen peering down at her. "It also looks like this injury was a few days old."

Before Jane had time to respond, Dr Johansen continued his conversation with Carl who acknowledged her with a wink before returning his attention back.

As she stood waiting to steal a moment, she picked up on their conversation. Carl explained there was a failure with the security CCTV this morning.

"Actually, the cameras are fine," she heard Carl reply. "It's the recording equipment that's failed." Jane didn't butt in. She figured they didn't really fail, this had something to do with the people behind the boy. She knew what they meant now when they said she was just one part of the picnic. *What if they had blackmailed Carl too?* she thought. She realised that to orchestrate something like this, it took planning and would involve more than just her. How many other people here did they blackmail? Who could she trust? She could trust Carl surely; she'd known him for two years. Dr Johansen continued to talk with Carl, but she was now oblivious to their conversation, their voices were just a parade of background sound, her glazed expression staring through them, fixing on the blue painted stripe that ran just below the wall rail opposite. She thought about her next move. She thought about her family and how alone she felt in all of this. All she wanted now was to call her husband and for him to tell her everything would be alright.

A dark cloud of doubt circled. She needed to talk to Carl, it was a gamble, but her options were limited, and time was not on her side.

Jane waited until Dr Johansen had finished with him. He had the file now, the one she was asked to dispose of, but that could wait, she could trace it later. She reached inside her pocket and felt the phone, she pulled it out and placed her finger on the dial button. She hesitated, pulling herself to one side, giving way to her busy colleagues. She'd been at work for over an hour now and completed none of her duties.

"Martha's looking for you," said a colleague in passing. "She doesn't look happy."

Jane placed the phone back in her pocket, noting another approaching colleague.

"Jane, you ok? You look like you've seen a ghost, you've been crying, what's wrong?" came a concerning voice. Jane was not in the mood for conversation, she didn't have time for awkward questions, her response was short and curt. "You'll have to excuse me I need to make an important call," she said pulling the phone from her pocket and turning away.

Her colleague ignored her rudeness. "As I said, Martha's looking for you, I suggest you don't keep her waiting," they said before walking off.

Ignoring the message, she took the opportunity to sit on one of the four blue visitor's chairs in the corridor, almost hiding to the side of the tall, white water dispenser, its large plastic container sitting slightly proud of her head. Wasting no time, she dialled the pre-programmed number. The phone rang a few times and her guts coiled tight. She now stood, pacing back and forth in the corridor, hoping Martha wouldn't appear before she had a chance to complete her conversation.

A voice responded. "I trust you have some news for me?" came the voice.

"Yes, it's not good news." She hesitated for a moment. "I'm afraid the boy didn't make it, there was nothing we—" She was interrupted abruptly.

"The details are not of importance any more, you know what you have to do, the boy will be collected, providing nothing has been compromised and the boy safely in our possession, your duty will have been fulfilled and you will be contacted, upon our call you will then place the phone in the bin to the right of the entrance, do I make myself clear?"

"Yes, but—" The call was ended, and Jane placed the phone back into her pocket. She checked her watch. 10:17am.

As she stood in disbelief, a flickering strip light above her became annoying. She hadn't noticed it before, just like she hadn't noticed which way Carl went. As she turned toward the double doors, a dark blue uniform approached. It was Martha. She wore a purposeful expression and she prepared for her wrath. She couldn't be any more nervous, but no one wanted to be on the wrong side of the ward sister. Martha bellowed her name with a tone that had all the traits of a mother scorning her child, maybe if she hadn't had the day she'd had, she would be cowering, but Jane had enough shit for one day, and Martha's warpath couldn't rock her world any more than it had already.

"Nurse Stevens, it has come to my attention that you have abandoned your duties, instead preferring to wander about the hospital in your own little world. Dr Johansen tells me you have not been available, is this right?" she asked, crossing her arms. "He personally had to arrange for the body to be taken to the morgue," said Martha, who's body language only served to emphasise her displeasure.

"I've been side-tracked by some personal news which I had to deal with first if you must know," snapped Jane. Martha didn't acknowledge her reply, not verbally anyway.

"I've called the police, they will be here shortly, they will want to ask you some questions along with Dr Johansen," she replied in a stern voice.

She had forgotten about the police, she had assumed since the boy had died, they would arrange to collect the body and she would be in the clear. How could she have been so stupid?

Martha dropped her scornful look for a second. She sensed Jane's anguish, enough for her to ask. This was Martha, tough when she needed to be but always appeasing when required.

"Jane, you're obviously preoccupied with your personal news, if it's that bad, then I suggest you take the rest of the shift off because you're no good here in this state," she said, gazing at her swollen eyes.

"I'm sorry, I might just have to," she replied thankfully.

"Take what time you need, go to the staff room. I will come and get you when the police arrive." Martha squeezed Jane's arm, the second time today Jane had been touched by someone with a caring streak.

She pulled off a smile, dragged her face through her hands, sniffed hard and whispered a thank you in return.

She hurried off through the double doors toward Dr Johannsen's office, she didn't hesitate or knock. Dr Johansen was slumped over his solid maple desk, masked by his laptop and straight placed paper trays. The light blue back wall, which was complemented by a dark blue tight cord carpet, galleried a collection of certificates and family portraits, all lined up perfectly, along with files and folders, edge to edge in a well-organised pile. This was a neat and precisely kept office. Dr Johansen was careful, focused. An organised individual. So she wasn't surprised he had asked Martha to call the police and request the security tapes.

"Excuse me?" scorned the doctor, lifting his head from the laptop. His blonde eyebrows raised.

"I take it you have a good reason for barging into my office like this?" he asked, sitting up from his desk.

"I need to know what's happening with the boy," replied Jane sharply.

"Nurse Stevens, I don't know what's got into you today, but you have shown no interest in his treatment so far and ignored my instructions along the way." He pulled his large tv framed glasses from his face, threw them onto his desk and slumped back into his sumptuous black leather chair. "For your information, the police want the body untouched until forensics have had chance to examine him due to the circumstances, and let's be fair here, they are a little strange. A teenage boy with a gunshot wound, and no one cares?" He swivelled from left to right in his chair, only the creaking leather interrupted his words. "I have to admit this is an odd one, no name, no relatives, not even a contact number, just dumped here, does that not seem strange to you?"

"Yes, I suppose so," replied Jane.

"You suppose so? Your behaviour has been more than flippant this morning Jane," he continued.

"Do you have the boys file?" she asked, still hovering awkwardly in his doorway.

"Yes, the police will require it and any other supporting information, this is now a criminal investigation and the boy's body will be held for evidence. Why the sudden interest now?"

"What can the file tell them now? it's just a body with no name or identification," she asked defensively.

Dr Johansen stood from his chair, closing his laptop lid and placing his glasses back on his face.

"What's got into you? You're acting like you have no idea about procedure, you know very well what happens in these cases. The bullet is still lodged in his brain, they will have their own forensic pathologist who will retrieve this for evidence, it's not our concern anymore, now if you don't mind, I have work to do."

Jane removed herself from his office, almost as abruptly as she entered. She hurried down the corridor toward the lift. As she stood waiting, she noticed an elderly woman with grey curls and over-indulgent makeup next to her. She caught her scent of cheap lavender perfume as she stood perched on an ornate wooden carved stick with a brass ball handle. Her large figure filled her emerald green floral dress. Jane felt a rush of tension, hoping the old woman didn't want to strike up any kind of conversation. She tried hard to make herself small, insignificant, if she didn't move or look at her, then the old woman wouldn't engage her attention. It felt like an eternity waiting for the lift to arrive, and when it did, she wasted no time stepping in. She pressed the "G" for ground, quickly letting the doors close before the old woman had time to enter. On the way down, she kept replaying her plan in her head, a crazy plan, foolhardy even, but she assured herself this was the only course of action left to her. Her blurred eyes acknowledged the time on her silver staff-watch which hung just below her right lapel. 10.41 am.

As the doors opened, she stepped out to a parade of people all going about their daily duties, for the second time this morning she bathed in the morning sun which was now a permanent feature of the foyer. She peered through the large double glass doors at the entrance, almost in jealousy of the outside world, its freedom and its sense of solace. Jane considered running to her car. Taking off down the road, picking up her children, calling her husband and just driving, fleeing the mess she was forced into, but she knew that decision lay only in fairy-tale endings.

She didn't really have the time to indulge such fantasies now, instead, an all-consuming rush of reality came over her. Turning left she made her way down past several wooden doors and green directional signs where the foyer narrowed into another single-lane corridor.

Stopping outside a door marked *'security'* she composed herself and rubbed her clammy hands down either side of her hips, a state they had been in for most of the morning.

She stood straight and knocked twice on the door, hoping Carl was there. Within a few seconds, he opened the door and his large hands gestured her to enter.

She stood facing the wall of security monitors, a long light wood-grained countertop ran the length of the wall just below the TV screens, a large black keyboard and control stick sat in the middle, yards of cables and wires weaved along the back walls and across the desktop, on the wall opposite, stacked in Meccano style frames, was the recording equipment, multicoloured lights flashed and flickered.

Jane took a moment to see which monitors might have caught her in the foyer talking to Max, but Carl's question caught her short.

"How can I help you, Jane?" he asked, sitting back down in his tall swivel chair.

Jane thought she was prepared for this, knew what to say, instead, she found herself randomly staring at his black socks which quite clearly did not meet his black trousers, not in the sitting position anyway. His white shirt which had a small yellow shield inscribed with *'security'* seemed to allow his large wrists to be permanently on display.

She pushed the door closed and pulled up a seat opposite him, the small room felt oppressive, made worse by the heat radiating from all the electrical equipment. She wondered how anyone could work in such an enclosed space.

She interlocked her fingers and lay them on her lap, her right leg seemed to have a mind of its own as it twitched repeatedly.

"Carl, I need to ask you something, something important. You're going to think I'm crazy and it probably won't make any sense, but I just need you to trust me and please, be honest with me."

She looked straight at him. Despite his hard chiselled features, his eyes were attentive and reassuring.

"Sounds intriguing, does it involve dinner?" He smiled. But there was no reciprocal smile in return, only a sullenness in her red, blotchy face, and her somewhat shifty, awkward posture that seemed to be relying on him in some way.

"I'm in trouble Carl and I need your help," she said.

Carl leaned forward, giving her all his attention realising now that this was a serious matter.

"Sorry Jane, you have my attention." He dropped his smile.

She thought about all the other people who she desperately wanted to tell but couldn't. She didn't really think too hard about what she was going to say, she just wanted to get it over with.

She looked at the monitors behind Carl for a moment, watching the world around her in black and white, almost bewitchingly, the herds of people scurrying about like tiny ants, their every move caught on tape.

She was about to lay bare her predicament and commit herself to tell Carl everything, she figured it couldn't get any worse now. Just as she was about to speak, the sound of a mobile rang out. She flinched, her eyes responded and simultaneously she felt herself blurting out.

"Don't answer that, please." Carl's response almost mirrored hers, halting his movements even before he had time to retrieve his phone from his pocket.

"Wow, do you want to tell me why I shouldn't answer it? You're clearly spooked, ever since you sat down you've been as jumpy as hell."

Jane felt like she was poised on the edge of a precipice now, a very deep and dark one. Whatever happens now, whatever she says to Carl, there is no going back.

"I think my family is in danger, earlier this morning, a man came into the hospital asking for me, I wasn't sure what it was about at first, he didn't seem to make much sense, and then he showed me photographs of my children and my husband, and said if I didn't do what he wanted he would harm them and, and—"

She broke down before she could finish. Carl leaned in and placed his arm around her and gave her some time before he replied.

"Let me get this straight, your telling me someone is blackmailing you?"

She felt stupid just listening to herself pour the words out, let alone what Carl must think.

He offered her a tissue which she took.

"Yes, I guess so."

"Can you describe this man?"

"Tall, black suit, smart I guess, and he had a Russian accent, but he was very well-spoken," she replied wiping her eyes.

Carl removed his arm and turned to the monitors, but a few seconds later he turned back.

"That's very strange because I was about to check the CCTV and realised it's not been working since this morning."

Carl gave her another tissue. "That's not a coincidence is it?" he finished.

Jane shook her head. "I think it's been sabotaged, Carl."

He sat motionlessly, his elbows perched on his knees, his head balanced on top of his clenched hands. Silence was the only immediate response, and Carl pulled more faces than a five-year-old at a birthday party, but all of them had a degree of seriousness.

"Ok, I wasn't expecting that," he replied, scratching his forehead. But what seemed like a long, awkward silence only lasted a couple of seconds before he responded.

"But why you, why here?" he exclaimed, settling back into his black swivel chair. "So, what exactly did he ask you to do?"

Jane felt the taste of fear slip from her throat, she sat, still awkwardly peeling her nails away, her long, delicate hands spoilt by the tell-tale signs of a bad habit, one she'd had since a child.

Today they had taken even more of a hammering, along with her face, where just a few hours ago there was an artwork of carefully applied makeup showcasing her turquoise eyes, there now appeared a face laid bare for anyone to see her anguish and despair, which Carl could see.

"Destroy the patients' file, don't call the police and after I explained the surgical procedure, he said we were not permitted to shave the head, I mean this man was cold Carl, he was really cold. He's got pictures of my family, who are these people?" she sobbed.

"Very bad people Jane, very bad people" he replied vacantly.

"Can you help me?"

"I'm taking it you don't want to go to the police?"

"I do but I can't, not if it puts my family in harm's way."

Either way, she had committed to sharing her story now, maybe it would be for the better, maybe Carl could still help her. She looked at the silver wall clock behind him. 10:57am

Chapter 9

Friday 27th 23.10

Putting off the inevitable and hanging on to fear did little to make her sprint to the car any easier. In fact, the longer she hesitated the heavier the burden of what she was doing bore down on her.

"You don't have to do this, not for me," said Gill, holding on firmly to the top of her arm.

"I'm doing this for both of us, we need our stuff, maybe the keys are still in the ignition, I could take them out and we could come back later for the car, when they've gone of course," replied Megan trying to raise her sister's hope.

"That sounds good. I don't really care about my car, but I do care about you," said Gill, sincerely.

Megan put her arm around her, pulling her close. The thickly spread canopy above had provided a welcome break from the continuous blanket of rain, if only for a short while. But just as she contemplated the brave dash to the car, a flash of light waving its way back through the forest impelled them to drop to the forest floor, hidden by the wild grasses they waited, watching the light grow nearer and with the frightening sound of deep Russian tongue.

The two men stopped by their car, circled the torches like a lighthouse, the beam sometimes only inches above their head. Minutes later they headed out toward the road and the sound of their vehicle pulling away brought some welcome relief.

"That was way too close for comfort, you ok Gill?"

Gill nodded, but the pain was clear in her expression.

"I'm going to get you some help soon, I need to see if our stuff's still in the car, wait here," she said.

Megan took advantage of the disappearing threat and sprinted to the car, her soaked trainers bellowing under the suction of the forest floor and waterlogged clothing felt uncomfortable. She gently pulled open the door, sat in the driver's seat and closed it again. She was still aware that they could return and took no chances with the interior light. For the second time today she felt more alive than she could remember, a strange concoction of fear and excitement washed over her. But a grounded voice, buried in her subconscious also told her this was no game.

Gill's anguish hung around her like a thick mist, demoralising her to the point of near surrender. Cold, tired, and the dull ache in her arm taking any precedence over being able to think straight, all she could do was wait for Megan to return and get as far away from there as possible.

She imagined what she looked like now, although vanity was not a priority, not like her sister who spent half her life run by impression and presentation, she did understand her job as a corporate hospitality organiser expected her to look her best.

Her senses were now highly stimulated, and she moved quickly, searching the car for any signs of their stuff. Their bags lay open on the rear seat, soaked by the deluge that came in through the space where the rear window once was. Just shards of jagged glass framed the back like a million teeth.

Gill wrestled with her tiredness, like a stalking demon it came and went. But she couldn't let that take over, not while her sister was still out there. Her lips craved the taste of fluid and the small drops of water which crawled down her cheeks only teased the need to quench her burning thirst. She placed one hand across her shoulder feeling for her own blood. Her tight coat which was firm around her swollen arm acted almost like a tourniquet and so far had slowed the loss of blood. She then caught sight of a piercing light, dancing in the distance beyond the next group of trees, not from the road but from deeper in the forest.

The unmistakable feeling of adrenalin was so powerful she could taste it in the back of her throat.

"Oh God, Megan," she chanted to herself.

Megan felt around the passenger seat, her cold, numb fingers grasping at discarded items from both their bags, she was not surprised they had been tampered with, the likelihood of finding their phones was looking slim.

"Shit," she cursed. Her hand moved down to the side of the seats, Gill's diary, makeup bag and a packet of unopened tissues were all she found. No phones. Things were not looking good. She leant to the side of the driver's seat and fumbled around for the ignition barrel. The absence of any keys was also another killer blow.

Gill stood on the very edge of the trees. She noticed the light getting closer, not one light, but two. Then came a faint rumble, a noise beyond that of the woods.

Megan continued to search; the rear footwell was covered in floating paper and leaves.

She raised her head from the seats and a flash of light caught her attention. So intense it stole the darkness, turning the inside of the car to a white haze.

She froze.

Gill was in no doubt about the source of the light. It was another vehicle, coming up the track toward her car. She considered calling out, but she was sure Megan would hear it.

The light and shadows continued moving around the inside of the car, followed by the noise. An engine noise. If she got out now she would surely be spotted, besides she would be running blind. There was no choice, panic gripped her so tightly she felt suffocated by it. She lay down across the back seat, like a blanket of gravel she felt the shards of broken glass eating into her torso, she thought about Gill, hoping she had the sense to run in pursuit of safety. She tried hard to limit the sound of her own erratic breathing.

The noise was only feet away now.

The car was now firmly caught in the approaching headlights, only a few feet behind.

Gill watched in fear as a large figure of a man exited the vehicle, cutting through the headlights and toward her car. She watched as he withdrew a hand-held object from his long-hooded coat, his right hand extended and pointing toward her car.

"No, please Megan, please be out of the car," she chanted, every bone in her body trembled, unable to do anything but look on hoping, praying her sister was out.

In desperation to help her sister, Gill screamed out, trying to cause a distraction, but to no avail. Her dry throat could barely muster a broken cry which was lost, soaked up in the damp and heavy atmosphere. Oblivious to her cry, the figure continued to move to the back of the car.

Megan tried to slow her nervous breathing. On her back looking up, she felt the presence of someone leaning over the back of the car. Flicking between light and shadow was an arm, protruding in through the rear opening, holding a weapon.

Gill dropped to her knees. A torrent of tears spilling from her. Now all she could do was listen as her sister was executed. She lay on her side, on the floor. Waiting for the bang.

Chapter 10

Friday 27th 10.57

Carl was motionless, his large frame still perched on the edge of his seat.

"Ok, so how do you want me to help you?" he asked, temporarily distracted by the flurry of activity on the monitors.

"I need to take the boy's body to them," she said, "but I can't do it on my own."

Carl glared. "Let me get this straight, you want to steal a body which, if I get this right, you say the police have impounded for their own investigations? Have you thought about what you're suggesting?"

"It's not like I have a choice."

"You're serious about this aren't you, does Dale know?"

"No, I don't want to involve him, besides they might know if I contact him, I can't risk putting him in danger, that's why I need your help. If the police take the body, then I'm done. If I take it, then this man gets the body back and my family will be safe."

"Didn't you say they're going to collect it?"

"Yes, but if the police get to it first then, then I don't want to think about what will happen. I know this sounds like a bad idea, but it's all I can think of doing, can you not see that?"

Jane pulled the phone from her pocket and showed him. "They gave me this, once they collect the body, they will call me. Then, well my part is over. Except it isn't because now the police are involved, I don't have the file and they won't have the body, so you see, I have to do this my way."

"That's why you jumped when my phone went off wasn't it? you thought I'd been blackmailed like you."

"I thought maybe they got to you, asked you to stop recording, I told you it's been sabotaged, now you see why I asked you that?"

"No one has approached me, rest assured," he replied.

"So, who else can gain access to your office?"

"Anyone with a master key, including cleaners. I guess it's not that difficult to get."

"Ok," replied Carl, picking up a pen and flicking it against his lips. "I just had an idea; I think I might be able to see who did."

"How?"

"Give me a moment."

Carl faced the monitors and began working the keyboard, the yellow biro protruding from his mouth like a lollipop.

"You see Jane, whoever stopped the recording had to enter this room, which would mean that it would still be recording right up to the point they stopped it, with me so far?" he asked, his fingers dancing across the keys.

"Yeah, but how will that help?" she asked watching the small screens in high-speed reverse.

"If we're lucky, they might have just stopped the recording, removed the lead and not deleted it, if they did, then the camera, the one pointing down this corridor will show them entering this room and..... here we go.... bingo!"

Carl removed the pen from his mouth and tapped the top left monitor. The time showed 8.56am.

She drew her chair closer, her eyes glued to the monitor. There were several people on the screen who passed by the security door, but Jane was concerned with one recognisable face.

Carl noted her reaction.

"Stop there," she hollered.

Carl stopped the tape, it showed a tall thin figure holding the door handle, the image was fuzzy and pixelated, but Jane knew straight away who it was.

"Dr Fuller? I don't believe it," she said.

"You know him?" he asked.

"Yes, well no, I've never seen him before, but I spoke to him this morning, he's a retired doctor, he was here to speak to Dr Johansen I think, it doesn't make any sense."

"Don't think I've ever seen or heard of a Dr Fuller," he replied.

Jane's realisation about the depth of this became frighteningly real.

"Do you think Dr Johansen is in on this too?" he asked rising from his chair and pulling his jacket from the back of the seat.

Jane watched him stand, his giant frame filled the room, she savoured the fact he was on her side, not just because of his size, but the status of his position which would only serve to aid her plan.

"I don't know now; I don't know what to think."

She leant on the desk and pushed herself to her feet. "So, will you help me?" she asked.

"Well it beats the monotony of this place," he replied with a reassuring smile.

"Thanks, I know it's asking a lot."

"Ok, but you sure you really want to do this?" he asked putting on his khaki coloured jacket.

Carl recognised her impatience, she had already made her way to the door. She played various scenarios in her head about how she was going to get the boy out.

"Do you have a plan?" asked Carl as they approached the stairs.

"Half a plan, I will think of something," she replied.

"Well, I kind of expected you to say that and I admire your guts, but I think you better have a damn good excuse for removing a body," said Carl, stopping at the top of the stairs, their voices resonating around the stairwell.

She gripped the rail as they descended toward the morgue. Carl followed. The small lighting did its best to illuminate the bottom of the enclosed stairwell.

Once on the lower ground, they were faced by two large stainless-steel doors, to the left was an intercom with a camera. Carl nudged Jane and indicated with his head to the camera above.

"Don't worry it's not recording, remember," said Carl.

Jane's hand wavered before pressing the intercom. "Here goes," she said, taking a deep breath.

After a short silence, a male voice crackled from the intercom and she replied, giving her name and position on the staff. She gazed up at the camera, Carl stood slightly to the left behind her. Although the two square windows in the door were opaque, it didn't stop Jane trying to peer through. A metallic clunk echoed like the gates of hell itself were opening, making her flinch nervously.

This was not like anywhere else in the hospital, it was a sign of mortal destiny, an undeniable reminder of our fate. She had seen plenty of dead bodies and some patients had even drawn their last breath against her own skin, but here death was just so clinical, all part of the process.

A slender dark skinned figure of a man stood before her; his blue coveralls had all the tell-tale signs of a recent autopsy. He pulled off his purple latex gloves and disposed of them in the bin to his left. She had seen him about the hospital, but their separate roles meant they rarely met.

"Can I help you, Nurse Stevens?" he asked, standing in the doorway.

"Yes, we've come to take the John Doe, brought down an hour ago?" she asked, trying her best to sound assertive and hoping her authority would hold some weight.

Carl butted in, sensing further explanation would be justified with his presence.

"We've come to take the body so the police can conduct a forensic investigation, I'm here to ensure that the body is not tampered with," continued Carl.

Jane was impressed by his interjection, she even salvaged a befitting smile to the morgue APT.

The morgue APT stood holding the metal door, glancing at Jane and Carl in bewilderment. His stance was firm and not inviting at all despite their best performance and confidence, which crumbled quickly with his retort.

"With all due respect I have strict instructions from Dr Johansen not to let the body out of my sight, and I'm told their own pathologist will examine the body here. This is secured evidence. Now unless you have signed paperwork I can't let you near the body, I hope you understand," he replied.

Once more she sank into submission, her plan had now been shot down in a blaze.

She didn't notice Carl move, not straight away. Her conscious mind was not yet ready to deal with any proactive intervention, she needed time to get her head together. Her body language was a signal of defeat, but before the awkwardness of her request sank in, she caught sight of an arm, a flash of dark jacket scouted past her and the sound of metal rang out as the half-open door swung back against the metal bin. The quiet room, free from the comings and goings of the living, a room buried beneath the bowels of the hospital was now stolen, in its place was now mayhem, ungainly and random.

She took a second before she realised what had happened, in that time, Carl had hold of the morgue pathologist, his large vice-like hands gripping the side of his neck. There was a small struggle, a lashing out, followed by a thump as his body dropped to the floor.

"Well don't just stand there, go get the boy," said Carl, the pathologist's body lying twisted before his feet. He then noted Jane's disapproving stare of horror. "Oh, don't worry he's not dead, just unconscious," he replied quickly.

She was surprised by Carl's sudden and seemingly violent actions. Had she in fact been a fool to trust him? Her emotional state at present was not a reliable one, and her judgments were not rational. But she was here, and a step closer to securing the boy into her care, and ultimately saving her family. She watched Carl from the doorway as he removed a mobile phone from the lifeless body and removed the SIM card. His actions were not interrupted by hesitancy and she could only paint a picture of Carl as she saw him.

"You've done this before haven't you?" she asked, moving into the room.

Carl stopped for a moment, straddled over the body and looked at her. "I had a life before this, let's just leave it there," he replied coldly.

She didn't want to press him anymore; this was not the time and definitely not the place.

The room felt repressive, lacking windows with only artificial lighting in which to work. In the middle, a white stone slab was the focal point, mid autopsy, the open chest of a corpse laid bare in a deep pool of blood and bodily fluids. To the side, an aluminium dish held the freshly removed heart and other organs, some still on the scales. Various shiny metal tools were laid out on a tall aluminium table, some still coated in flesh and blood. Even Jane found this place uncomfortable, carrying its own unmistakable odour.

She made her way toward the far end of the room, to the steel body lockers, four on the top and four underneath, looking for the label that said *'John Doe'* she pulled open the stainless casket and there, covered in a white sheet lay the boy, she respectfully pulled back the sheet, his white skin a contrast against his raven black, curly hair. She wanted to get this over with, sensing an overpowering feeling of dread which came over her.

She stood to the side of the body looking at his innocent face, wondering how this boy's life had been and now even after death, a careless death, he was important. She thought about the callous men who brought him in and gently stroked his hair.

"You sure you want to do this?" asked Carl, standing the other side of the gurney. "You know there's no going back after this."

"I don't see that I have any other choice, it's already too late for that, I can't have this threat hanging over my family.

"Just be careful, these people won't take kindly to blackmail, I just hope you've weighed up the odds," replied Carl, looking at the boy.

"What do you mean odds? I'm not blackmailing them," said Jane inquisitively.

"I mean I just hope the boy's importance to them is outweighed by their need to punish you for trying to barter with them, for the safety of your family, they will see that as blackmail, it's something you need to consider," he replied.

"If I let the boy fall into the hands of the police then I *will* be punished."

She continued stroking the boy's hair. "So, I don't actually have a choice," she replied, pulling a tissue from a box and dabbing her teary eyes.

"There may be another solution," said Carl.

"Ok, what's that?" she asked, laying eyes on the still lifeless body, incapacitated by Carl's hands.

"Later. We need to move the boy first, I have somewhere you can lay low for now," he replied, handing her another tissue.

Carl pulled a pen from his jacket pocket and then took Jane's hand. He wrote an address on the palm of her hand and the location to the key.

"Take my vehicle, in case they're watching yours, it's a white van parked around the side, use the emergency exit, it's not alarmed, just make sure you're not seen, I will grab your keys from your locker and take your car, that way I can take alternative steps to get to you."

"I thought we were both doing this?" she quizzed.

"It will buy you some time, besides, the police will be here soon."

Jane was puzzled by Carl's intentions and the sacrifice he was clearly making. She took Carl's hand this time and shook it. "Thank you," she said with sincerity.

"I never liked this job anyway; besides, I have other plans." He smiled. "Now go."

Jane wheeled the gurney across the room and entered the lift reserved for the movement of bodies. She surfaced towards the back of the hospital and pushed the gurney a few yards to the emergency exit at the side of the hospital. She peered through the glass, spotting the white van parked against an adjacent hedge. There was a small amount of hesitation before she dashed with the gurney across the small area reserved for deliveries and security. She was oblivious to her surroundings, instead focusing on the white van. She took his keys, quickly swinging open the rear doors. She slid the body off the gurney and into the back of the van, abandoning the metal gurney by the exit.

She jumped into the driver's seat, instantly overcome with nerves. She took a moment to gather herself, catching a glance in the rear-view mirror before twisting the key. She didn't recognise herself now, once a mother, kind, caring, even sexy and self-assured. But now all she saw was the face of a devious criminal. But she needed to stay focused on why she was doing this.

Chapter 11

Friday 27th 11:53am

Carl hoped that Jane had managed to get the boy out of the hospital. He didn't really think too hard about why he helped her. He was baffled by the extreme circumstances she described, especially when she identified a doctor, tampering with security equipment.

He dragged the pathologist body onto a chair, despite his earlier actions he didn't want him to be in any discomfort when he came around. His attentions though were stolen by approaching footsteps, echoing down the stairs. Acting quickly, he found a suitable place to hide, a small walk-in cupboard to the side of the morgue which was used to keep clothing and other medical items. He was not prepared for any visitors just yet and feared the discovery of the unconscious pathologist would raise some alarms. He switched his phone to silent and turned off his walkie talkie.

As he stood listening in the semi-darkness, he wrestled with images of his past. His mind served up images of war, the bloodshed and the sound of bullets whistling inches from his head. Comrades screaming and the helplessness of just watching as their lives slipped away in front of him. He saw the face of a woman and young child, standing under a half-ruined arch, her face contorted with panic, begging for help. He knew these were brought on by the current situation, his counsellor had told him to avoid prolonged periods of stress, and here he was in the middle of a drama, but he managed to push these to the back of his mind. For now, at least.

The door was already open when he heard someone enter. The footsteps were erratic and impatient. Various metallic noises and the sound of aluminium lockers could be heard, echoing around the room.

The footsteps stopped for a moment.

"Hello, its Fuller here, I've got some bad news, the body has gone. I'm convinced the nurse must have him."

Carl remained motionless, disturbed by the call.

"No sign of the nurse or the security guard, do you want me to find her?"

There was a pause. "Ok, no problem."

Carl had heard enough, deciding intervention was required. He appeared from hiding to find Dr Fuller pulling a phone similar to the one Jane had from his pocket.

"I wouldn't if I were you," said Carl glaring at him.

Carl was intimidating enough given his size, but Fullers late years and gangly build made Carl's assertiveness more poignant.

His sudden appearance sparked a flash of worry across the doctor's face, leaving him open-mouthed.

"You have no idea what you're interfering with," he snarled, his saggy cheeks blemished with red.

Carl moved toward him. "Hand me the phone," he instructed, extending his hand.

"What have you done with the boy?" asked Dr Fuller.

"That's not your concern, you need to tell me who you're about to call," he demanded.

"She has him, doesn't she? The nurse."

Carl reached for his throat, pinning him against the steel body lockers. "I don't have time for games, I need to know what the hell is going on in this hospital," he seethed.

The doctor's face turned to a rich shade of red before he released his grip and he fell to the ground holding his throat.

Carl took the phone from him. "Tell me what's going on before the police arrive," he asked.

Dr Fuller cleared his throat. "Someone was already on their way to collect the boy, they weren't happy when I told them he's gone," he said, still rubbing his throat.

"So how exactly are you wrapped up in all of this, who's pulling your chain, because this isn't the behaviour of a doctor."

Dr Fuller glanced up at him. "I could ask you the same thing, you're going to have a lot of explaining to do, especially when *he* comes around." He nodded toward the pathologist slumped on the chair in the corner.

"Let me worry about that, you need to tell me what's going on or you'll be spending the night in one of those body lockers. I know it was you that sabotaged my equipment, so tell me, why would a retired doctor be doing something like that?"

"You have no idea what you're sticking your nose into," said Fuller.

Carl said nothing, he reached toward the nearest shiny locker against the back wall and opened the square stainless-steel door, exposing the cold empty metal container, as he grabbed his shirt, Dr Fuller held his hands up.

"Ok, stop. I'll tell you, but you won't win against these people."

Carl pulled him up onto a chair with little effort. "Ok, start talking," he said impatiently.

He straightened his shirt, loosening another button in a hope his breathing would be less strained. "I'm not a doctor," he started. "My name is Jack Fuller, I'm a private investigator."

"Ok, go on," said Carl.

"I had a visit yesterday morning, at my office, by a man who called himself Max, nicely dressed, well-spoken, Russian accent." Fuller rubbed his throat, still sore from Carl's grasp.

"So, he blackmailed you as well?" asked Carl.

"No, he didn't, he offered me a job, one day's work for ten thousand pounds, I nearly choked on my coffee. Now I've had some weird and unusual requests over the years, but I knew this was going to be something underhand and illegal. You don't get that kind of money for one day's work unless it's dangerous or illegal."

"But you accepted it anyway because you're unscrupulous," replied Carl.

"I don't have any family to blackmail, I have one grown-up daughter, she lives in South Africa. I lost my wife four years ago and my business is not exactly thriving. It would take me months of work to earn that and I want to be able to see my daughter before it's too late. The money is for her," he said.

"So, it's ok for you to destroy other people's lives, as long as you get your money?" snapped Carl. "So, what exactly did you have to do for this money?" he continued.

"I had to do surveillance on some staff, you know, take pictures of their families and stuff, then the photos were collected from me at the end of the day, I had to disarm the surveillance system, stealing a master key was pretty straightforward. Then I followed Nurse Stevens and the other staff to retrieve information on the boy's condition and report any problems. I was their eyes. I stole staff ID, changed the picture and just wandered around the hospital. I felt sorry for the nurse, we spoke in the lift, I knew they had shown her the pictures, I saw her pain. I even tried to get her to talk," he said, gazing up at Carl's towering statue.

"You're no better than them."

"Like her, I didn't have a choice, yes, they bought my time, but they put it in such a way that I couldn't really say no, otherwise I might have been in one of those lockers already."

"I heard you on the phone, what was that about?"

Fuller smiled. "I offered to find her, but they said I don't need to, it won't be a problem."

"And me?" asked Carl, sideways glancing the pathologist in the chair.

"I followed you both, I knew she had told you, I watched her go into your room, I told them and they said I had to keep an eye on you two, they already had someone on the way to collect the body. They're going to be very pissed off, she should have just let things go and not interfered," said Fuller angrily.

"She's trying to do the right thing, to protect her family."

"You need to know they're going to call a guy called Felix, I understand he is the one tracking her down."

"You mean he's going to kill her," stated Carl.

Fuller shrugged. "Probably, I didn't really ask, they're not the sort of people you ask questions of. It's too late, they know she has the boy, they've probably called him by now."

"What about her family?" asked Carl.

"They're not interested, they just used the photos to blackmail her. But they will kill her, especially now."

"She intends to hand him over, she was just taking him before the police did," he said still casting an occasional eye on the pathologist. "Why is the boy that important to them, especially now that he's dead?"

"I don't know, they didn't say why," he replied.

Carl pulled up a chair opposite, rubbed his chin and brushed his short spiky hair back and forth. "This doesn't make sense; I mean they only brought the boy in this morning."

"So?"

"Don't you see, if they asked you yesterday to do the surveillance on Jane and whoever else here, that means this was planned in advance, which means that boy must have been shot more than a day ago, and yet they leave it until this morning to bring him in. I just don't see why they would go to all this trouble and planning, even less so now that he's dead."

"They didn't say he was shot to me, they just told me a boy was being brought in today needing treatment and I was to follow their instructions, that's all."

Carl sat back in the chair and gave another flash look to the still unconscious pathologist. He was direct with his next question. "So, what's your daughter's name?"

Fuller frowned. "Emily. Why?"

"Do you have a picture of her?"

"Yes, why do you want to know?" he asked cautiously.

"Curious, you said you want to go see her."

Fuller removed his wallet from his back pocket and gently removed a folded picture of his daughter, standing next to a large disfigured tree.

"She's pretty. How old is she here? Where in South Africa does she live?" he asked.

"She sent me that picture six months ago, she's thirty-seven now, we had her late in life," he said, sharing the picture with Carl. "She lives in a small town called Montagu, near Johannesburg. She's a teacher, started out doing relief work for the UN and ended up staying. I miss her a lot," said Fuller, his eyes glazing over.

Carl folded the photo and tucked it in his top pocket, then stood from his chair and handed the phone back to Fuller.

"Can I have the photo back, please?" asked Fuller extending his hand.

Carl shook his head. "Nope, I will tell you what you're going to do now. You're going to disappear before whoever is coming turns up, and in one hour, you are going to call this Max and tell him that Jane has the body at this address." Carl took his pen and wrote the address on Fuller's hand, just as he did with Jane. "If you phone a second earlier or this Felix arrives at this address before I do then I will make sure this picture gets to them with her name and where she lives, telling them exactly what you told me," he said sternly.

"You bastard," said Fuller rising from his chair to face Carl.

"And I thought you were the private investigator, sucks when someone messes with your family doesn't it?" he replied, making his way to the door. "Remember, one hour. Maybe we'll both come out of this."

Chapter 12

Friday 27th 12.38pm

As Jane drove away from the hospital and the busy streets of Blackwater, she couldn't help but allow some of her emotions to spill. Tears rolled down her face and gathered on her chin. She was now placing her trust with Carl and by doing so, maybe her life.

As the town disappeared from the rearview and closer to the lane he was sending her to, it all became a little scary. She questioned her judgment. Could she trust Carl? Was the place she was heading to safe? But she took some comfort from at least having the boy, and a step further to relinquishing her family from any harm. She felt a mild but reassuring optimism.

She noted the address, loosely scribed on her hand. She knew the road vaguely, a narrow lane, a few miles off the main road, it led down to a small loch, often used by local anglers and sightseers.

Halfway down the narrow road on the left-hand side stood a three-story Victorian house, the bleakness of its location gave the impression of safety, but at this moment she did not feel anything like safe.

Set back slightly from the road and surrounded on two sides by a natural hedge line and bare fields all around, it's red brick and charming architecture looked welcoming enough but not the sort of place she envisaged Carl living in.

She pulled the van on to a small concrete drive which wound to the right of the house. She entered with a key which she retrieved from a nearby drain cover, just as Carl had instructed her to.

She entered a large hallway. The original ornate decretive floor and period features you would expect to see in a Victorian house remained, but decor beyond that was very much a mix of dated modern and shabby antique. Only a couple of dark oak carved bookcases to the left of the stairs in the hallway looked period. She turned left and into the lounge, the large full-length sash window appeared tired, its timber frame barely hanging onto the ageing paint and came with its customary rattle every time the wind made its presence. The window was framed by floor-length red velvet curtains and centred by a fine weaved cream net and looked out towards the lane, giving her a viewpoint of the road and more importantly approaching people.

She scouted the room, the deep red matching velvet sofa looked inviting, but she was too nervous to sit. She took the opportunity to explore a few of the rooms. A stale smell touched her senses as she wandered from room to room and something odd occurred to her. There were no photos anywhere in the flat, no evidence of a life spent, no family portraits. Only a few old-fashioned prints framed in tacky gold gilded frames hung around the gold and cream floral wallpaper. She thought this strange. The decor had seen better days, the large feature wall towards the back of the lounge displayed yet another neglected feature, its corners falling back revealing the presence of black mould. The high Victorian skirting was original as was the twisted patterned coving above.

She opened the door to the rear of the lounge and wandered into the dining room beyond. Again it was stifled and possessed little furniture, other than a round dark, oak carved table and matching chairs, all requiring fresh upholstery.

She felt more than slightly uncomfortable. Here she was in a strange house, having driven someone else's van that contained the body of a dead teenager. She could not be more removed from normal if she tried.

Her curiosity was justified for a moment, her reasoning for infiltrating personal space was driven by self-preservation and a need to put some trust in Carl, so she rifled through a few drawers and cupboards, a tall light wood sideboard occupied the space towards the back of the lounge, its contents contained only old paperwork and household oddities. Her nervousness did not stall her attention and she focused back on the large bay window where she peered out again, moving the heavy stained net curtain to one side. With her anxiety rising, she glanced at a silver wall clock which hung above the large white marble Victorian fireplace. It was 13:25. She decided to give Carl thirty minutes, then she would call Max and take her chances in delivering the boy.

After exploring the rooms, she took a moment to freshen up. The downstairs bathroom off the kitchen was large and still had the original iron bath and large square Victorian sink, complemented by a dripping tap. Its small square frosted window was suffocated by tangled foliage from the garden which engulfed the rear of the house. It was clear this house lacked recent attention and maintenance. She looked bewilderingly into the mirrored cabinet above the sink wondering how much further she would be consumed by this surreal situation. Her face was not the one she left home with this morning; her turquoise eyes had lost the sparkle, even bathing her face in warm water did little to hide her anguish.

She could not imagine how such a place like this could be occupied by an ex-military man. His previous life in the army would have been controlled by meticulous order and routine, even to the extent of being OCD. Something didn't sit right with her, it gnawed away at her. Maybe it was her subconscious telling her not to trust him. She decided, when the time was right, to question him on this.

Feeling refreshed, she paced the lounge once again. Each time towards the bay window, glancing out toward the lane, which was narrow and seldom used. Other than access to the loch and local beauty spot, traffic here was rare, so any sound outside brought her attention back to the window.

She glanced the clock again, 13:35. This time, as she looked out again, Carl's large figure approached swiftly up the drive and she dashed to the door.

"Jane, you ok?" he asked, his lungs yearning for oxygen and his words erratic between breaths. "Glad you made it here alright."

She frowned. "You ran? Where's my car?" she asked.

"Parked up the road, didn't want it spotted here, I'm betting they know your car."

He wasted no time in ushering her to the small dining room beyond the lounge.

"Did you manage to sort things out at the hospital?" she asked as he gestured her to sit.

She pulled out the heavy carved chair and sat, her hands on the table nervously picking at her nails.

Carl removed his khaki jacket and flung it over the back of his chair, his face was a layer of sweat and she could feel the heat radiating from him.

"We don't have long so it's very important you do exactly what I tell you," he said leaning on the table.

"I already know what I'm going to do, I need to call this Max, hand them the boy."

"Not that simple Jane, you need to hear me out," he said.

She removed the phone from her pocket, placed it on the table in front of him and folded her arms.

"Tell me why I shouldn't call Max and just hand over the boy. I mean that was the idea all along wasn't it?"

Carl leant back on his chair, the dark wood frame creaking under his stocky frame. He had to be frank with her, frighten her even, but there was a woman consumed by a need to save her family and to that end, oblivious to the trappings of the world she thought lay only in stories.

"Go on then," he replied, pushing the phone towards her. "But, you might just want to hear what I have to say first before you do."

She rubbed her hands down the sides of her uniform, her leg twitching, enough to vibrate the lose wooden floor underfoot. "I've had enough of games, I just want this nightmare over with," she replied. "Either you want to help me, or you don't," she finished scornfully.

Carl changed the direction of conversation; he was cautious about the time he had before Felix could show up.

"Look, just after you left, I bumped into Fuller."

"Dr Fuller?" she asked, her eyes widening slightly. "What did he have to say?" Her voice a pitch higher with surprise.

"Well to start with, he's not a Doctor, his name is Jack Fuller, he's a private investigator. Long story short, he was also blackmailed, well to a degree by these people whoever they are to watch you and other staff. He's the one that took the pictures of your family."

She placed a hand over her mouth, surprised by his revelation.

"They paid him to find out about your family, then they collected the pictures, but they don't actually know themselves where your family is, it appears they just used the pictures to blackmail you."

"Are you kidding me?" She stood from her chair and started to pace the room.

"They are not interested in your family, it's you they want, but that's not going to happen. I don't think just handing over the boy now is quite as straight forward as you might think."

She gave a long exhale. "I don't believe this, this is ridiculous, so what now?" she asked, still pacing the small room and eyeing the large oak wardrobe in the corner.

Despite the rather worn burgundy rug which lay shy of the full wooden floor on all sides, her pacing had the floor beneath creaking with each step.

Carl looked at his watch. "Look, I need you to listen carefully, one of them is coming here for you," he continued, his eyes following her as she continued to pace back and forth.

She turned on the spot. "You're joking, right?"

"Let me finish. Fuller also had a phone, like the one they gave you, he was under the impression they would send a guy called Felix to hunt you down, and I don't have to tell you how that supposed to play out."

Carl was still seated; his grey eyes following her movements.

"Oh, this just gets better and better. I can't do this, I'm sorry."

Carl stood from his chair, his large hands reaching for her arm, but Jane's impatience had her already out of the room and approaching the door.

"Jane, wait," he shouted, following her. He grabbed the top of her arm as she drew open the door, tears forming once more on her cheeks.

"Jane, I can't let you leave. I'm sorry it's too dangerous. If this Felix sees you, he will kill you, as far as they are concerned you interrupted their plan, regardless of your best intensions. According to Fuller they already had someone coming for the body, I'm guessing before the police. He won't care about any sob story you have to offer. They just want their boy. Period. You need to understand these are not reasonable people, they don't live in our world."

She removed his hand from the top of her arm.

"Look, I appreciate you trying to help me, I'm confused and feel like I'm going to wake up any minute with my kids jumping on my bed telling me they're hungry, but that's not going to happen, is it?" Jane let go of the handle and leant back against the door, resting her head against the frosted pane. "I need to make a couple of phone calls."

She noted the white wall-mounted phone in the kitchen, nestled under the yellowed pine cabinets.

"I need to use your landline to call the school. I need to get my children to somewhere safe."

In all the commotion she had failed to make sure her children were out of harm's way. She was angry with herself, she had let the situation override her instinct to protect her family. She turned the watch pinned to her uniform and checked the time. 14.10.

Carl's attention was focused beyond the kitchen and to the lane outside. He was unusually quiet in thought and clearly unresponsive to her. Realising his mind was occupied, she asked again. "Did you hear me, Carl?"

She mirrored his behaviour for a second and found herself staring out of the window.

"You're waiting for this Felix guy to come here aren't you? To kill me." She shivered at the thought. Her arms were an explosion of goose pimples and she rubbed them quickly.

Carl withdrew from his thoughts for now and slipped into the lounge, ignoring her momentarily. It was clear to her that he was preoccupied with something. She followed inquisitively and watched as Carl's size made small work of moving the red velvet chair across the lounge and facing it dead centre of the doorway, lining it up with the hallway.

"What the hell are you doing?" she quizzed, watching him play furniture charades.

He stopped for a brief second and responded. "Make your calls, make them quick and don't say anything about your situation."

Jane shook her head, more than slightly annoyed at Carl's comment, assuming all blondes lack the intelligence to decipher what is appropriate to say and what not to say. "Oh, I was going to call the local paper and tell them my story," she retorted.

Carl smiled. "Sarcasm, least you still have that, not sure I would."

"It's not humour, it's an attack on your intelligence, to assume I'm an idiot. Don't worry, if you're confused, I will explain it to you slowly."

Carl grinned. "Now that was sarcastic."

She left the lounge and picked up the phone in the kitchen, planning to secure the safety of her children.

Carl didn't ask about her calls, besides, he heard most of the conversation and knew intervening between a mother and her children was going to be a dead-end, instead, he just asked if they were safe.

"I have a relative picking them up, they will be safe," she replied quietly.

"What about your husband?" he asked.

"Oh, he's away on business, I don't want to involve him, I don't even know what to say to him. You going to tell me what you're up to?" she asked, changing the subject and trying not to dwell on her family.

"Something's been bugging me since I got here, something Fuller said they were going to do," he remarked, moving a tall thin brass lamp across the lounge and plugging it in by the bay window.

"What's that?" she asked, still watching him manoeuvre the furniture about.

"Something Fuller said, I didn't think too much about it at the time, remember I told you he had a phone like the one they gave you?"

"Yes, why?"

"He called this Max, offered to find you, but he told me they already had someone on it."

"Yes, so you keep reminding me. What about it?"

Carl stopped for a moment, grabbed his waistline and pulled his trousers up, it was clear he had lost some weight; the black trousers presenting some fitting issues.

"Hand me the phone they gave you please," he said, holding out his hand.

Jane, looking puzzled, pulled the phone from her uniform pocket and handed it to him.

"Who are you calling, Max?" she asked.

"Nope, no one. I gave Fuller this address, told him to call Max in one hour and let him know you're here. But if I hadn't, how would this Felix know where to find you?"

Carl pulled off the back of the phone, his large fingers prying something from inside. Jane moved closer and looked on as he removed a small round silver disc from inside the phone and held it up in front of her. "Just as I thought," he exclaimed.

"Is that a bug? Have we been bugged all this time?" she asked staring at the silver disc.

"Not exactly, it's a locator, not difficult to get hold of, they can track you to within a few feet, that's how Felix will find you." Carl placed the locator back in the phone.

"What the hell are you doing?" she asked trying to snatch the phone from him.

"It's ok, I'm going to use the phone as bait, set Felix up, maybe get some answers."

Jane crossed the lounge to where Carl had positioned the sofa, this time she embraced its soft offerings. She was conscious of her swollen, heavy eyes, and could have easily surrendered them to sleep, but she didn't. Carl sat on the arm of the sofa.

"What are you planning Carl?" she asked.

He ignored her question and handed back the phone. She was hesitant about taking it at first but eventually took it from him.

"I want you to call Max, tell him you have the boy and you want to meet, tell him where you are, but he will know that anyway."

There was silence. Not the usual ambient lack of sound. Sure, the house was quiet, apart from a ticking wall clock and the sound the wind made against the ill-fitting window, but this was a different silence, a calm before a storm that told her she was playing ball in a different league. This was now Carl's territory, she knew that Carl was more than capable of dealing with situations like this, but still found herself asking questions of him.

She leaned forward, her hands rubbing nervously on the tops of her legs.

"What did you do in the army? Why did you leave?" she asked directly.

Carl dropped his gaze and stared at the kaleidoscope of worn coloured threads in the carpet. "I was wondering when you were going to ask about me, and I guess you deserve some answers, being that I expect you to trust me," he said, returning eye contact.

"I was part of a reconnaissance team, set up to withdraw priority targets, government officials, political

VIP's. It was unofficial, below radar stuff, even now I'm not allowed to say who sanctioned these missions. One day we were in a high alert military zone, Afghanistan, me and two other colleagues were sent to extract a local diplomat who had Intel on an underground bunker which supposedly contained bomb-making equipment, it looked like a regular mission, we agreed to meet him, it was dusk, we had an armoured vehicle parked just around the corner, it was supposed to be a snatch and grab. Anyway, we get to the safe house, he's there waiting, but as my two colleagues went to escort him out, he told them his wife and new-born son would come with him, they weren't part of the deal."

"You left them?" interrupted Jane.

"I didn't want to, I tried to persuade my colleagues to take them too but they just spouted orders are orders, she wasn't a British citizen. I had no choice. We grabbed our man, who wouldn't stop begging us to take her, but we had to leave them. I remember her face, holding their son as we dragged him away."

"What happened after?" she asked.

"We got the intel eventually, but we learnt three days later, that they tortured and killed his wife and baby. I left shortly after, even now I have flashbacks of her face. I learnt that day that sometimes it's not the enemy that make victims, we make our own victims by our own actions. That day we tortured them, not the enemy."

"How long ago was that?"

"Just over two years now, shortly after my mother died. I'd already lost my father when I was young. You see, this is my mother's house, I have a place a few miles north of here, but I stay here because it's close to work, it needs work, one day I will restore it."

Jane smiled at him, feeling relieved that he included to tell her about the house. She responded with sincerity.

"I trust you Carl; I want you to know that."

He stood quickly, without saying anything, he moved into the dining room, his large, black boots did little to make his pace quiet. She looked on as he bent down and lifted the corner of the large rug in the dining room, exposing the dark, oak flooring. She watched intently as he lifted a loose board from one end of the room and withdrew an object wrapped in a light grey rag. More than slightly curious, she sat upright and edged forward from the sofa as he returned to the lounge and placed the object on the glass-topped coffee table. He then sat on the edge of the chair he had previously moved. She didn't have a chance to ask what the object was. Before she even considered asking, Carl had unwrapped the object from its oily, discarded t-shirt and revealed a handgun, complete with a detachable suppressor. She was more than shocked. This was the second time today someone had revealed a gun to her. Admittedly this was not for the purpose to threaten, but still, it gave her a feeling of uneasiness. She combed her fingers through her hair, its tangled strands resisting on occasion, she felt sticky, uncomfortable, her uniform felt tight, and she craved a hot shower.

She cleared her throat; it was a nervous action. "You going to use that, on Felix? This is way too deep for me, I don't want to get involved in this, no way am I going to be involved in murder, I will take my chances with the boy, I will call Max like you asked, see what he says. No one needs to get hurt Carl."

Jane's statement fell on deaf ears as he fiddled with the firearm, pulling the clip from the handle, exposing the gold-tipped ammo before snapping it back into place. Every metallic click and operation of the firearm had her flinching. Although she trusted him, she didn't bargain on killing anyone. As he embraced the gun, wiping its black surface religiously with the rag, he remained quiet for a time. He was a little frustrated by the naivety of her and her perception of this other world she was now thrust in to.

Carl placed the gun on the table and clenched his hands.

"Jane this is not a reality you're used to, I know. We're different, you fix people, I just... well, get rid of bad people, or used to." His voice was not condemning or judgmental. "As I said before, these people don't play by any rules, if you're lucky they will kill you instantly, if you're unlucky they will torture you first, they don't show compassion, they see that as a sign of weakness. You're a small cog in a big wheel, these criminals planned everything around making sure this boy's identity was kept a secret, from manipulating a private detective to controlling and blackmailing. That takes planning and money." Carl did not once raise his voice, he spoke directly, hoping his message would get through. Jane listened to Carl, occasionally glancing at the gun on the table, a stark reminder of something very serious. "They had everything under control until you took the boy. We took that control. I had no idea at the time how big this was. Doesn't matter that you thought you were doing the right thing, it's too late for that now, Felix will come here, and he will kill you," he said softly.

"I know what you're doing Carl," she replied, responding in an equally direct manner. "You're trying to save me, not from them but from yourself, you think by saving me your guilt over not saving that woman and child will vanish. It won't Carl. I'm not your answer."

Carl shrugged his shoulders, he did not try to defend her statement, perhaps she was right, but he still needed to conclude this mission, that's how he saw it now, a mission. Not just helping a colleague. He would be more focused that way.

"Either you trust me, or you don't. It's your call Jane. But I would rather you didn't leave."

He waited for her reply, he didn't push, just sat in the silence of the house. Occasionally the wind whipped the tangled bushes that lay pressed against the dining room window, its scraping sound breaking the intervals of silence.

She quickly realised that in order to get through this she would need to surrender to his plan, but the thought of someone's life possibly being taken in the process left a bitter taste in her mouth.

She surrendered. "Ok, so what am I supposed to do in all of this?"

He checked his watch as he stood, realising the hour he gave Fuller to call had been and gone. He couldn't be sure where Felix would be coming from, but he doubted it would be far, and it would be with silence and stealth.

"Ok, I want you to go to the first-floor bedroom on the left and remove your uniform, you will find some clothes in the wardrobe, then bring me your uniform."

Carl moved towards the side of the bay window, staring out toward the lane and the field beyond. Access to the house was difficult without being spotted. The rear entrance was blocked by years of neglected garden. At least for visitors.

She entered the bedroom and was greeted by a large, brass-framed bed filling the room, three drawer cabinets on each side, nothing on top other than a black anglepoise lamp. The room had an all too familiar smell that old houses have, stale and damp. A large, oak wardrobe with ornate legs and a carved arched pelmet presented an assortment of clothes, some were floral beyond belief, but Jane ignored an urge to have a one-woman discussion on the art of a dead woman's fashion. She didn't want to spend a minute longer in here than she had to. She picked out a pair of black trousers and a long, cream coat. Remarkably, they fitted perfectly.

With uniform in hand, she returned to the lounge, her anxiety rising, but this was nothing compared to the shock she felt on discovering Carl, manhandling a shop mannequin onto the sofa. The life-size plastic mannequin was naked, but unlike any other mannequin this had black circles drawn on in various places, each had several numbers scribbled next to them, almost mathematical. More unsettling, there was what looked like bullet holes, centre right around the chest and several in the forehead. She could only guess now why Carl wanted her uniform.

"You need to get a real girlfriend," smiled Jane, nervously, even in this tense situation she felt a little humour might just help things along.

Carl turned to see her dressed in his mother's clothes, he didn't want to spoil the moment by making any remark, but instead just replied to her light-hearted comment. "She's nice, not as chatty as you though," he chuckled. Jane handed him her blue uniform which he then proceeded to dress the mannequin in.

"I know what you're thinking," he said pulling a blonde wig from a carrier bag. Carl was still too preoccupied with dressing the mannequin to look at her.

"The only way you stay ahead of the game is practice. My commanding officer was not the usual run of the mill textbook trainer, he said anyone can shoot at a round target, but the human body has shape and form, and depending on where you hit depends on whether they stay down or shoot back. Each number represents a distance I have shot from, it also enables me to calibrate my weapon which is equally important. There, that will do," he said standing back from the mannequin and admiring its effectiveness.

She couldn't help but feel humoured by the model of herself.

Carl placed the blonde wig onto the mannequin and then sat it on the sofa making sure the head and shoulders were above the height of the sofa, which he had previously positioned with its back to the window.

Jane approached the mannequin, removed her hairband and tied the wig back, just like her own hair.

"We don't have much time, call Max now. Do exactly what I say."

She nodded, biting her bottom lip. She picked up the phone from the table in readiness.

Carl was stood by the side of the window, periodically looking back to her with instructions.

"Tell Max you have the boy. Tell him you want to meet him, it's very important you tell him you are at this address."

She was struck by nervous tension, it had been a while since she spoke to Max, he had a way of intimidating her. She didn't know whether to stand or sit but pacing seemed to be the thing she did best under stress. She pressed the call button, several rings later, his voice haunted her once more.

"Nurse Stevens," said Max calmly. "Where is my boy?"

"I have him," she hesitated. "He is with me, I will give you an address, I can explain—"

He cut her off, she looked at Carl, still rubbernecking between her and the window.

A few seconds later the phone vibrated in her hand, and she jumped.

"Hello?" she said timidly.

"You will not negotiate with me, do you understand?" he said in a stern voice.

"Yes, sorry," she replied quietly, looking down at the intricate patterns in the carpet.

"Pines Café, be there at 8.30pm."

The phone went dead. She placed it back on the table.

"What did he say?" asked Carl still guarding the window.

She told him what Max had said.

"I don't like this, I'm not happy about you going."

She didn't feel like arguing, there was no point anymore, she just focused on the end result.

She couldn't wait to leave this house; she paced the lounge again.

Carl picked up the phone form the table and placed it on the sofa next to the mannequin.

"Why are you still going ahead with this charade?" she asked, watching him put the finishing touches to the mannequin. "I have my ending," she stated.

Carl stood back from the settee and took her hand, leading her into the dining room and sat her down again, her clammy hands fidgeting in her lap.

"Ok, here's the deal." Carl placed the van keys on the table which he had retrieved from her uniform. "You can take the van now and do this on your own, leave here, do what you want, or you can stay here, trust me and end this my way. I don't want your blood on my hands. I can't change who you are, you're trusting of people, and only see good intentions, you're a nurse it's your job, your disposition. I get that," he said as softly as he could.

"I'm just confused, I don't know what to think anymore." She picked up the keys and played with them in her hand, flicking them between her fingers, then handed them to Carl.

"Ok, you want me to trust you, I need to know what you're doing, moving the furniture, the mannequin, why I shouldn't meet Max? What's going on Carl?"

"Ok, firstly Max was just buying time, he'll call Felix, that's a definite. If Fuller didn't get a chance to tell him where we are like I asked, he will trace the phone, more than likely he will wait until darkness, he knows he has about five hours to do this and assumes you will just stay where you are until around seven-thirty. I moved the sofa towards the window so he will see what he believes is you. The head and shoulders together with the uniform should be enough to convince him, the phone trace confirming your location. He won't need to ask you where the boy is because we've already told him the boy is here. He will then do one of two things. Either he will shoot you through the window, I mean the mannequin, that way he doesn't have to worry about any confrontation that might go wrong and leave undue evidence. Or he will make it a personal kill and enter the house to kill you on the sofa. Personally, I would do it from outside, that way if anyone else was in the house I could avoid being seen or caught. After killing you he will then wait to see if there is any other movement or anyone else. Either way, Felix will come in here and check that you're dead. But what Felix doesn't know, is I will be sitting in this seat facing the door, which incidentally he can't see from the window outside.

"And then you just kill him I suppose," she spouted.

"Not if I can help it, I want him alive, incapacitated but alive. I want to know why they want this boy so much, why all the drama at the hospital."

Jane sat back and sighed, playing with the silver buckle on the coat.

"You sound very sure, what about me, where do I figure in this?" she added.

Carl folded his arms across his large chest and raised a half-smile. "Go to the top floor, lock the door, get a shower, have a kip. But stay up there. I need to collect some items once I have dealt with this situation, I will call you when this is over."

She shook her head and pulled her clammy hands down her face. "How am I supposed to chill out knowing there's someone coming to kill me, what if it goes wrong, what if he kills you?"

"It won't, this is what I do remember. Now go upstairs, take some time out," he replied.

"I can't do that Carl, I have to feel like I'm still in control, maybe I should just go home, I've got a few hours," she replied, watching him rise from his chair.

She became aware of Carls presence, standing behind her, his hands placed on the top of her chair. She felt slightly uncomfortable as he said nothing, his warm breath on the back of her neck, the next moment she felt his hands around her, but before she had chance to react, she felt a darkness come over her.

Chapter 13

Jane's eyes felt sticky as she forced them open to the background noise of ringing. It faded a little before returning, but this time even louder as she regained consciousness. She felt sick and disorientated for a moment before realising she was lying fully dressed on top of a bed in semi-darkness. Two square, skylight windows above her provided no light, but a dim single lamp was bright enough to highlight the angled ceiling and play shadows across the bed. She sat up and silenced the small plastic alarm clock on the bedside table to her left. For a second she had almost forgotten about the whole event in the few seconds of waking. But then she remembered with horror the last moments with Carl, his hands crushing down on her. She focused her eyes on a note next to the lamp. *"Sorry I had to do this it was for your own good I will be watching you at the café, good luck, take care, Carl"*

She flicked on the light. Three small round ceiling lights had her squinting for a few seconds. The room was small and the ceiling steeply angled, she realised she must be on the third floor, the attic room. It was neutrally coloured, a single bed with a plain brown duvet and a pillow. A small, white chest of drawers lay at the far end of the bed. There were no wardrobes due to the restricted height.

She sat on the end of the bed, realising she had left her mobile in her locker at work. She turned to the clock again. It was ten past seven.

A chilling thought occurred to her. What if Carl failed, what if Felix was still in the house? The boy. What if Carl had taken the boy, what now? A multitude of scenarios came and went. She waited a few minutes, listening, but there were no sounds to be heard. She opened the bedroom door slowly, its rigid mechanism felt louder in the silence. The open door allowed the light from the bedroom to illuminate the small area to the top of the stairs and a door opposite. A steep, narrow staircase to the left ran to the second floor below.

She dashed across the landing into a small bathroom opposite with just a single sink and toilet. She searched a pine vanity unit under the sink. Amongst the aged toiletries was a small plastic box with plasters, bandages and a pair of long silver nail scissors. She took the scissors in hand and descended the narrow stairs to the floor below, stopping occasionally to listen. She didn't want to waste any time exploring the second floor, her objective now was to get to the ground floor and find out if she was alone.

Outside, the light had faded, dark, rolling clouds smothered the evening light, but Jane was reluctant to switch on any lights just yet. As she moved carefully across the second floor, the house woke, orchestrating various noises as she descended. It was not a quiet house.

She descended the last staircase to the hallway and toward the kitchen, catching sight of a yellow glow emitting from the lounge.

She was apprehensive. The side door now lay only a few feet away and she made a dash to open it.

To her relief, the van was still parked in the same spot.

She returned to the house. Still, there was silence. She held the scissors tightly as she moved cautiously toward the lounge doorway, the tall lamp in the corner providing light as she peered in.

The lounge was empty. No bodies, no blood. In fact, it was eerily normal. Even the mannequin had gone, no sign that anyone had been here.

She dropped the scissors into her coat pocket and returned to the kitchen, picking up the white wall phone and called the hospital, curious to know what mess she had left. The call was answered by the reception and she requested to speak to Martha. As she was placed on hold, she eyed the cupboard above her. A half-consumed packet of biscuits stared her in the face, she was hungry, she didn't have time before to think about it but now she needed food. She ripped open the packet and stuffed a couple of chocolate biscuits into her mouth.

"Hello, Nurse Stevens?" Came a voice.

She swallowed quickly.

"Yes, Martha?"

"Jane, where are you? We've got the police crawling all over the hospital," she snapped.

"I can't say right now, I'm sorry. Why are the police there?" Curious how much they knew.

"Dr Raj is missing and so is a body from the morgue. We can't find Carl from security either. I know you were speaking to him earlier, I'm sorry but I've given the police your details. They want to talk to you urgently, you're not answering your phone, Jane."

Martha waited for an explanation.

"I need you to do me a huge favour, please?"

"What favour, Jane?" she asked sharply.

"I need you to take my bag out my locker, then meet me in the staff car park in fifteen minutes. Please, Martha," she begged.

"What the hell is going on with you today? You really need to come and speak to the police, it's serious."

There was a small pause.

"If you bring my bag, I will explain everything to you, please?" she pleaded.

She heard a deep sigh down the phone. "Ok, my shift finishes at seven-thirty. But you really need to talk to the police, I'm not covering for you anymore after this," she replied.

"Thank you, Martha. Oh, and I will be in a white van."

She replaced the receiver and stood for a second in the kitchen, catching her reflection in the window. The blackness outside turned the tall narrow window into a dark mirror. She felt confused and deceived, she considered Carl's reasons for risking his career and life to help her, only to bail out at the last moment.

She scrambled around the kitchen seizing a bottle of coke and stuffing the remainder of the biscuits for a quick fix. She had presumed that Carl had taken the phone that Max had given her, but she remembered the last phone call she had with him. Pines cafe 8.30 pm. Maybe this was her best option now. With no way of contacting them, she took the decision to go ahead and trade the boy there.

She turned to see the silver wall clock. Realising she had slightly more than the hour to meet Martha and be at the Pines cafe. She grabbed the van keys perched on the edge of the worktop and exited the house.

The early evening brought with it a sharp bite. It was non-the less a welcome relief from the claustrophobic interior of the house.

In the van, she turned to see the lifeless shape in the back. She felt guilty for the boy. Someone somewhere was missing a son. It wasn't his fault; these men clearly had no compassion for human life. But here she was, returning him back into their sordid hands, an act which left a bitter taste in her mouth, but she instead focused on the bigger picture. Her family free from threat.

She turned the key and started off, back up the narrow lane and toward Blackwater. She was conscious of the body in the back, making her journey into town filled with paranoia about being stopped by the police. She was careful with her speed, her eyes glued to the speedo. The blurry, yellow glow of the town drew close and she reached the hospital entrance without drama.

As she pulled into the staff car park, the green quartz clock on the dash showed 19:35.

She sat waiting, picking the corner of her nail, feeling its sharp edge, hoping that Martha would not ask too many questions. Her concerns also turned to the now slightly irritating smell of the corpse; its odour had gained in strength since she was last in the van. She lowered the window halfway, feeling its cool touch on her warm cheeks and hoping the damp air would somehow dilute the presence of a decomposing body. She then watched the variety of people coming and going, chewing softly on her nails, occasionally glancing at their roughness in disgust.

She only had to wait a few moments before Martha emerged from the entrance, the vibrant lights of the entrance picking out her colourful purple coat and scarf.

She flashed the lights and Martha raised a hand in recognition. She made her way over and parked herself in the passenger seat sighing loudly. Martha didn't say anything until she had unwound her scarf.

Her presence felt as intimidating as the man she spoke to this morning.

"Isn't this Carl's van?" asked Martha.

She forced her already stretched brain for a suitable excuse. "I needed to move some furniture, he lent me his van, he has my car," she replied, hoping Martha would buy it.

"Do you know where he is now? Because right at this moment he's missing. I don't know what's going on with you Jane, but it's been a long and intrusive day, to say the least," fired Martha. "You've been behaving rather oddly since you took that call this morning. We have police here now and we have two missing staff and a body stolen from the morgue. I can tell you it's quite an affair."

She felt uncomfortable, knowing she couldn't tell Martha, so she played the ignorance card and did her best to fake surprise.

"What do you mean missing? You're joking."

She didn't look directly at Martha, she felt more respectful about lying to her if she instead studied the light drizzle distorting the busy view through the windscreen.

Martha removed her glasses and rubbed her eyes before returning them. "Look, Jane, we have several witnesses that say they saw you talking to a gentleman in the lobby. Apparently, you took him to the family room?"

This caught her off guard, she had not considered the extent of Martha's knowledge of events, or that the police were already in the mix. She picked her nails, tucked her hair nervously behind her ear for the hundredth time and tried to convincingly answer her question. She felt unscrupulous, like this was an awful betrayal of friendship. Martha was more than just a colleague, ok, she was a straight talker, unscathed by what other people thought about her shoot from the hip attitude but the upshot of this was that you knew where you stood, she didn't dress things up. Most of the time she was right, she ventured where others failed in a war of words, but she was also very sympathetic and would help anyone who asked for it. Herein lay her problem.

"It was one of my husband's colleagues, Josh, he had an accident. Nothing serious," she added quickly.

Martha didn't say anything straight away, she tilted her head away from Jane, watching a mother escort her young son hobbling ungainly up the steps toward the entrance. "Your husbands' colleague, is he British?" she inquired. Still following with interest, the toddler and his mum.

"Yes, why do you ask?" replied Jane curiously.

Martha's attention returned to Jane. Pulling her glasses to the end of her nose she dealt a killer reply.

"Well, that's strange, because the receptionist he spoke to said he had a Russian accent."

Jane knew when she was beaten, she couldn't stretch the truth any further, and more importantly not deceive a friend and insult their intelligence.

Knowing how much Martha knew already and the fact her emotional reserves were on empty, she decided that Martha would be more useful as an ally than a deceived friend.

She gazed at the quartz clock on the dash, her head running some calculations, realising she would need thirty minutes to drive the twenty-odd miles to Pines cafe. Giving her ten minutes to give Martha enough information to satisfy her curiosity and win her support. She wound the window back up and wiping the side of her cold wet face with her sleeve.

She looked down at her ravaged nails. "Ok, he's not a colleague. I'm in the middle of something, the man from this morning, in the lobby, he's, well he's blackmailing me," spouted Jane.

Martha removed her glasses. "I'm sorry Jane, I'm struggling to follow you, blackmailed for what?" she interrupted.

Just as she did with Carl, she felt compelled to spill the story, the instructions she was to follow, even the fake Dr Fuller, but not the full story, not the part about how she is sitting less than a few feet away from the dead boy, and certainly not the involvement with Carl.

Martha watched her spill the difficult words from her lips, she was speechless. "My goodness, you're not joking, are you?"

Jane shook her head, more tears dripped into the coat.

Martha pulled a tissue from her bag.

"You need to go in there right now and tell the police what you told me."

"I'm not telling the police, not yet. I have a plan, please don't tell me the police will protect me and all that, if you knew what I knew you'd understand."

Martha shook her head in disapproval. "Have you listened to yourself, Jane? You're a nurse not a have a go hero," she added.

Jane picked again at her nails and shifted a few loose strands of hair from her face. "I know the police have procedures to follow. I've watched enough films to know how much time they waste playing cat and mouse with these people, I'm not putting my family's safety in the hands of anyone, I'm sorry," she added.

"So who has our missing John Doe?" asked Martha.

"I presume these men that brought him in," she lied.

"And Dr Raj, he's the one that could confirm this, and he seems to have disappeared off the face of the earth."

Jane shook her head. "I don't know, I haven't seen him today," she said spinning more lies and deceit.

"I wish I could get my head around this but to be honest, I'm struggling. I don't know what it is you want from me, Jane."

"A friend?" she asked.

"We are friends, but what you're doing is ridiculous."

"I'm not asking you to lie, I'm just asking you not to repeat anything I told you, please."

"You're putting me in a tough spot, I'm sorry Jane I can't do that. If it came out I knew all this I could lose my job, let alone be prosecuted." Martha handed Jane her bag. "I'm sorry," she said reaching for the door handle. "Whatever you do I wish you luck." Martha left the van and made her way back to the hospital, leaving Jane to wonder if she would tell the police.

She noted the time once more, just over half an hour to drive out to Pines cafe and end all this

Chapter 14

Saturday 28th 00:15

As the last of the SOCO team packed up and left, along with the local uniform, McBride stood in the doorway of the café trying to piece together the information he had. Relishing momentarily in the silence, he watched O'Connor hurry off toward his squad car dancing around the deep puddles which littered the car park. McBride smirked and stuffed his hands into his pockets. The sweet smell of the midnight rain filled his nostrils, and the crisp air plunged even lower.

Mary Tripp finished closing the café and fiddled with her keys.

"Can I help you any further?" she asked locking up behind him.

"No, thank you. I've finished here now, you get home. We may need to speak to you again," he continued.

Mary stood next to him, with a bunch of keys in one hand and a flowery coloured shopping bag perched between her feet. She couldn't help but make one last attempt to pry.

"Do you have any leads yet?" she asked.

McBride turned to her and smiled. "I know you're curious, after all, it's your cafe it happened in. Unfortunately, as I said before, I'm not at liberty to discuss the case. Just keep a watchful eye on the news."

"I understand," she replied placing one hand on his arm.

"Just a quick question, have these men ever been here before, do you know?" asked McBride.

"No, not to my knowledge, I don't recognise them, but ask Frank Gibbs, he's a regular, he might know."

"Thanks, I will be sure to ask. Oh, I'll send in our team of specialist cleaners in the morning, hopefully, we won't keep you closed too long," he added.

"Thank you, Sir. I appreciate that." She smiled. Mary patted his arm and checked again she had locked the door behind her.

As he watched Mary dash to catch her lift, he became aware of his phone ringing. He fumbled quickly and pulled it to his ear.

"DCI McBride," he answered.

O'Connor had barely settled in his car when he caught sight of McBride under the entrance waving his hand at him to stop. He cursed and returned to his boss.

McBride was still glued to his phone and O'Connor hoped it was important enough to keep him from his bed, especially given the early hour. But that would be unlikely as he knew McBride only too well. If there was a lead to follow up then no matter what the hour, he would tie it up first, and by the sound of the conversation he was having, this was going to be one of those times.

The quiet was now only trumped by the sound of Mary's lift disappearing into the distance, that and the deluge of rain cascading from the apex roof above. O'Connor shuffled from foot to foot impatiently.

After a couple of minutes, McBride returned his phone to his jacket.

"That was control, they say the alarm has been raised in the forestry commission cabin."

"Yeah, and?" replied O'Connor, pondering the importance.

O'Connor frowned. "So now you're thinking it's something to do with what happened here?"

McBride pulled his hands from his pockets to help emphasise his thoughts. "Think about it. One, we have a woman on the run. Two, she's on foot as far as we know, and she needs shelter and a place to hide. And three, we have two armed men who are probably just as eager to catch her as we are," he replied, stuffing his hands back into his pockets.

"How far is it from here?" asked O'Connor.

"Not sure, but the online maps will know," chuckled McBride

He whisked his phone out and scouted Google Maps, his fat fingers making awkward work.

O'Connor just stood and humoured in McBride's inept ability with technology.

"Think that's it, looks like it's at the end of a small track through the forest," said McBride, pointing to an oblong shape. "Less than a mile from here."

"You are calling this in?" quizzed O'Connor, placing a cigarette between his lips and lighting it.

McBride looked up and watched the water hang from the wooden apex before dropping in a small explosion just before his feet as he rocked from toe to heel. "I see your point O'Connor, but we could be in danger of warning her off. I was hoping we could do a quick reconnaissance, assess the situation and then decide. Besides, by the time we put in a request and ten over-enthusiastic armed police arrive in a barrage of noise, they'd be long gone."

O'Connor raised his brows before puffing out a sigh. "Your call boss, but I'm not happy, not with two-gun wielding lunatics wandering around," he replied. "What if it's not her but them?"

"Window of opportunity, O'Connor, remember that. Could be our best chance of catching our suspect."

O'Connor rushed his cigarette before dropping it into a nearby puddle. Reluctantly he decided to indulge his boss's curiosity and experience.

Chapter 15

Saturday 28th 20:10

Jane felt the witching hour approach. That's what it felt like. The green quartz clock in front of her blinked away as a constant reminder. She was eager to vacate the van. Its tinny cocoon smothered her. The longer she drove, the more repressive the sense of occasion. She was not an overly religious person, in fact, she could count on one hand the number of times she and the house of God had made acquaintances, but at this moment in time, like most of us faced with life-threatening situations, she prayed to God this would work.

With the cafe just a few hundred metres ahead, she checked her rear-view mirror, with an absence of any headlights behind, she was confident she had not been followed.

Conscious of the conversation she had with Carl, she wasn't going to drive straight into the car park. That would be foolish. She needed some insurance.

As she brought the van to a crawl, now opposite the café, a wave of dread washed over her, fiercer than she had known before, more than the dread of being shown the photos of her family even.

She crawled past the cafe, hoping to find a spot big enough in which to hide the van. She spied a small track on the left, leading off from the road. She checked her mirror again. Nothing but the distant glow of the cafe lights.

The track ascended slightly from the road and the tail of the van wavered under the slushy mud. She descended and weaved her way along the track, barley squeezing past an abandoned car and into the overgrown arms of large, green fir trees which dusted the sides of the van as she pushed on through. Eventually, the track came to a sudden end, restricted by a large aluminium gate, with a sign saying, '*Forestry commission. No access*'

She turned and headed steadily back up the track spotting a small gap in a line of thick shrubbery. She manoeuvred the struggling van off the track and through a bush but didn't anticipate the deep slope the other side and lost control, the van careening down the slope. She gripped the wheel with gritted teeth as it crashed to a sudden halt on a large tree root at the bottom of a deep gully.

"Shit," she uttered.

The van was going nowhere now.

With time running out, she forced open the door against the branches and climbed out. Her feet instantly submerged into a muddy bog. She grabbed her bag, abandoned the van and made her way back up the track. There was little elegance in the trek back to the road, but it gave her time to think about how she was going to do this.

She approached the café, the light above the entrance was strong enough to make her entrance visible from inside.

Pulling open the door, there was a sickening sensation in her stomach as she was met by the dazzle of bright lights and a strangely quiet ambience. Her scrambling in the forest had become obvious looking down at her ruined shoes, even the black trousers did little to hide her battle with the woods and she felt aware of this. The rain fell from her hair, pooling on the shiny black and white tiles underfoot. The café was strangely empty, and she couldn't for one moment imagine trading a corpse with a gang of criminals in a place like this.

She approached the counter. A coffee would offer only a small satisfaction now.

A quick glance reassured her there was no one here looking remotely like the one she met this morning. Only a young family and a middle-aged man, with a slightly gaunt look, and grey stubble, wearing a tatty, red cap pulled low. All the same, she acknowledged his smile as he drew his attention away from the paper to notice her.

The larger than life waitress welcomed her with a grin, her bright red lipstick overemphasised her smile.

"What can I get you?" she asked.

"Oh, err coffee please."

"Milk or cream," asked the waitress.

"I'm sorry, what?"

"Milk or cream."

"Oh, what, sorry, just a little milk thanks," said Jane, clearly distracted.

She focused her attentions on the entrance, occasionally breaking away to glance the clock which signalled her judgment hour.

"One coffee. Help yourself to sugar," said the waitress.

"Thanks," she replied, pulling out some loose change.

Jane took her coffee and sat in a booth facing the door. She cupped the mug of coffee and sipped. Refreshing as it was, it did little to occupy her mind with calmer thoughts and her gaze was now fixed firmly on the entrance.

She watched the wall clock work its way slowly past half eight. Then eight forty-five. Every second felt like a minute. Judgment hour had been and gone. She started to question if she had the right time or even the right place. Still, she watched the door. Then moments later a flash of light flickered through the blinds followed shortly by the presence of a well-built man, in dark jeans and a black leather jacket, un-zipped halfway exposing a thick gold chain against his black shirt. His receding hair was jelled back to a small stubby ponytail.

She fidgeted in her seat; her hands clenched tight to the point where her knuckles turned white.

He approached with no polite greeting or facial response. Everything else in the room seemed to stop. At least that was how she felt as he sat beside her in the booth.

A flash thought entered her mind but exited almost as quickly. What if Carl was waiting to save her? The note from earlier, maybe he's waiting for them to make a move, yes that would be it, she told herself. She dispelled her thought as nothing more than a desperate fantasy at that moment.

She avoided eye contact and any conversation. Despite her seemingly assertive plan, she realised she was way out of her depth. She could run but her legs were too shaky to carry her. She was beginning to realise that this was a bad idea.

His scent that invaded her nasal passages wasn't after-shave but a sweet sickly scent of perspiration and stale cigarettes. He didn't even look to her before striking a conversation.

"You have the boy?" he asked abruptly, in a deep Russian accent.

She had underestimated the level of intimidation, and her confidence flattened. It soon dawned on her she wasn't in any position to take control.

I'm going to die, she thought.

She tried to speak, but only a rattle immerged. She cleared her throat. "Yes, yes I have him," her voice breaking.

The man reached inside his jacket and pulled out his phone. He held a conversation in Russian before snapping it shut.

Staring down at her cup she tucked her hair back behind her ears, she did this several times. Within a minute, two more men had made their entrance. Both dressed in dark suits and blemish-free leather shoes. They nodded to the man next to her before taking up a booth on the other side of the cafe.

He reached inside his jacket again, this time not for a phone. Suddenly she felt a hard-blunt object in the side of her ribs. She knew what it was straight away. She was getting used to people pulling guns on her. If this was any other situation, she might even laugh about it. But this was not one of those times.

"In a few seconds, you will follow me out of the cafe and take me to the boy. Do not attempt to run, you understand yes?" he uttered.

She nodded.

She knew they were never going to let her leave here alive. Carl was right about them. If they can be as cold as ice over the life of a child, then her life would be even less significant to them.

She prayed for a miracle.

The man stood from the booth. She knew she had no choice but to follow. She felt sick, beyond frightened now. The rest of the patrons carried on their social niceties, oblivious to her otherworldly nightmare.

She followed him from the booth, the man put his arm around her waist and walked her out. A pure facade.

As he walked her past the other two men in suits, they exchanged a few words in their native tongue before leaving the security of the cafe. Her last chance to shout for help. She didn't know why, but she stalled her execution with a last desperate attempt.

"I really need the bathroom first," she muttered.

He grabbed her arm and marched her towards the toilet. Holding her tight he pushed open the door and peered in, making sure there was nowhere for her to escape. One small square window high up was made of thick glass blocks, clearly too tough and too small to break out of.

He removed her bag.

"You have a minute," he said releasing her arm and pushing her in.

"Come on Jane, think of a plan," she muttered to herself as she stood in the middle of the toilet.

It wasn't large. It had three cubicles and two sinks on the opposite side with a small square mirror above. In between was wall to wall white tiles.

She felt suffocated by panic. As the minute neared, she still had no idea what she was going to do.

"Hurry up," came the voice the other side of the door.

"Ok, just washing my hands," she shouted. She went to the sink, turning on the tap.

She glanced into the mirror above, not recognising herself. There were no more tears to come, no more fight or bright ideas, just a lasting image of a broken woman. She was done. Tonight, she was going to die.

As she moved away from the sink, she was oblivious to the water which had cascaded over the edge and soaked into her coat.

She brushed her hands down her coat to dispel the water, as she did so, she felt something sharp dig into her hand, causing her to flinch. Curious, she placed her hand into the right-hand pocket and felt the long silver nail scissors she had picked up from Carl's place.

She was not a violent person but backed into a corner, her absolute need for survival left her with only one option. She knew what she had to do. The miracle she had prayed for was there all the time.

She stepped behind the door, the long sharp nail scissors poised in her right hand, ready for a killer blow, her breathing almost as loud as her heart.

She waited.

"You have ten seconds to come out, otherwise I drag you out," he said impatiently.

She did not answer.

Only a few seconds passed before the door flew open, almost against her. As the man entered, she took her chance and plunged the scissors into the side of his throat.

The man instantly dropped to his knees clutching his throat with his hands. Only a gurgled sound came from his mouth. She was overwhelmed by the blood, its deep red almost black colour exploded over the white tiles, made worse by the dramatic writhing movements of his last desperate attempts to breathe before finally crashing to the ground.

She stared at the bloody stains, still wet enough to trickle down her hands.

The realisation of what she had done kicked in. She grabbed her bag and left the toilet, staggering down the corridor towards the entrance, crashing through the double doors and out into the night.

She braced herself against the entrance pillar and spilt her breakfast, the stinging taste of bile catching in her throat.

She ran from the car park toward the road. All she could think of was to run as far away as possible. She reached the road running with little idea of where she was going. Then the familiar sound of a car grew ever nearer, slowing as it neared her. She saw the female driver, staring back at her before speeding up and disappearing toward the café.

She felt alone, abandoned by Carl and now with a terrible act infesting her conscience. She felt the man's blood on her hands, its sticky residue. She dragged her hands through the wet grass on the verge, desperate to remove any trace.

She took a second to consider her options; she had her phone but who would she call? She couldn't call the police, not now she was probably wanted for body snatching, and she didn't have Carl's number. *"Yes, where was Carl, why had he not turned up?"* she thought.

With the night gathering pace, cold, wet and confused, she decided to trek back to the van.

She didn't know how she got there, she couldn't remember scrambling through the woods, but she arrived, pulled open the driver's door and fell exhausted into the seat.

Inside, the silence was only broken by the patter of raindrops which fell from the canopy above, crashing on to the tinny roof. As she sat for a short while, a wave of post adrenalin rush was soon replaced by nervous exhaustion. She placed her head against the seat rest, and It wasn't long before she succumbed to sleep.

Chapter 16

Friday 27th 23:28

Megan turned in the back seat to find she was staring down the barrel of a gun. But instead of hearing a bang, she heard a voice.

"You're not Jane," came the voice. "What you are doing out here?" he asked, looking at her terrified expression.

It took a few seconds for her to realise she was being questioned and not shot.

As she pulled herself up from the seat, the dark figure loomed over her from the gap in the rear window. He opened the door and replaced the gun for a helping hand.

"It's ok, I'm not here to harm you, I was just expecting someone else when I saw the movement."

Megan looked at the huge figure, still outlined by the headlights, his hand of help still offering.

"I'm Carl, want to tell me what you're doing here, especially at this hour on a night like this?"

Megan looked up at him, his large hood hiding his face, but she didn't feel as scared anymore, as he holsted his weapon back under his coat.

"It's a long story," she said, trying to suss him out.

"What's your name?"

"Megan."

"Ok, Megan. So why you here?"

"Hiding I guess, anyway what are you doing here, why do you have a gun?"

"Hiding from who?"

"Not sure, some really bad men, look it's a long story, I need to get to my sister."

Megan looked towards the trees, hoping to see her.

"This your car?"

Megan nodded. "My sister's."

Carl ran his hand across the boot edge, feeling the round crater below the badge. "You've been shot at, haven't you?"

"What? Why do think that?"

He pointed to the left-over glass in the window frame. "Been shot out, plus I know a bullet hole when I see one, I'm going to take a wild guess here and say you've had a nasty encounter with a couple of Russian goons."

Megan frowned. "Hold on, how do you know, I mean you know about them? And who is Jane?"

"Sorry?"

"Jane, you said I'm not Jane, is that your wife?"

"No, not my wife, but It's important I find her, like you it's a long story, one which can wait for now, look, where's your sister, I'm not sure having a convo here is the best idea, there's a forestry cabin down the end of this track, I was heading there until I can figure out how I'm going to find her. You and your sister can come with me if you like. You look like you could use some shelter."

Megan stood thinking for a moment, just as the sound of breaking twigs snatched her attention toward the trees.

Carl reached for his weapon.

"Megan," shouted Gill. "You're alive, thank goodness."

Gill threw her arms around her sister, ignoring her pain at that moment.

Carl made an appearance from the side of the car. "I hate to break up the reunion, but I need to move on."

"It's ok, his name's Carl, he helped me," explained Megan, watching her sister step back.

Carl picked up the broken pieces of glass from the rear of the car and rolled them in his hand before throwing them down.

"Your sister tells me you were shot, you ok? I'm guessing the bullet that came through the rear window. Your shoulder?" he asked looking at her hand braced around the top of her arm.

"Yes, it kills."

"So, you're undercover police, is that why you're armed. Did you find the body in the cafe?"

Carl dropped his hood, his eyes and mouth reacting simultaneously "Hey, hold on a second, what body?"

"The body in the cafe, in the ladies toilet," said Megan.

"I need you to tell me more, but we need to move on from here, I think my friend and you may have run into the same people, come with me to the cabin."

"I need to know who you are first," asked Megan. "We've had one hell of an evening and I'm a little picky who I trust right now."

Megan explained to Carl what had happened, as briefly as she could.

"The woman you saw at the side of the road. What did she look like, what was she wearing? Which way did she go? Did you speak to her?" Carl wanted to save the conversation until they were in a safe place. The middle of the woods with a few gun-happy Russians on their tail and a thirst for revenge was not a clever idea. But he was desperate for some answers and anxious to find Jane.

"Black trousers and light-coloured coat if that helps, didn't really notice her face only that she looked scared," said Megan.

"I need to find her," he said.

Carl noticed Gill's pain, her face painted a picture of suffering and it was obvious she was struggling to stand.

"It's because of her we are in this mess," snapped Gill.

"No, it's because we both stuck our noses in." Megan's voice was raised higher than Carl was comfortable with.

"Hey, keep it down, we'll discuss this later."

"Not till you level with us, you still haven't answered my question," said Megan again.

"Ok. I'm a security guard at Blackwater Hospital. Jane is a nurse who needed my help. Like I said It's a long story and one for later. Now I'm leaving, if you want to come with me, you're welcome but I'm not standing here any longer, I need to find Jane.

Megan was unsure about trusting Carl but given there were bigger threats, she didn't have much of a choice. Gill followed her sister to his vehicle and realised how awkward it was to walk in her broken shoes.

Carl waited for them to squeeze into the small cab of the Land Rover.

He drove down the narrow track to the bottom, the less than adequate lights and the undulating surface made in an uncomfortable drive, occasionally catching the steep bank throwing them around in the process.

He came to the iron gate, nudging it with the front of his Land Rover until the small chain snapped and the gate swung back with force.

Megan moved the heater knob to full, placing her icy hands over the meagre heater.

"Aint much good I'm afraid."

Megan felt for her sister, trying to imagine how much pain she was in. Emotionally and physically. Part of her wanted to apologise for dragging her sister through this terrible ordeal. Because she was always looking for that exciting moment, the unpredictable, risk-taking adventure. An opportunity to feel like she was living, rather than surrendering to her bland self-destructive life. But she couldn't. To do that would be to admit her selfish motive. Anyway, her sister was just as inquisitive as she was about the woman. It was there she left that thought.

"He saved me, remember? I trust him."

"Just around this corner now. How are you both doing?"

"She's been shot, how do you think she's doing?" snapped Megan.

"This is all to do with your friend Jane, how's she involved?" she asked.

"She's as much as a victim as you two before you start playing the blame game."

"You want to elaborate?" asked Megan.

"That's a story for another time," he replied.

"Looks like we've got a lot of stories to catch up on then," said Megan.

Carl chuckled. "Indeed, we do. But let's just get to shelter, for now, your sister needs medical attention and there's a medical kit in the cabin."

"What cabin?" asked Megan.

"Belongs to the forestry commission, it's the only other shelter around here for now."

Carl pulled up past the cabin and parked under a large group of fir trees a few yards behind it.

Megan stroked her sisters face. Her large brown eyes were barely open. "You go, just leave me here."

"Don't you dare give up now, you hear me, now get up."

He opened the door and lent his hand to Megan. "I'll carry her, don't worry."

"Thanks."

She watched as Carl carefully lifted her sister from the back seat. His strong frame made light work of her, even though Gill was a little larger than Megan. Megan had always been slight in build. She put this down to living with anxiety and anger. Not all the anger was directed towards their mother for leaving them so suddenly. Some, just a little, was toward her sister for moving on so quickly and perusing her own personal goals. She found that tough. She was always emotionally weaker than Gill. But here, right now, in this situation, she was the stronger one and for the first time in a long time felt useful.

Megan didn't wait to be asked before following Carl, feeling their way in the darkness until finally appearing in the open, opposite the cabin. Megan grabbed for the handle. It was locked. Carl barged the door, the wooden frame cracking under the brute force. A second attempt had the door open.

A damp, squalid smell was the first thing to greet her. Carl grunted as he manoeuvred Gill through the doorway and carefully placed her on the floor with her back to a cupboard.

"We should lie her down," said Megan scouting the cabin.

"No, she has a shoulder wound, we need to keep her upright. Less chance of her bleeding out so quickly. Wait here I have some supplies in the Land Rover."

"How do we know we're safe here?" asked Megan. "I mean if you found this place, then they can as well."

Carl turned back and placed a reassuring hand on her shoulder, her body shaking. "We don't. But It's safer than wandering around the woods. We will figure this out. You're a tough girl, most people would have folded by now. You have the strength of a survivor."

She pulled away from him. "You don't know what I've been through, how dare you tell me what I'm capable of," she scorned.

"I didn't mean anything by it." Carl turned to the door and pulled up his hood. "I'm sorry, it was a compliment, not a judgment," he replied, leaving the cabin.

Megan explored the place. The darkness didn't quite steal her capacity to pick out objects and familiar shapes. The vinyl-covered floor was like most porta-cabins and had the lack of firmness. At the far end were kitchen worktops running across the back and halfway up one side towards the door. Four large, square glass cases sat on top of the worktops, each containing a stuffed bird of prey. Although Megan could see the outline of a bird, it was still too dark to read the label or recognise the breed. Not that she knew her birds that well. Under the countertops were old kitchen cabinets but each one she tried was locked. Next to that was a small bookcase with assorted files and magazines. Around the walls were several posters, all of which, she guessed would be information about wildlife and such related paraphernalia. Again, the darkness made it difficult to make out any detail. The cabin had one small oblong window high up at the far end and another similar one on the opposite side. A larger window ran along the side toward the door. All had metal bars attached. Although Megan found a light switch, she was reluctant to turn it on, not wanting to attract attention.

She sat next to her sister perched against the desk. She began to take stock. Her body had been preoccupied with keeping her alive and her senses in full working order. She had no time to feel hungry or thirsty, cold, or tired. But now as she sat there, her body slumped, like it was coming down from a big high. Megan noticed her cold, wet clothes. The cuts on her hands from fighting through the bushes were now beginning to sting and of course, the need to eat and drink was present. But as Megan sat nestled into Gill, it was her tiredness that she noticed most.

Megan jumped suddenly as Carl entered the cabin. She realised she had started to fall asleep and told herself she would not let her guard down again. Not until she could be sure both she and her sister were safe and well.

Carl removed his hood and dropped a rucksack on the floor. Reaching into one of the pockets he took out a large hunting knife. Megan instinctively shifted but Carl was quick to settle her.

"You don't have to worry. It's not for you. I'm not here to hurt you, I'm here to help you, I keep telling you that," he said moving towards the middle of the cabin.

"Yeah, well, maybe I'm just cautious. You can't blame me for being wary."

"Take a look in the front pocket of my bag, there's another knife much the same as this one. Take it out and keep it," instructed Carl.

"For what?" asked Megan.

"I want you to feel safe. Now you have a knife as well."

Megan unzipped the pocket and took out the knife. She held it firmly in her delicate hand, running her finger carefully along the top edge. It was heavy, and it did indeed make her feel safer. "Thanks," she replied.

Carl reached up toward the light in the middle of the cabin. Using the knife, he prised off the plastic cover from the strip light.

Megan watched curiously as he took the cover in hand and left the cabin. He returned and the light cover appeared to be filled with something.

"What are you doing?" she asked, staring at the light cover.

"We need some light, I need to give Gill first aid, but I don't want this place looking like a lighthouse. It's an old trick I picked up. I've filled the light cover with mud and leaves." Carl reached up and pressed the cover back in place.

"Do me a favour, flick the light switch to your right will you?"

Megan flicked the switch. The cabin was now lit in a dull glow. Colours were weak but recognisable. It was enough to manage, but not to cast any shadows.

"I need you to remove your sisters top to expose the wound for me," asked Carl kneeling opposite Gill. "Then I want you to take out the bag from the rucksack and I want you to eat and drink something." Carl looked at her. Even under the low light, he could see the exhaustion written all over her. "You need to refuel, please just eat and drink something while I attend to this."

Megan took out a small carrier bag from the rucksack. Inside was a bottle of water, a banana and a bar of chocolate. "Hey, what girl doesn't like chocolate?" smiled Megan.

Carl used the knife once more. This time to prise open the filing cabinet. A small square green sticker with a white cross in the middle told him inside would be a first aid kit. After several attempts, the drawer gave in and Carl took the green first aid box.

"Can you pass me a bottle of vodka from the rucksack please?" asked Carl as he opened the box.

"Chocolate and booze." Megan grinned, handing Carl the bottle.

"It's for the wound, I need it to be sterile. You have a nice smile," he continued. "You should wear it more often."

"It's been a long time since I wore a smile," she replied.

Carl lent towards Gill and dousing the lint with vodka he wiped her wound, removing the excess blood. His attention toward Gill did not deter from his conversation with Megan.

"So, is there a story about your absence of smiles?" he asked.

Megan sat cross-legged, watching Carl help her sister. She watched the concentration on his face. "I'm trying to figure you out. You're not just a security guard, are you? You're resourceful and calm," said Megan.

Carl stopped for a moment giving her a glance. "You're very observant."

Carl finished patching Gill up, she groaned momentarily as he pressed on her shoulder.

"You're close to your sister, aren't you?"

"We're twins, so yes. We've been through a lot together. We're still going through a lot. Truth is, Gill is actually the stronger one." Megan peeled the banana from the bag and stuffed it in her mouth, there was no etiquette in ceasing her hunger.

Carl closed the first aid box and sat opposite, leaning against the other cupboard.

Megan watched her sister sleeping. "Is she going to be ok, I mean she won't die, will she?"

Carl took Gills arm and felt her pulse. "She's going to be ok. She has a strong pulse. Ideally, she needs to be treated in case of infection. She was lucky it was only a flesh wound. It missed any major arteries and the bullet passed through."

Carl phased out briefly, thinking about how he had failed Jane. Thinking how she would know what to do for Gill and if he had done enough.

"Can you tell me what happened in the cafe earlier, you mentioned a dead body?" he asked with curiosity.

"Tell me about your friend Jane first. Why are you so keen to find her?"

Carl raised his brow and nodded. "Ok, Jane was being blackmailed, actually she wasn't the only one, but they got someone to take pictures of her family and used them to manipulate her. Some Russian guy called Max wanted her to help a boy that had been shot. They didn't want the police involved or a paperwork trail. I think you can guess why. So, they threatened her family."

Megan tried to imagine what Jane had gone through, the woman both her and Gill had been so quick to scorn.

"So how did you get involved?"

"She came to me for help. I ended up getting involved as much as she did."

"How come?"

"I guess I felt sorry for her, plus if I'm honest I'm bored with my job, especially after my time in the forces."

Carl unzipped his camouflaged coat, took out his wallet and produced a photograph. The picture showed an Asian woman dressed in black, holding a baby.

"Three days after that picture was taken, she was tortured and murdered along with her baby. My job was to extract her husband for Intel. I wasn't told we would have to leave his wife and child behind."

Megan raised her hand to her mouth; she felt his anguish. "That's so wrong, couldn't you have taken them?" she asked.

"There was plenty of room in the chopper, but all I could do was watch her husband scream, begging for us to take his wife and child. But those were not our orders. A while later I came out of the forces. War is not just about good versus bad, it's sometimes good deeds turning bad."

Megan handed back the photo. "So, you punish yourself every day by keeping that photo as a reminder?"

"Yes, I guess I do," replied Carl, taking one last look before returning it.

Megan broke an awkward pause. "I lost my mum. We lost our mum, June, when we were fifteen. She committed suicide. Hung herself. There didn't seem to be any reason. Dad couldn't handle it and we lived with our auntie for a while. Dad folded up and moved away. That's where we are going, were going, whatever, to see him after twenty years. We lost contact but our auntie was still in touch, she never talked about dad and we never asked. He knew how to contact us if he wanted to. Then one day she told us he needed to see us, and soon." She stopped talking for a moment. "That's why I'm angry. Not because she decided to take her own life but because I didn't know she was in that frame of mind and maybe if I had, I could have stopped her." Megan lifted her head and looked across at her sister. "It was Gill that found mum. But it was me that couldn't accept it. She made a good life for herself, own business, nice car, nice house."

"You jealous?" Interrupted Carl as he played with the toggles on his hood.

"Jealous? No. I'm not jealous. I'm angry with myself because I let my anger and my emotions get in the way of my life. I've dragged twenty years of pain around with me, So no I'm not Jealous, I'm proud of Gill." Megan sniffed hard, fighting back her tears.

"I guess we're both carrying our demons with us then."

"Yes, I suppose we are."

Megan changed the conversation quickly, realising she had just shared her intimate memories with a stranger. "So, Carl, how do you intend to find this Jane?" asked Megan twisting the lid off the bottle of water.

Carl took a mobile device from inside his jacket and held it in front of her. "With this. You see I fitted a tracker so I could keep an eye on her in case she ran into trouble, which is another long story. I knew she was going to the cafe and tracked my van here, that's when I stumbled upon your car but it's on the blink now and I'm having trouble getting a signal."

Before Megan could answer, their attention was snatched. A gunshot rang out in the distance.

Megan flinched. "Shit, it's them, they're back," she screeched.

"Hey, don't panic," said Carl, raising his hand to her. "It sounded like it was some distance away." Carl flicked off the light and pulled the pistol from his jacket and cocked it.

Megan flinched again. She looked at her sister, but she was just a shadow in the dark.

"Gill, you awake?" Megan stroked her cheek. Its coldness concerned her.

"Carl? I'm worried about Gill, she's really cold."

Megan lifted the bottle of water to her sister's lips.

Carl placed the gun on the worktop to check on Gill.

"It seems to have stopped bleeding, but she's cold, she could go into shock."

Carl stood and removed his camouflaged jacket. He placed it around Gill, swamping her.

"That should help," he said, picking up the gun.

Megan gazed at him; she admired his physique. The way his black t-shirt hugged every contour. She felt safe with him, something she hadn't felt for a while.

Carl's gaze flickered to the door, then to the desk, then back to the door.

"Okay, I need you and Gill to move further up. Away from the door."

Megan didn't question him. She knew whatever he had planned would be in their best interest. As she moved, her damp clothing became uncomfortable. She placed her hands under Gill's arms and dragged her down the end of the cabin, resting her against a cupboard. Gill was barely conscious but groaned on occasion. She perched next to her sister with her arms tightly crossed, hoping the shivering would stop.

Carl tucked the gun in the back of his camo trousers and then pulled the wooden desk from the wall, positioning it a few feet from the door. He then opened the door. Its position only allowed for the door to be open a couple of feet. Closing the door, he pulled up a chair opposite and sat with the gun firmly clutched but resting on his lap. Although only a few feet away, his form was barely more than a shape in the corner.

"I suggest you get some sleep while you can," came Carl's voice from the shadows.

"You really think I'm going to sleep now? Not until we're a long way from this place," she replied.

She listened to the sound of the branches skipping across the thin flat roof and the whistle of the wind squeezing through every gap.

"If anything happens, I will wake you."

"No, I'm staying awake, anyway, why don't you just drive us out of here? And why are we here?" she quizzed.

"Do you trust me or not?"

"You didn't answer my question."

"Look, you're safe here, we wait a few hours and then I'll take you where you need to go, they'll be long gone by then."

"What about your friend Jane? You going to just leave her out there?" asked Megan.

"You think I got her into this?" he replied defensively. "She wanted to get involved, she asked *me* for help." Carl fiddled with the barrel of his gun. "I warned her about getting involved. She chose not to listen."

"You pig," replied Megan sharply. "You left her to do this alone and then you have the balls to blame her when your egotistical adventure goes tits up."

Megan was cold and tired, her frustration clearly directed at Carl.

Carl snapped "I saved *your* ass, didn't I?"

Megan said nothing more.

Chapter 17

Saturday 28th 00:15

Jane flinched as she woke to a loud noise. She was instantly thrust from the calm piece of sleep to a heightened state. Unaware of how long she had been asleep, she put the keys into the ignition slot and flicked it on. The green dash-clock flashed 00:15.

She cursed under her breath and turned to see if the body was still in the back. A large dark shape confirmed, along with the smell, now stronger in odour. She knew this would eventually turn to a deep putrid smell as the body's organic material broke down further with each passing hour.

She was convinced the loud noise she heard was a gunshot. Unsure of which direction the noise came from and unable to drive the van out of the ditch, she decided she would be safer in the sanctuary of the woods, in case the white van was spotted.

She turned once more to the lifeless shape in the back. After all, here was the body of a boy who had been at the forefront of her nightmare and the nucleus to everyone involved. She was not religious but carried a valued set of morals which she believed made her a decent human being. She couldn't, of course, forget her guilt about committing the ultimate sin and taking the life of another human being, but sitting just as equally on her other shoulder was the voice of justification.

She spoke to the lifeless black body bag. "Do you realise how much trouble you've caused me?"

For a tiny moment, all her fears were paused. There was a calm in her empathy for the boy.

She stepped out the van to the rear and opened the rear doors as quietly as possible and dragged the body bag from the back. She muttered a "Sorry," as its weight brought it to the floor with a thud.

Although the van was buried in the overgrowth and somewhat off the beaten track, she felt it would still be vulnerable. She feared staying in the van until morning, especially with the body in the back would be risky.

Her confused mind was a spinning roundabout of uncertainty, but she took the decision to move the body away from the van. The farther it was from the van the less likely it could be found.

The forest floor was not forgiving, and she found her feet sinking into the thick tar of mud with each step. She dragged the body bag down into a gully, its smooth plastic surface sliding easily down the slope. she grunted rhythmically to her movements until finally leaving it to rest in the gully at the bottom.

She sat, catching her breath, her hands camouflaged by the black stain of the ground, only then did she notice the lack of one shoe, buried somewhere in the bowels of the forest.

She laughed. Not loud but all the same it was a laugh, maybe it was a nervous reaction and maybe it was because it was the only emotion left to give which hadn't been spent.

She composed herself, pulled her shoe from the boggy ground and placed one hand on the body bag and spoke. "I will be back, I promise."

There was a certain tension in the soundless background. Beyond the usual array of stretching and creaking timber.

She wiped the thick mud from her hands, it's deep odour and rich texture was offensive.

She continued to follow the track, unsure and unaware of its direction.

She arrived at the large metal gate she drove to earlier, only this time she noticed it was open. she continued warily to follow the track.

It was obvious now, an exchange was never going to happen the way she envisaged. It could well have been her body lying somewhere in these woods, just as Carl tried to tell her. She didn't want them to have the boy now. They didn't deserve him. Not now. Her agenda for the boy had changed. She would lay low until morning and then contact the police, explain everything, accept the consequences and hope they can provide protection for her family.

She stopped walking for a second. In all the rush to hide the body, she had forgotten her bag which she had gone out of her way with to retrieve from Martha at the hospital. More importantly her phone. She turned and looked back; the track was visible for only a good thirty yards before it vanished into the darkness. She contemplated returning for her phone but decided she had come too far, so she would return in the morning.

As she rounded a corner, a small clearing became visible. The track now split, left and right. The left fork was narrow and was more of a footpath, not wide enough for any vehicle except maybe a pushbike. The right fork remained wide, still with two tracks cut in. Jane took the right track, hoping it would lead to the edge of the forest or maybe a farm. There she could summon help.

As the shadows of the wood became thinner, she noticed a porta-cabin. It's dark exterior almost covered with the wild growth of the forest. She knelt in the long grass. observing the cabin, her face twitched as the patter of rain fell from her hair, watching for signs of life. Nothing. Nothing but a voice in her head yelling shelter. She hesitated, wondering if she would be walking back to her pursuers.

She watched the cabin for several minutes from a canopy of trees nearby before moving toward it. A carved sign to the side reads *"Forestry commission"* She mounted the wooden steps slowly and reached for the handle. The anticipation of a locked door was short-lived as she encountered little resistance in its opening. She eased the door ajar cautiously, inch by inch.

Halfway in, the door became obstructed. She felt around with her left hand, the other still firmly gripped on the handle. As she shifted sideways into the narrow gap she felt a solid obstruction against her leg.

Chapter 18

Saturday 28th 00:15

As they left the café in McBride's squad car, O'Connor felt uneasy about investigating the cabin without backup. Having only transferred to the murder squad in the last year from organised crime, he was still learning, but he relied heavily on his judgment. His respect for McBride as a lead detective conflicted his own intuition. He wasn't a hero and had seen the results of many colleagues who had dared to take the dangerous route in order to pursue the camaraderie of being a hero but failed, leaving their families to pick up the pieces.

Tonight, he was not a hero, but entrusted the experience of McBride, despite some of his procedures being questionable. O'Connor none the less felt the urge to make known his opinion all the same.

"You think maybe it would be better if we called in for backup? We could cover more ground, might be safer as well," stated O'Connor, watching McBride scout the side of the road for a suitable place to pull over.

"You think too much O'Connor," he said, eying a spot on the left.

O'Connor decided on a more obvious tact. "Just thinking of our safety that's all boss."

"I understand your reserve, but sometimes you have to take the bull by the horns, embrace the opportunity, police work is all about seizing the opportunity."

McBride cut the engine and with the last forward momentum, steered up onto the grass bank coming to rest just a few yards from the track entrance.

"Those goons aren't going to spend all night pissing in the dark for a woman who could be god knows anywhere."

McBride undid his seat belt and slipped more gum into his mouth.

O'Connor realised his opinion had gone unnoticed.

"I'm willing to bet a Big Mac she's in there," said McBride chomping down on his gum.

O'Connor could smell the sweet scent of peppermint drifting around the car. A scent he was familiar with when working with McBride.

"I could kill for a Big Mac now," grinned O'Connor.

"When we've cuffed this woman, you can buy me one as well."

"And if she's not?" he asked watching McBride's cheeks make hard work of his gum.

"Then I guess I will buy you one. It's a win-win."

O'Connor removed his fluorescent jacket as he left the car.

"Turn off your radio and phone, don't want any unwanted noise."

O'Connor grabbed a long black-handled torch from the glove box. There was a mixture of excitement and fear. It wasn't often he ventured out into the wilderness, most the crimes he'd attended were in the concrete jungle of big cities, so a murder on the outer edges of civilisation made it a change, if not a strange one.

A short trek found them partway down the track. McBride was clumsy in pace, and certainly not dressed for the occasion, especially in leather shoes and casual trousers. But he wasn't about to let inappropriate clothing put him off a valuable lead.

O'Connor didn't want to undermine his senior, but he felt compelled to reiterate his concern. O'Connor's experience on the murder squad was in its infancy but already his time with McBride had left him questioning some of his methods. But here he was, indulging in his less than by the book practices. Despite all this he trusted him. Trusted his experience.

"Maybe this is more complicated than we thought," suggested O'Connor. "We can't even be sure they haven't caught up with her, or if they're the ones in the cabin, not to mention how heavily armed they are. I don't want to sound like a rule book, but we need armed backup, Sir."

McBride sighed, loud enough for O'Connor to pick up his displeasure and turned on the spot, placing a friendly hand on his shoulder.

"I like you, Daniel, I do, but you're too focussed on the procedure, leave that to the guys who aren't working in the field. Sometimes opportunities present themselves for you to act on gut feeling. If we wait for back up now that's another hour and in this game, the opportunity could of sailed off into the sunset, ergo she'd of fled the cabin or been caught by those goons. Now keep moving because I'm not staying out in this pissing weather any longer than I need to."

O'Connor once again was drawn into his senior's way, it was clear they had different views about how to play this, but given McBride was as stubborn as he was logical, he decided to run with his plan.

"Ok, we'll do it your way, but for the record, this scares me."

If O'Connor could see McBride's face, he knew he would be wearing his usual you know I'm right look. O'Connor couldn't argue with McBride's logic. So for now, he was willing to go along. His boss was not a man easily swayed by the opinions of others. A result tonight might just turn out to be a career boost. So, he focused on the positives for now.

McBride yanked on his collar, pulling it up around his neck. "Try to keep the pace sensible will you."

O'Connor's six-foot frame and standard-issue police boots made light work of the terrain, compared to McBride's shorter and less than nimble movement.

The post-midnight sky had now lost its blackness and transcended into a sombre grey. The September rain changed tact and was now more of a fine mist but no less cool in its touch or invasive in its presence. Dark angular shapes were more visible, the treetop owl still gracious in its calling was the only welcoming sound in the forest.

Both made cautious progress, soon coming to a dark shape on the track. O'Connor Shone his torch, catching the reflective silver BMW.

"Well there's their car, looks abandoned."

"Windows' gone, hole in the boot lid, that explains the shots that were heard," said McBride moving up behind.

"So, this is Gill Carter's car, the women who called it in?"

"Apparently," replied McBride opening the door and searching the inside.

McBride focused his light on the top of the driver's seat, furrowing his bushy eyebrows. "Someone's injured, there's blood on the seat, hopefully not too bad."

"Shall I run the plates anyway?" asked O'Connor.

"No don't waste your time, it's their car alright."

"Well, that's a stroke of luck. I don't get why they drove down here. If I was being shot at I'd want to get as far away as possible," said O'Connor, redirecting his torch to the forest for a moment.

"I guess they had their reasons, maybe we'll bump into all three, now wouldn't that be a jackpot," smiled McBride, patting O'Connor on the back.

"Well, nothing useful in the car, only their bags, someone's rifled through them, all their makeup and shit's just been emptied on the seat. come on, let's move on, see if we can't wrap this up tonight."

"Something's bugging me about this," said McBride, dodging the thick mud and dancing around the water-filled ruts, cursing the state of his shoes.

"What's that?"

"The way Marry Tripp described the two women, she said one was immaculately dressed, nice jewellery, well-groomed and polite manner, maybe middle class if you like, the other one, was dressed more casually, jeans and hoodie, but clearly they were good friends, possibly related, and then there's our suspect, who was also well dressed, nervous but articulate."

"Your point, sir?'

"Well, they're not the sort of people who would you associate with these goons, let's face it they're on opposite sides of the social spectrum which leads to one of two possibilities. Either they were witnesses to a crime and therefore they want to silence them, or, they have something they want."

"Something else is bugging me as well," commented McBride pulling his jacket tighter for warmth. "Our suspect didn't arrive or leave with the two women in the BMW. So, how the fuck did she get here given that the nearest town is twenty miles away? It doesn't fit," said McBride shaking his head.

"That is a bit of a mystery, but there must be a connection between these three, considering this Gill Carter and her friend were asking questions about her."

They've crossed paths at some point in time, how else would they know what our suspect was wearing and why the interest?

"Look, we can ponder these mysteries later, we need to move on, I don't want to be out here any longer than I have to," said O'Connor moving away from the car.

O'Connor left his boss to ponder the scene and drifted forward to the bend, curious to where the track leads. Realising he had probably wondered a good fifty yards up the track, he turned back, anticipating his clumsy torso to be groaning his way toward him, but nothing.

He waited a few minutes, then convinced himself he heard a noise. Not an animal, but a low muffled sound, coupled with a deep voice which carried in the wind. Then the unmistakable sound of a gunshot. His heart fluttered and panic moved in.

He scrambled up the bank and threw himself under a nearby bush, ignoring the tearing brambles against his face, now so close to the ground he could taste the mud on his lips.

This was the exact situation he feared, the very reason he so desperately tried to warn McBride about, but here he was.

The rain returned, only now it was heavier, but even against the sound of it crashing on the trees, he could hear the approaching voices. They were now below him, on the track, their torches slicing through the darkness. An exchange of Russian dialogue raised and abrupt only added to his fear.

After a few minutes, they disappeared back toward the road.

Still, he waited, even after their departure. With fear and relief in equal measures, he eventually raised from the cover of the bush.

He sat up, his head nursed in his palms, realising how close to death he'd probably come. He had never experienced anything as close to those last ten minutes. His time on the force had never placed him in the middle of a life-threatening situation, but now he had been in the devil's mouth itself.

He wiped away the dirt ingrained in his face and stood watchfully. His legs trembled and the taste of adrenalin still clung to the back of his throat. He took a moment, then deciding if he should retrace his steps back to the car, in the hope his boss may be alive and hiding like he was, but the gunshot only reminded him of the level of danger he was involved in, and his courage to return evaded him for now.

He reached for his radio on the shoulder of his vest, his finger paused over the button. He knew the right thing to do was to call for backup, get in the armed division, but something made him stop. He would have a lot of explaining to do, the responsibility of McBride's possible death weighed heavy. An internal investigation was the last thing he needed now, not exactly a career booster and again he cursed his boss.

Still trembling, he took stock and considered the original plan. He pushed on toward the cabin. Maybe some good can come from this, if he can at least help this Gill Carter and run into the suspect, then he may still be able to salvage something from tonight.

The sour weather continued to make things difficult and he found himself scrambling ungainly. He deliberately avoided the track, too open and exposed, so tactfully he cut through the forest.

Immerging from a line of dense fir trees, his attention was drawn by a flash of white, nestled amongst overhanging branches. A white van wedged against a large tree, its wheels submerged in the soft ground. *What the fuck*, he thought.

He pulled open the passenger door, a weak light did little to the interior, but he spotted a large bag in the passenger footwell. Dropping onto the seat, he riffled through the bag. Discarding the usual female items. In the bottom was a mobile phone and a letter headed piece of paper with "*NHS Blackwater Hospital*" at the top with the name Jane Stevens. He realised that this was the woman they had been seeking, not only that, but it answered the mystery that perplexed McBride so much. She did arrive and leave by a vehicle. Albeit not very far.

O'Connor was side-tracked by another niggling thought, the coincidence of both the BMW and as it turns out the suspects' vehicle all in the same vicinity.

As he searched her bag, an irritating smell surfaced, its stench sitting awkwardly in the back of his nose. He placed the phone and paper in his pocket and rallied around the back of the van, pulling open the double doors. He pulled a small pocket torch from his jacket and scanned the inside. The plywood panels which lined the van we're not surprisingly battered and marked but nothing looked unusual. Only the stench. He replaced the torch and closed the doors. He returned to the van leaving the door ajar. The sweet smell of the damp forest was more tolerable than the retching smell from the back.

He grabbed his mobile from his top pocket and turned it on. At some point he would have to face the music, so he gave in to his conscience, which had been chipping away at him, and could hold out no longer. He would call it in and accept the consequences

The phone beeped and two messages instantly came through, his watery eyes struggling to focus. The first a text from his wife asking how late he was going to be. The second was from McBride, but the time of the message didn't make any sense. It was five minutes ago

O'Connor stared at the text. He read it again. Only this time he realised he was already in way over his head.

"We have the detective, do not inform anyone. We want the boy. Jane Stevens has what we want. Find her. Find the boy. You have until 6am. Break any instruction he will be executed. If we don't have the boy, he will be executed. We will be in contact."

His heart skipped. His thoughts presented in no order. The ensuing weight of the situation and responsibility was more than he could bear. The name, Jane Stevens. It all became clear. He had her phone and work address. He smiled, but it was the smile of an idiot as he realised it was of no use here. He exited the van, scrambled up the bank and continued toward the cabin for now.

Chapter 19

Saturday 28th 00:50

Carl sat patiently opposite the door, his fingers rhythmically rubbing the rough grip of his pistol which he held on his lap. Occasionally he would peer at Megan, resting her head on Gill's shoulder. He could only guess if she was asleep as their figures were just a merged black distorted shape vaguely darker than the background they sat against. Her comments about Jane weighed heavy on his mind. They were hurtful but true. Yes, there were circumstances out of his control, but he should have planned for such contingencies. He knew if he was on a mission for his unit, he would have every angle and outcome covered and planned for. So why was Jane's life worth less? he asked himself. Being in civvy street had made him complacent. But then much of the necessities which were an integral part of being one step ahead in battle are completely removed from the world outside of war. Carl needed control and structure, hell he couldn't even cook breakfast without a plan. It was in his DNA.

He sat in anticipation of the door bursting open and being confronted by someone as menacing as him. But all was calm. Minutes ticked away, and the only distraction was the day's events playing out in his head.

He shifted his chair in line with the doorway, and in doing so, convinced he saw movement through the window out the corner of his eye. This shadow was much darker and closer to the window, its movement different from the stadium of waving branches. Given the height of the window from the ground, he knew instantly this was not an animal, so he readied his weapon.

A metallic spring action sounded, and he knew it was the noise of the handle. Only seconds passed but like most heightened situations of dramatic anticipation, it felt much longer.

Like an automated machine he had assessed, acted and rendered the situation safe. He now had the intruder inside and on their knees with the cold hard barrel of his suppressor firmly pressed against the back of their head.

A textbook manoeuvre.

It took him longer to realise who he was holding than it did to be proactive. He recognised the pale coloured coat and the tone of the scream.

"Jane?" he said, surprised. He removed his hand from her mouth and placed the gun on the table. It was at that point he felt her displeasure as she struck out, wielding her arms like a frenzied cat backed into a corner. He took several strikes.

"You asshole! What the hell are you doing here?" she shrieked.

"Hey, keep your voice down."

Carl stepped back giving her some room.

"I trusted you, Carl, you left me in your house, just left me to do this on my own. Where the hell have you been?" she yelled catching sight of two shadowy figures on the floor at the far end.

Carl stood awkwardly.

"So, you're Jane," came a voice from the end of the cabin.

Jane stepped closer to the voice, now just visible in the faint light.

Megan stood, feeling the blood rush back into her legs. "I owe you an apology."

"I recognise you," said Jane, frowning at the familiar face.

Carl interrupted. "I think we all need to take a breath here." But his attempts to engage fell on deaf ears.

"You're the woman in the car," frowned Jane.

"I know I'm sorry, we're sorry, we should have stopped." Megan could still see the remnants of smeared blood on her face, despite the more obvious appearance of mud. "Look if it makes you feel any better, we asked about you, back at the cafe, after my sister and I drove past you." Her gaze fell to the floor.

"What the hell, it doesn't matter now. I'm sure looking at me I would have done the same thing," she said, too tired to argue.

"I'm Megan," she said, offering a friendly hand and eyeing the state of her clothes.

"I'm not in any worse state than you by the looks of it, crawling through the woods in this weather isn't recommended." She smiled warmly.

Megan hesitated, then fired a question. "Look, I know you probably don't want to help me now, but my sister, Gill, she's been shot. Carl told me you are a nurse, is that right?"

"Yes, I am. Well maybe not now, not at Blackwater anyway, not after what I've done."

Jane looked at Gill, hidden in the oversized jacket of Carl's, limp and lifeless. "Yes, of course I will."

She knelt in front of Gill and carefully pulled away the coat. "I'm going to need some light," she said, turning to Carl.

Carl peered through the window, waiting to catch more moving shadows, before handing Jane a small silver pen torch.

"I *am* sorry Jane," he said as she snatched the torch from him.

"Sorry for what? Rendering me unconscious, robbing me of a choice? leaving me in a house with a killer on the way or allowing me to end up in this situation? Take your pick."

More tears made their way down her stained cheeks. "I killed someone Carl, I killed someone," she cried. "I thought I was going to die."

Carl was shocked, his tough ego descended into a pang of guilt. He was not good with emotions or expressing feelings, these were no good to him outside the rigid mechanical actions of war. But the last twelve months had chipped away at this barrier, especially working in a caring environment like a hospital.

"Jesus Jane," he stuttered. "I'm so sorry, I can't believe how stupid I was."

His cool assertive stance and rock-solid look faded, and his eyes fell to the floor. "What happened?" he asked, avoiding eye contact.

Jane slid down to the floor, her eyes filled with a watery glaze. She knew he was sorry and being angry at him now wouldn't help. "I don't want to talk about it now, not yet," she said.

"Look, let me at least explain," he began.

"Not now Carl, ok?" she said turning away.

He made his way back to the chair by the door. He didn't blame her for being angry, he was just glad she was alive. "Just keep the torch beam away from the windows," he instructed.

Megan assisted Jane, aware her hands were less than dexterous, shaking from shock and numb from the cold. They were also no less stained and scarred than her feet.

"You must have been really scared?" asked Megan watching her gently attend to the wound.

"You have no idea."

"So what happened?" she quizzed.

Jane didn't take her eyes off what she was doing. She reeled off the events like she was reading a sentence from a novel. "You mean how did I kill him?"

"I'm sorry I shouldn't ask, that's the bad side of me, always delving into people's business, I'm just curious I guess, forgive me."

"I stabbed him in the neck with a pair of nail scissors," she said matter of factly. "They say it takes a certain person to take the life of another, but I disagree. Anyone is capable, given the right set of circumstances, your life or theirs. You just act. It was him or me. I foolishly got involved in a situation I couldn't get out of, not prepared for. I thought I was doing the right thing, but Carl was right, he told me back at his place how foolish I was, I should have listened really."

"If you thought you were doing the right thing, that's all that matters," said Megan watching her.

"Finishing what I started matters now, making my family safe. This has to be done right but handing over a dead child like a piece of meat doesn't sit right with me."

Megan frowned. "What dead child?" she quizzed, shifting around on the hard floor of the cabin.

"It all started with a young boy admitted to my hospital, it spiralled from there, he died but the animals that brought him in now want him back."

"So, you have him?"

"Yes, before the police did, that's how I involved Carl. I've known him a while, he's the security guard there."

Megan watched her tentatively dressing the wound, aided by the torch held by Megan's less than steady hand, not once did she look to Megan, but she knew it's easier to express a traumatic event when you don't have to face the person you're pouring it out to.

"I can't imagine being forced into a situation like that," said Megan softly.

"So how did you and your sister end up here?" she asked, still focusing on the job of being a nurse.

"As I said, we asked about you at the cafe, we felt guilty after leaving you, it just happened so quickly, except we weren't the only people in there with an interest in you apparently. There were two menacing-looking men in suits, at first, I thought they might be businessmen, but I realised after hearing them speak and the way they kept looking at us that something wasn't right with them. It was just a feeling, a hunch. They thought we knew you because they overheard us asking about you, they followed us, chased us and the next minute we were shot at, not something you expect when you just pull over for a coffee in a quiet roadside cafe. That's when Gill got hurt, a bullet came through the rear window. We drove in here to hide but they found us in the woods, our car at least."

"Those men you mentioned, they were there with me, there was a third, the man that was going to kill me." Jane stopped what she was doing for a second, now she was saying it out loud, it started to feel real.

"I know how you felt, you know," added Megan. "I hid in the car after going back for our belongings, as this figure approached the car, I closed my eyes waiting for the shot. I was convinced I was about to die but instead It was him." She pointed to Carl, now sat by the doorway. "That's how we ended up here."

Jane sniffed back her tears.

"Your sister is lucky, it's a flesh wound, although I'm concerned about infection setting in if she doesn't get to a hospital soon. She just needs to rest and plenty of fluids," she finished.

"Carl bandaged her up," said Megan.

"He did ok. So, you local around here? I'm guessing not, you don't have the accent," asked Jane.

"No, we're from Devon, we're on our way to visit our father, we've not seen him in twenty years. It's complicated, like everything about today, and you?" she asked.

"Yes local, my husbands an architect but he's away now on business, not sure how the hell he's going to understand all this," she replied, trying to wipe the dried mud from her hands.

"It's my two children I fear for the most, luckily they're with my mother in law, she has no idea either, she must have thought something was wrong as I never ask her to pick up the children from school, I can't even remember what excuse I gave, my head was just a blur."

Jane rested against the cupboard fronts, staring at the innocence of a stuffed tawny owl in a Perspex box, she couldn't help feeling the relevance of a once free, beautiful creature, hunted and killed for no apparent reason. There was an irony about her own predicament. She eyed her hands in the torchlight, her nails, most had been picked away until they bled, blacker than the night and filled with a disgusting mixture of rotten plant and damp clay.

"So where is this body now?" asked Megan pulling pine needles from her hair.

"The woods, in a body bag, sounds bad when I sit and think about what I've done," she said staring at the vivid colours of a kingfisher in the next cabinet.

"He wasn't dead when he was brought in, but his prognosis wasn't good, even less so when our protocol was interrupted and questioned by someone who could only be described as a psychopath. That was the strangest thing about all this. They were prepared to let him die because they didn't want us to follow the surgical procedure to remove a bullet from his head. He died but seems they are still keen to retrieve the body. Carl helped me get the boy out of the hospital before he was ceased by the police for evidence. Seems foolish now when I think back, but I just acted on the spur of the moment, like you do. I was going to use him to trade for my family. I dug myself a huge hole and ended up in the middle of it. The disconnection got to me, the way he referred to the boy, almost like a disposable item and certainly not a human being, I just don't understand why they are so desperate to get him back now he's dead, and they're prepared to sacrifice further lives for it."

Megan looked at her with sad eyes. "How the hell did you manage to keep it together? You can't feel bad. You did what you had to do," she said, placing her arm around her. "We're in this together now by the looks of it. I just need to get out of here somehow, but I've got a feeling I'm going to be spending some time in hospital with my sister first. I'm worried our father will be trying to call us, maybe our auntie as well, but they took our phones from the car."

Jane shared in her predicament giving her a smile of acknowledgement, but that moment was short-lived, startled by Carl's sudden gravelly voice. They hadn't noticed him stand.

"Ok, look sharp I think we have company." Carl reached for his weapon and stood opposite the door. Megan and Jane were both stabbed with fear once again. "Quick, throw me the torch." he snapped.

Jane rolled it toward him, he held it above his gun and aimed it at the door. He was unsure if their voices had carried beyond the four walls, but it didn't matter. His eyes were now glued to the door, waiting once again for the sound of the handle. Megan and Jane were braced in the corner at the far end, sharing the panic.

Jane reached for Megan's hand, squeezing it tight.

A moment of silence passed; Carl's gaze remained focused. Then came the sound of the handle, only this time it wasn't subtle. Carl was poised ready to disable the intruder momentarily with his torch, like a rabbit frozen in a car's headlamp. As a gap appeared, a cool brisk wind barged in and circled the cabin and he felt its presence on his face, instantly bringing his eyes to water. A large man stood before him, covering his eyes, and Carl pressed the gun to his head.

"I need you to put your arms behind your head and kneel on the floor. Slowly," he ordered.

"Ok, look I wasn't trying to be a hero. I'm looking for Jane like you asked me to," came the voice.

Carl looked at him confusingly, almost a DeJa'Vu moment he had with Jane. "What the hell are you talking about?" He still had the torch directed at his distorted face, squinting so hard his eyes sank into their sockets.

"You're not Russian," exclaimed Carl, noticing the distinct lack of accent.

"Russian?" came a confused voice. "No, my names Dan O'Connor, I'm a police officer," he replied quickly. O'Connor sank to the floor like he was asked, still conscious of the barrel pressed against his head.

Jane and Megan looked on in disbelief. Carl stepped back from the doorway and ushered him up.

"Carl, he's police, he can help us," yelled Megan.

"Let me handle this, I don't trust anyone tonight."

"What do you want with Jane?" he asked.

"Do you know where she is?" asked O'Connor, opening his eyes.

"I need some answers first."

"Yeah well, you're not the only one."

"Well I'm the one holding the gun, so I guess I get to decide who asks the questions."

"I don't know what trouble you got yourself in, but I can guarantee I'm not your problem tonight," replied O'Connor, hands still locked behind his head.

"Tell me what you want with Jane," he demanded.

O'Connor could still feel the barrel against the side of his face, even though he concluded his life was not in immediate danger.

"I need to speak to her about the events of tonight, but it transpires that this has now gotten way beyond that, in fact, we believe she's a victim." O'Connor sighed. "It's gotten personal now. Jesus what a mess. I know she's around here because I found her van in the woods."

Jane's head shot up on hearing the mention of her van.

"I'm guessing I'm not the only one caught up in this," O'Connor said.

"You said it's personal now, how?" asked Carl.

"Because my boss has been snatched, not far from here."

Carl replaced his gun and lowered his torch.

O'Connor lowered his hands. "I need to find her, it's important."

Before O'Connor could say another word, Jane appeared from the shadows.

"I'm Jane," she said stepping into the soft light. Her sudden introduction had O'Connor startled.

Carl held up his hand to halt her from coming any closer.

"I don't know who you are or how mixed up you are in this, but all I need from Jane is the whereabouts of a boy?" said O'Connor giving Jane a side glance.

"What do you know about the boy?" she asked.

"My boss and I responded to an alarm in this cabin, but halfway here he was abducted, possibly shot, I definitely heard a gunshot. Then shortly after I received a text message." O'Connor opened the message for her and Carl to see.

"It's been the weirdest night, and I'm still trying to fathom out what's going on, it couldn't get any more fucking complicated," he remarked.

"I killed the man in the café," blurted Jane. "As far as the boy, that's for me to take care of."

"Who is this boy? Where is he now?" asked O'Connor.

"He's dead."

"You don't have to explain anything to him," said Megan stepping forward.

"Let me finish," she continued. "I know how badly they want this corpse and I have no idea why but I'm not about to just hand him over now."

"Seems to me from where I'm standing that doing just that would put an end to this and you lot can go home," stated O'Connor sitting on the edge of the desk.

"You don't come into the game last-minute and start dictating the rules, you have no idea what it's taken to get *this* far," she replied assertively.

"Keep your voices down," said Carl watching Jane stand her ground.

O'Connor's powers of persuasion were being tested, so he decided to revisit this later.

"I didn't abandon you," said Carl, taking advantage of the silence between the two of them. "Your car broke down leaving me with no alternative but to leave it and hitch a lift to mine to collect the Land Rover. Not a contingency I planned for. Frustratingly I knew where you were as my van has a tracker. I'm sorry."

Jane listened to him this time.

"And this Felix? Did he show?" she asked, accepting his explanation.

"Felix made his appearance, just as I had anticipated," he replied.

"What happened? Did you kill him?" she asked coldly.

Carl was grumbled by her un-sympathetic response to a deed he clearly saw as necessary for her survival. "He won't be troubling you, but thanks for the gratitude."

She huffed. "I appreciate your help, but I'm not used to being with someone who leaves a trail of bodies in their wake, and don't you dare compare my actions tonight with yours. I had no choice, I did what I had to do to survive," she replied angrily.

He remained quiet.

"I bet you wish you could record all of this; you'd be a hero bringing this evening to a close," said Megan.

O'Connor frowned at her comment. "Hero? No. Like all of you here I'm a survivalist at this moment in time." He raised his hand and pointed to Carl. "Him. I'm not so sure about, I recognise a military man when I see one."

Carl reacted instantly. "You got some balls; you wear the uniform but it's pretty fucking useless tonight. You're as much a prey now in this mess as we are. You don't know jack shit about what they've all been through."

He raised from the desk, expressing his physical prowess like an alpha male. "Maybe I'll just kick your ass out of this cabin and leave you to sort your own problem out," he continued.

O'Connor scorned at him. "This is just an excuse for you to play action man."

Carl didn't bite.

Before the testosterone-fuelled atmosphere could peak any higher, Jane stood between them, facing Carl.

"Jesus, guys come on. We have bigger problems here. Carl. Help us out of this please."

Megan didn't say anything, she agreed with Jane. Yes, Carl might be a bit of egotistical jerk at times, but she knew if it wasn't for him, she could have been just a corpse. Plus, he was the only person right now who had the skills to get them through this. She'd been reading him closely. Calm and decisive under pressure. O'Connor was right, you can spot a military man a mile off but when your life is in the balance its a man like Carl you want on your side. She was also quietly smitten with him, but those feelings could stay buried for now.

Time was pressing on and the likelihood of them being caught in the cabin was intensifying.

"Ok, I think I've got a plan. O'Connor, I need to know a few things first."

"Like what?" he replied sharply.

Megan checked on her sister.

"Tell me where you were when they took your partner; how close to this cabin were you?

I need to know if you called it in. I need to know if we can expect the cavalry."

Carl reeled off the questions faster than O'Connor could think, but he needed to know exactly what was going on outside. O'Connor explained the event as it happened, interjected by the experiences of the others, and Carl began to build a picture and form a plan in his head.

Carl leaned on the desk in front of him, addressing the others, O'Connor was still feeling insulted by Carl's lack of respect for him as a representative of the law, but for now, he had a higher agenda and that was to save his partner. Even if it meant playing to the tune of a man he disliked already.

"Ok, O'Connor, according to you we have until morning, that gives us about five hours, let's use that time to our advantage. They want Jane to get to the boy, so we have the advantage of knowing where the boy is. Is that correct Jane?" he asked.

Jane bellowed her objection. "Surely you're not suggesting we hand over the boy now. Not after all I've been through, you just going to give in to these people?"

"Hold on, am I missing something here, wasn't that your plan, isn't that why I helped you in the first place?"

"Yes, so they would leave my family alone, not to give him away to save someone we don't even know, no disrespect officer," she replied.

"I think formality went out the window a long time ago, just call me O'Connor, and I understand what you're saying, but surely handing him back will save my boss and they won't have a reason to go after your family."

Jane folded her arms and huffed.

Carl placed his hands on his hips, hinting his authority. "There are lives at stake here. The boy is dead, he can't be saved twice but we can save the life of O'Connor's boss," exclaimed Carl.

"It doesn't matter who gives him up, as long as they have what they want then they'll just move on, and so can we," replied Carl.

He turned his attention to O'Connor. "So where is your backup? I passed the café earlier and it was crawling with police, you had two, possibly more shooters in the area and you and your boss just decided to wade into here on your own knowing all this? In my book that would be called a suicide mission."

"That's exactly what should have happened, but McBride persuaded me it would be a simple job. I trusted his experience. He's a good detective and in twelve months of knowing him I have never questioned his judgment, well not to this extent."

"Until now," added Carl.

O'Connor accepted that Carl was right, he did question tonight's call but felt he owed his partner some loyalty.

"You know what's funny?" asked Carl. "I knew this cabin was alarmed, I knew the minute I barged open the door, I'm not sure why, there's nothing here worth stealing. But I figured at least the police would turn up and flush out the bad guys, use them as a decoy to get Jane to safety, and it turns out Gill and Megan, which I hadn't bargained for, but like you heard first hand, they've also run the gauntlet tonight," said Carl, removing his pistol and cocking it again like a toy you never get bored of. "Looks like you're joining us then."

"And what if I'd been an armed officer entering, you could have been shot."

Carl laughed. "You serious? They'd make more of an entrance than you, there'd be helicopters, flashing lights, the whole lot. That's what should have happened here."

O'Connor grunted.

"You want your colleague back don't you?"

Megan interrupted. "Are you really just going to hand him over now?

Carl nodded.

"Megan, they will kill his partner, you were nearly killed, your sister was shot and you two had nothing to do with it. We've been caught up in something that is not our business with ruthless people."

Megan yawned in a wave the tiredness.

"Aren't you just a little bit curious why the dead boy is so important?"

"Oh, come on Megan. There could be a thousand reasons why, but only they know the answer," he replied.

Megan didn't reply. She just sat trying hard not to let the tiredness take over.

Carl ushered Jane over. "I need to speak to you." Jane struggled to raise herself from the wooden floor.

"What do you want, Carl?" she sighed.

"I need you to take me to the boy. But before you object, just hear me out?" he asked.

She perched herself on the end of the desk. "Ok, I'm listening."

"I'm going to use the boy to our advantage. Your efforts to save him may not be totally in vain, the tracker that's on my van. I'm going to remove it and place it in the body bag, that way I can track them to wherever they take him."

"Then do what?" interjected O'Connor folding his arms.

"First, you're going to hand me your phone, so I can contact the captors," said Carl.

O'Connor unfolded his arms and took out his phone. "I hope you know what you are doing."

Carl raised his eyebrows. "Do you want my help or not?" He was not used to people questioning his motives or his strategy. In the field, you either give the orders or you act on them but never question them. However, Carl accepted he was not working alongside highly trained operatives.

"Are you asking me to go back out there to get the boy, alone?" she quizzed.

"No, I'm coming with you," said Megan.

"No, you won't," Carl said sternly. "Just me and Jane. Those guys will have gone now. They have O'Connor's partner as a bargaining tool. They have nothing to gain by camping in the woods now. Danger's over for now."

"You seem sure of that," remarked O'Connor.

"Common sense, they won't be standing around in this climate on the chance we might be wandering about in the dark, they will have taken your boss somewhere secure."

"I hope so," said Jane.

"And what about my sister?" asked Megan.

Carl's patience was running a little thin with the repetitiveness of which Megan and Jane challenged his every word. Carl scratched his head in frustration. He was beginning to feel that the conflict inside the cabin was worse than the threat outside. He placed his hands around the top of Megan's arms, momentarily he felt like shaking her. "Look. I can't move everyone at once," he said, looking at her weathered expression. "I'm taking Jane with me in the Land Rover to retrieve the boy and the tracker. When I return, I intend to set up refuge in the cafe. There is food, water, light and a place to lie down. From there you can call an ambulance and you and your sister can go to the hospital."

O'Connor butted in. "You know the police will ask questions, anyone with a gunshot wound is automatically questioned. Could get messy, I'm just saying," he replied raising his hands. "Something you need to keep in mind."

"No way. I'm not leaving Gill to face the music."

Megan threw a glance at Jane. There was a desperation in her eyes. "Can you help her? I can't have the police asking questions, what if they arrest us?" she pleaded.

"I could go with her," suggested O'Connor. "To the hospital, I can say I'm with her to make a statement, that way we can avoid any suspicion. I'm your perfect cover." O'Connor waited for his suggestion to be accepted. He wanted to feel like he was contributing to the group, after all, they were helping to find McBride.

"Sorry to be the voice of despair but the hospital is crawling with police. I would imagine being a small community your colleagues might have some questions for you as well," said Jane.

"She has a point."

Megan glared out the window. Was Carl right, had they gone? What if she made a break for it? She was restless now, tired hungry and irritated by her waterlogged clothes which had now given her a coldness she couldn't shake. "Why can't we all go in your Land Rover?" she asked, watching the water zigzag down the glass.

"There's no room, single cab plus all my gear in the back as well, sorry. I can take Jane and take your sister with me," said Carl standing by the door. "O'Connor you stay here with Megan until I return. It's the best solution all round."

O'Connor had begun to think like a detective, he had watched McBride more than enough times to understand the importance of observation and hang onto snippets of information. He approached Jane, who was sat with Gill. He crouched before her.

"Jane, I don't mean to bring up your experience at the cafe and I'm not interested in questioning you as a suspect, but I am interested in the man you overpowered." He was delicate in his questioning and evaded using the word killed.

She was surprised by O'Connor's sudden interest in her experience. Nervously she picked at her fingers. They may all be in this together but at the end of the day she had taken the life of another, and O'Connor was still a police officer.

"What are you after? A confession?" She was short with her reply.

"I told you I don't care about what you did, you're a brave woman. I just want to know about the man."

"What do you want to know? What he was wearing? What he sounded like or what he said to me? Because all I can remember is being so petrified."

"I need to know if he had any identifying marks or unusual jewellery," he asked.

"Are you fucking kidding?" said Megan. "The woman's been through a terrible ordeal, you think for one minute she's going to remember stupid little things like the colour of his fucking socks?"

Carl butted in. "What are you doing, O'Connor?"

"I'm trying to establish which corner of the criminal underworld these lowlifes are from because that will tell me a lot about who we are dealing with and exactly what their MO is." O'Connor just looked straight up at Carl. "You of all people should understand that, surely. Know your enemy."

"They're bad fucking people. That's it," said Megan, waving her arms. "What difference does it make?"

O'Connor pulled out a mobile phone." I believe this is yours, I took it from the van, when I was looking for you."

Jane scorned. "What? Why did you take my phone, what for?"

"Actually, I'm not sure."

She grabbed the phone from him. Straight away she noticed several missed calls, one from her husband, and several from the hospital. She hovered over the call button to Dale, staring at his missed call.

"You ok?" asked O'Connor, seeing her staring at her phone in silence.

"I want to call Dale, my husband, but it's late and I have no idea what to say to him or even how to start the conversation."

"I think we'll leave this, for now, O'Connor, don't you?" Carl said. "We need to retrieve the boy. Jane, you ok to come with me?"

She popped the phone into her pocket. "Yes, I suppose so."

"O'Connor, you ok to stay with Megan?"

"Like I have a choice," he answered sarcastically.

"This isn't a prison barrack, you're free to leave, walk out, do what you want but if you want me to help you get your partner back then you need to follow my plan." Carl was short on sympathy and heavy on impatience.

O'Connor remained quiet again.

"I will be back for you both."

Jane pulled her coat tight, tying the waistband and pulling up the collar.

Carl flung his rucksack over his shoulder and removed the car keys from his pocket. Making light work he pulled

Gill from the floor and placed her across his shoulder like a lifeless doll, just a hint of raucous exhalation reminded them she was still alive. Before any more questions could come his way, Carl had pulled open the door and made his way to the Land Rover just a few yards away. The sweet smell of the forest was carried in on a chilling wind. For a single moment, Jane closed her eyes, just long enough to embrace the freedom she had been yearning for. She didn't mind the rain now. In fact, she relished every drop, feeling its touch on her beaten brow.

Carl placed Gill in the seat, sitting her against his large rucksack and Jane squeezed in beside her.

He pulled out from a fir tree, flicked on the lights and immediately a barrage of insects filled the beams.

"Ok, Jane, it's down to you now. How far up the track do we need to go?"

"Not sure, just keep driving and I will tell you," she said, peering over the dash.

Carl negotiated the track; the dancing beams were less than subtle. Jane sat forward in the seat, gripping the handrail tightly on the dash.

"You do know what you're looking for, right?" he asked.

"This is harder than I thought, I just dumped the van and ran. I didn't take much notice, sorry. Anyway, don't you have a tracker on the van?"

"I do but it's only accurate to around a hundred yards."

As the vehicle rounded a bend, Jane noticed a familiar sight. A high bank with broken foliage near its ridge. "There," she shouted, pointing to the bank. "I drove the van in there somewhere, if we find the van, I know where the boy is."

Carl pulled up.

"Ok let's go," he said quietly. For the few seconds it took for her to clear the vehicle and disappear into the bushes, she felt the paranoia of being caught, so stayed close to Carl.

He swept the vicinity with his torch, hoping to catch a reflection somewhere down in the gully.

"You ok?" he asked, noticing her limp.

"It's my feet, just sore that's all."

Carl offered his arm and they descended the bank. Within a few yards, the beam picked out a reflective shape buried amidst a canopy of branches.

"Well there's my van, so where is the boy?" he whispered.

She approached the van and pulled open the passenger door, she felt around for her belongings, scattered on the footwell.

"Forget your stuff for now, just find the boy."

"He's down there, in that gully." She pointed.

Carl shone the beam to a gully at the base of the bank. Jane sat, exhausted and out of will. She removed her shoes and massaged her toes hoping the pain would somehow rub off. Carl was now at the base, but she had no desire to help. His voice echoed from below, but she ignored him.

She was then stirred by the sound of breaking twigs and heavy breathing as Carl emerged from the bottom, dragging the body bag up the bank.

She looked on, feeling repulsion in her gut and ignoring him, she turned and made her way back to the Land Rover and sat in thought.

He returned, lifting the body onto the flat bed behind the cab, the thud was not subtle and she sensed there was no dignity is his handling.

Carl had his fingers poised on the keys.

"Ok, so what's bugging you now? I appreciate this is not easy for you but Jesus you could've given me a hand down there," he replied, dropping his hood.

"You know how I feel about trading the boy now, especially after all we went through to get him out. I don't have a choice though do I because more people are going to die if they don't get him back."

"Jesus, you like to pick and choose, If you remember we got him out that hospital so you could trade him for your family. Now suddenly you have a conscience," he spat, shaking his head.

"At least I have a conscience, you just shoot people who get in your way, I don't think you value human life at all, this is a child's body we're bargaining with, trading it like a piece of meat," she angered.

Carl sat opened mouthed. "So why the hell did I save Megan and Gill, come to think of it why the hell did I bother trying to find you and save your sorry ass."

"Because you like to play the hero, but all you do is trade one life for another."

Carl didn't react, he didn't know how, he felt his intelligence belittled, but unless anyone had seen and been through what he had, they could never separate personal feelings from duty or survival.

"The boy is dead, we didn't kill him, they did. We can't bring him back; his life can't be made more painful, but we can save O'Connor's partner," he replied.

Jane dabbed her eyes with her coat sleeve. "So they get what they want now, even after what they put me through. It could have been me lying on that toilet floor."

"You know the truth in all of this? You're bitter because they were going to kill you. This is revenge, isn't it? Pure and simple. This isn't about saving the boy, it's about you getting one up on them."

She slapped him across the face, punched at his chest and yelled before sobbing into the wing of his arm.

He let her sob for a few moments.

"It's ok, Jane, I'm sorry, I shouldn't have said that, I can't imagine how hard this is for you, or how petrified you must have been," he replied softly.

"No I can't save him, I can't put him to rest, but I also don't want them to have him, this just goes way beyond fair. I'm just so confused right now." She pulled back to her seat. "I'm sorry Carl, I shouldn't have hit you. But you're right, I don't want them to get away with what they've done, and now, seeing the way that poor boy is being traded like a piece of meat makes me angry. I don't know what to do anymore."

"Let's just get you to the café, some hot coffee and you can warm up. We will figure this out."

Chapter 20

Saturday 28th 02.10

O'Connor paced the cabin, but there was no rhythm or set pattern to his movement. Occasionally he would stare at the stuffed birds in their cabinets wishing he had enough light to see their beauty and detail.

"My wife used to like birds," he said randomly.

Megan sat on the worktop, fidgeting and tapping the door fronts with her feet.

"Is that all you got to say? Look, I'm sorry but I'm not up for small talk. I just care about getting out of here with my sister."

O'Connor shot her a glance. "I bet you wished you'd not stopped in the café now, I know I should have listened to my own instincts, instead of my pig-headed superior. This is going to cost me my career now. It's possibly going to cost him his life," he mumbled, feeling the glass boxes.

"What's your first name then?" she asked. "O'Connor seems rather formal."

"Daniel," he replied. "But everyone calls me O'Connor."

"I'm curious," he said. "Why do you put so much faith in Carl? Do you not stop to think he has a higher agenda? A man with an ego as big as his needs feeding. I mean why not just drive you out of here, to safety, tell the police?"

"I guess he had his reasons. Besides, involving the police would jeopardise Janes' family. That's the whole point of blackmail. I'm sure even you can work that out," she said sarcastically.

"You know the police are equipped to handle this kind of situation."

"Yeah? What if it was your family O'Connor? Besides, I don't see you calling for back up."

"Well yeah, it's gotten way too complicated for that now."

Megan jumped from the worktop, turning her attention to the cupboards below. Nothing more than boredom and the chance to avoid O'Connor's annoying suggestions. Her thoughts turned inward as she opened and closed the cupboard doors, still desperately trying to block out the chill which she struggled to shake. She was hungry too, more than she was tired. She pictured the vending machine in the café, but for the moment she was stuck here.

Lost in mid-thought, a loud crackle made her flinch, turning to O'Connor quickly. It was his police radio.

"Control to three seven one. Do you copy? Over."

His manner changed.

"You going to reply?" she asked.

"You kidding? I'm already in the shit for coming down here without backup as it is. I shouldn't even be here."

The radio crackled again. *"Control to three seven one. Do you copy? Over."*

His pacing increased.

"Odds on they tried McBride's radio, but they will have destroyed that. They may try our mobiles." O'Connor shook his head and laughed. "Of course, action man's got mine," he mused. He then stood gazing out the window as the same message was transmitted.

Megan joined him at the window, pondering the chances of just running.

"So why don't we just leave, I mean Carl said they've probably gone now," she suggested.

"It makes sense, they won't have my partner in the woods, they'd take him somewhere secure. They can't afford the risk of police turning up and sweeping the area." O'Connor rubbed his face. "Why the hell did he have to be so pig-headed, always chasing the danger. What the hell am I going to tell his wife?" He kicked at the cabin wall with his large black boot. Even Megan felt it's tremble as it rippled through the less than sturdy walls.

She sat on the desk by the door again, still contemplating making her own way to the cafe, and her sister. She watched O'Connor, haunted by the guilt of his partner, but then she knew all too well about guilt.

"Don't know about you but I am not staying here any longer, I'm worried about my sister, I need to be with her. Carl could be dead for all we know."

"What? You sure it's safer out there than in here, Carl will be back soon, let's wait," he suggested.

"Really, O'Connor, listen to yourself. You don't even like the bloke, now you want to follow his orders?" she replied directly.

"I don't like the bloke," he said defensively. "But it seems the sensible solution, plus if his plan with the boy goes well, I might be able to save my boss, that's all I'm worried about. You're welcome to scramble through the woods in this pissing rain."

He walked to the window again, his hands in his pockets, watching as the forest changed shape like an ever-moving picture, but he wasn't really seeing, just thinking about what may have happened to his boss, and if he was actually still alive.

"Something puzzles me," he said turning to Megan.

"What's that?"

"These people, the ones after us, Russian accent, organised and ruthless, all points to a Russian mafia, but that just doesn't feel right, out here arse end of nowhere, I mean there's nothing here."

"What makes you say that," she asked, pacing the cabin, her hands wedged tightly under her armpits for warmth.

"The body in the toilets, McBride said they had no fingerprints, this was something I came across a while back, it's so they can't be identified, highly organised, but I need more information, I need to talk to Jane again."

O'Connor turned from the window to find Megan now sat in the corner embracing the foetal position for added heat. His observation did not extend to a courteous acknowledgement of her obvious distress.

"Didn't you see the body?" she quizzed.

"Only briefly, McBride examined the body, but we didn't really get much chance to discuss it. I questioned some eyewitnesses in the cafe but nothing significant came of that. To be honest, we were more interested in Jane, you and your sister."

"You really trying to solve this? I just want to survive this."

"I'm trying to figure out who we're dealing with."

"What does it matter, they're still scumbags," she spat.

"I don't expect you to understand, I get that you're angry."

"Oh, and you're not angry. They have your boss for fuck-sake."

He withdrew a cigarette from his padded vest pocket and lit it, inhaling the calming effect it brought.

"Yeah, I'm angry but I'm also trying to save him and the best way to do that is to do what I'm trained for, that's why I wanted to question Jane, she saw one of them close up, maybe she noticed something about them, that's what also confuses me. Why up here, there's nothing up here."

He drew on his cigarette, the bright orange tip glowing in the dusky light.

"Why can't it just be a few scumbags chancing their luck, maybe the boy was for a ransom and it went wrong, these things are usually about money. Aren't they?"

"Not these, they're too organised, besides, a dead boy is no use in a ransom."

Megan stood from the floor, hoping some movement might make her feel warmer.

"Jane said they went to great lengths to blackmail several people in the hospital, that takes a lot of background work and organising. They manipulated people which takes planning, they are smart people, ruthless and kill without restraint. This is not a kidnapping gone wrong, because they are not stupid enough to take the boy to a hospital if he was someone's missing child. So, if he wasn't missing and not needed for a ransom we come around to the same question. Why do they want him now that he's dead? Why not walk away and leave him in the hospital, disappear back to where they came from? They need him for something, and I'm going to find out. I'll admit I'm out of my depth on this and haven't worked a case like this for years."

"Maybe it's drugs, there's a lot of money in drugs."

"How is that relevant to the boy?"

"Maybe he was made to swallow them, you hear of people doing that to smuggle them."

O'Connor shook his head. "No it's not drugs, there is no way anyone could swallow the amount of drugs to justify the lengths and organising these guys are going to, not to mention the risk of taking him to hospital."

She accepted what he said made sense.

"You ok?" he asked after a few moments of silence.

"I just thought about something," she said, ignoring his question. "We saw the other two men in the cafe. I remember as me and my sister walked past them in the cafe, they were sat in a booth, the large man, he had a tattoo of a fish behind his ear. The other guy, the skinny one I couldn't make out but he had one, in the same place, I think. Does that help?" she asked.

O'Connor turned to her with a deadpan expression. "Are you absolutely sure about the tattoos?"

She clocked his surprise. "Pretty sure, why?"

"That's a problem, that's a big problem. Shit. What the hell are those guys doing in this neighbourhood." O'Connor paced the room stroking his face.

Megan felt a sense of dread. "What? You know what that means? What do you mean a big problem?" she asked worryingly.

O'Connor took up position on the desk again, his fingers drumming against the wooden top. Megan couldn't settle, she didn't like the way he reacted to her description.

"Part of the Russian mafia, I came across these guys a few years back, but that was in London, think of them as more of a Mafia separatist group, very dangerous people, some serious shit, but they are so far from home, it doesn't add up."

Megan's stomach tensed. "Oh shit. This isn't going to end well, if they'd have caught us—"

"You'd be dead. No two ways," he interrupted.

"What about your boss?" she asked anxiously.

O'Connor shook his head and took a last drag before stubbing it out. "I doubt he'll be returned alive," he said pessimistically.

"What, you know that for sure?"

"They don't leave loose ends; he can identify them. It doesn't matter if they get the boy or not. Also, I hate to say it, but Jane has stirred a hornet's nest. Taking the boy and then trying to bargain with them, no wonder they want blood, and we all better hope we don't cross paths with them again," he said.

"Ok, that's beginning to really scare me now. Let's just give them the boy, I mean that's all they really want, let's leave him in the cafe and get the hell out of there, tell them where to find him."

O'Connor raised from the desk and moved back to the window. His attention disengaged.

"Hey, O'Connor. Did you hear me?" she said impatiently.

He approached her, closer than she felt comfortable with. "We need to get to the cafe; I need to warn the others."

"What now?"

"You coming?" he asked, making his way to the door.

"When I wanted to leave you said to wait for Carl"

"Yes, but that's before you told me about the men in the café"

"You want to wait for Carl?"

"No, I don't."

O'Connor held the door and she left the cabin.

Chapter 21

Saturday 28th

Carl exited the woods. Poised parallel to the road, lights and engine off, and waited a few minutes.

"What are we waiting for?" asked Jane.

"Shush." He gestured as he wound down the window.

"Stay here."

Carl exited the vehicle and stood by the road, listening. There was a stillness that was only experienced when the world was asleep. There was no city lights, just bleak and empty wilderness. He peered toward the direction of the cafe, again no lights, not even a faint glow. After a few moments, he clambered back in.

"Ok let's do this," he said quietly.

"What were you looking for? Them?"

"Yeah. A part of me thinks they might have the same idea about the cafe, but I can't see any lights. It's the only building around here for miles which kind of makes it an ideal place to lay low. I'm going to run with no lights just in case, so keep an eye out."

As Carl pulled onto the road, she sat forward, her face almost pushed against the windscreen. His pace was slow and cautious, straddling the middle of the road, allowing for space while running dark. Within a few moments, the cafe spawned into view. Carl shifted into neutral and the slight downhill gradient was enough to reach the Cafe without any more engine noise than was necessary. He rolled into the car park, narrowly avoiding a large police sign that read '*Incident closed*'

"Wait here until I check it out. I will leave the keys in the ignition, if you hear anything other than me, drive out of here," he ordered.

"But that's not going to happen, right?" she asked.

"I hope not," he replied, leaving the vehicle.

She moved across to the driver's side, watching as he approached the cafe. It was a very different scene to earlier. Yards of police tape stretched across the building's entrance was a kick in the teeth reminder of the horrific ordeal she'd been part of earlier. As he disappeared around the side of the café, she couldn't help feeling insecure, she was not ready to be left alone, raising her anxiety to an uncomfortable level.

A few minutes later, he appeared from the entrance, breaking the Police tape.

"It's all clear, doesn't look like anyone's been here since it was sealed up. I'm taking Gill in. You coming?" he asked looking at the worried expression on her face.

"Yeah. I guess so."

"You, ok?

She nodded.

"Look I know this seems hard for you, but in there is the best place right now. At least until I figure this out."

"Carl, what really happened back at your place?" she asked, stalling.

Carl leaned against the open driver's door. He removed his hood, rubbed his crew-cut hair, and repositioned it back up.

"I told you."

"No, you told me he wouldn't be a problem anymore. I just need to know what you did to protect me that's all. Did you kill him?" she asked directly.

"You want to feel more guilty, punish yourself, like you have over the boy. Look I'm not going to tell you what happened, you don't need to know, just put it to bed, Jane. You've been through more than enough already. Sorry but I'm not going to add to that."

She knew in her heart what he had done, but she wanted to hear it. Maybe to punish herself for taking a life, a polar opposite to her oath as a nurse.

Carl carried Gill into the café, and Jane limped in behind him.

Inside the main entrance, the smell of bleach was overpowering. It was not just the smell that triggered a flashback. But the long, dark corridor directly in front of her. Shivers ran from head to toe as she faced it again, the place where she had not so long ago fought for her life.

"Damn this place," she said under her breath.

A glow from the vending machine in the corner provided adequate light, as well as the small emergency lighting above the fire exit at the back of the cafe. She watched as Carl went from window to window, making sure the blinds were shut, not wanting any of their movements to be seen from outside. She stood by the counter, staring across at the table in which she was forced to sit earlier. Only a deep hum from the fridges and vending machine made any noticeable background noise. No passing traffic, no clattering of cups or cheerful voices. Just silence.

Carl took stock, unzipped his coat and surveyed the room. "You ok?" he asked.

"What, being here?"

"You know this will end Jane. I will do my best to make sure your family are safe."

She slumped into the nearest seat. Eclipsed by exhaustion. "And O'Connor's boss?" she asked.

Carl sat opposite. "Yeah. Just when I thought saving your ass was not testing enough. I'll be honest, I'm not sure how this is going to play out," he confessed.

"Thought you had a plan. I mean the boy. You're going to track the boy, right?"

Carl sat back. "That's the plan. Find out where they take him."

"Then what?"

"Pass on the information to the police. Hopefully, catch those bastards." Carl leaned forward, his eyes still on watch. "This is no military operation though, they're not predictable. Maybe they'll just kill him anyway. You got to understand, Jane, I can't be held responsible for everyone, especially McBeth... McBride... whatever his fucking name is."

"It's ok, Carl, I don't expect you to be responsible for anyone, especially me. I'm sorry I gave you a hard time back in the car, I know it wasn't your fault. I realise I roped you into this mess," she explained.

He checked his watch. "Shit, I need to go pick up the others. Look, why don't you see if you can make some coffee, I bet you could use one," he said.

Carl spotted her subtle smile, even under the tangled web of once blonde hair.

"You're safe here. If they were coming here they'd be here now. Besides I need you to take care of Gill, you're the nurse, right?"

Carl's reassurance had little effect, but she had no choice, she knew that.

"Please don't be too long," she said.

Carl drew a large knife from a leather sheath under his coat and offered it to her. "Here take this, it's more effective than nail scissors. Just in case," he grinned, trying to lighten her spirits.

She failed to see the funny side but accepted what he was trying to do. She took the knife, caressing the cold reflective blade which felt large and deadly in her small hands. Heavy too.

"If I'm not back in thirty minutes, call the police, tell them everything that happened, and about me. Oh, and lock the front door behind me."

Carl zipped his coat and disappeared through the front doors.

She remained in the chair, staring at the large knife she held in her right hand, she didn't even see him leave.

She continued caressing the knife for a few moments. The black, shapely, ivory handle felt comfortable in her grasp. She felt empowered, and gently placed the knife under her belt, not wanting to be separated from it, and then checked on Gill who was still laid on the seat. She was pale but her breathing was steady. Gently rolling Gill onto her side she checked the entrance and exit wound, both small raised holes capped in congealed blood. She was happy that no infection had taken hold. At least not for now. As she sat with her, quietly and peacefully, she felt the weight of emotional exhaustion. Again, for the second time, she resisted.

The quietness was the worst. Now that Carl had gone there was a level of vulnerability that she found hard to ignore. As a precaution, she made her way around the cafe, checking the security of the doors. She contemplated freshening up. But that meant venturing down the long corridor to the toilets, and that now was a feat too much.

Chapter 22

Saturday 28th 02:35

There was a sense of freedom as Megan left the cabin, and the potential danger on the outside was less of a worry than the thought of being cornered inside.

As she took a moment to get her breath, she realised that O'Connor was not behind her. There was a temptation for a moment to shout his name, but self-preservation was the stronger urge. She knelt in the long grass, waiting and watching for him to appear, but each minute she was motionless was a minute more she felt exposed, so she moved on, looking back to see if O'Connor had caught up. But there was no sign of him. There was, however, the sound of a vehicle turning into the track. She dropped quickly into the long-wet grass but instinctively knew this would be Carl, recognising the distinct sound of a Land Rover, the same sound she remembered from their parent's farm.

As it rounded the corner, she leapt in front of the bright lights, waving her arms.

Instantly, the Land Rover slid on the wet ground before coming to rest just inches from her.

She raised her hand against the blinding headlamps.

A large silhouette exited the vehicle.

"Jesus Megan," cursed Carl. "I could have run you over. What the hell are you doing out here? Where's O'Connor?" he added, looking beyond her.

"I don't know, I mean we both left the cabin and I thought he was behind me; I don't know," she replied.

"Ok, get in."

She sat, peeling the soft mud from her hands. "I need to tell you something," she said, still catching her breath.

Carl frowned. "What's that?"

"O'Connor told me just before we left the cabin what the tattoos meant, he said he knows who they are."

"How?"

"Only because I remembered seeing the tattoos, that's why he wanted to talk to Jane earlier. He didn't know I'd seen them as well; he was just rambling; I didn't pay too much attention."

She fiddled with the heater, trying desperately to warm her aching hands.

Carl shoved it into gear and set off.

"Where are you going?" she asked, as he continued toward the cabin.

"To find O'Connor, he's probably not far behind you, hopefully, he'll be as stupid as you and jump out in front," he humoured.

Megan didn't respond.

"Tell me what he said."

"About what?"

"The tattoos, you said he knew?"

"Russian mafia, something like that."

Carl brought the Land Rover to neck-snapping halt.

"You're shitting me right?" he glared.

"That's what he said."

"Nah, can't be, that's way off-grid for them, London maybe, but up here where sheep outnumber people, I find that hard to believe."

"Well if we find him you can ask him yourself. No way he's this far back. I don't understand," she said.

Carl drew to a stop, a few yards from the cabin, and leant across the steering wheel, peering at the cabin, the lights centred on the doorway.

"It doesn't make any sense," she muttered.

"You sure he left behind you; I mean did you actually see him behind you at any time?"

"I just remember running for my life, I assumed he was right behind me, he let me go out first, it's only when I stopped to get my breath, I realised he wasn't with me. But why? Why would he not run with me?" she asked.

"Maybe he was caught, or had other ideas."

"Ok, we'll head back, get you warm, should be some coffee waiting at the cafe, I left Jane to sort it, keep her occupied."

She was not really paying attention to him and certainly not as upbeat as he seemed to be. Thoughts about O'Connor's whereabouts concerned her.

"What were the tattoos?" he asked, navigating the ruts.

"One had a fish behind his ear, the other had a bull, something like that, I didn't get a very good view, you have any idea?" she asked.

"No, I don't, but it's probably some kind of alliance," he suggested. "if it is Russian mafia, like O'Connor suggested, then it's not something I would actively get involved with, but now we're up to our necks in it, we just have to finish this the best we can."

"What about O'Connor's boss, you still banking on an exchange?"

"That's a tough one, sounds callous I know but if O'Connor's right, then he's dead anyway. Like I told Jane earlier, I can't be responsible for everyone in this mess, looking out for you three yes, but can't help anyone else who gets into this."

"Sounds fair I guess, I know I probably wouldn't be here if you hadn't shown up, or Gill."

"Yeah, I'm not sure Jane would share your appreciation, I really thought I was helping her at the start, but I feel bad for her, she could've been killed," he said, still negotiating the undulating track and wrestling the steering.

"At the end of the day she involved you from the start, she asked for your help, Carl, if it wasn't for you, she would be dead anyway by now by the sounds of it."

Megan fiddled with the heater again, eager to feel warmth but to no avail.

"It's not very effective."

"No shit."

He smiled.

On the final push to the road, he killed the lights again, taking no chances. The northern rain had picked up the pace and the inefficient wipers did little to help his visibility.

He pulled once more into the cafe, this time at the top of the car park.

"God, I hope they're not there," said Megan.

"If they are, then it's game over." Carl pulled a gun from his jacket. "Stay here till I've checked it out."

Megan's blood ran cold with the thought of them being in there with her sister.

"Like I said to Jane, if it isn't me coming out that door, take the Land Rover with the boy and just get the hell out of here, ok?"

Megan nodded and a second later Carl was halfway towards the front entrance, gun poised. But her worst fear soon evaporated as Jane appeared at the door and wasted no time in running to the entrance.

"Am I glad to see you." Megan smiled, wrapping her arms around Jane. "How's Gill? Is she ok?"

"Yes, she's fine, she's sleeping still, best thing she can do, let her body recover."

Carl locked the door behind them. "You ok, Jane?" he asked with puddles of water draining off his camo-coat.

"I guess. Just a bit scared, but I got some coffee on."

She went behind the counter and brought out a large glass coffee pot and some white mugs. "This all seems a bit false Carl," she said, pouring the coffee. "I'm not sure what we're doing here now, I keep expecting them to just burst in." She stopped pouring for a second. "Where's O'Connor?" she asked, looking up.

"I don't know, I thought he was behind me when I left the cabin."

"Oh, this just gets worse, why would he not come with you, what if he's also been caught?"

Megan shrugged. "I don't know, my heads too full to think about it."

Megan grabbed a mug of coffee, swallowing slowly to savour the taste, her earth covered hands relishing the warmth.

Carl unzipped his coat and placed himself in the booth opposite her, placing his gun on the table.

"Here's your knife back," offered Jane.

"Keep it, at least until this is all over."

She didn't argue, it had certainly aided her feelings of security.

After checking on her sister, Megan made her way to the room behind the counter. She needed to get out of her wet clothes and thought maybe there would be some chefs uniform out the back, but again luck was not favouring her tonight. She searched the room, looking for anything that might help, not really focusing on anything. She needed a distraction. On the back wall was a sink with a hot water tank and to the left hung a few white aprons. Megan opened a wall cupboard above the sink, only tea, coffee and an assortment of condiments could be found. To the left was a tall thin set of three lockers and a door which only led to the single staff toilet. Megan was nosey and proceeded to open the lockers, but they were all locked.

Apart from a drawer which had a variety of knives and kitchen implements, there was not a lot in the room. She felt a selfish streak peaking its way through her conscience. She could just take herself and her sister away from here, continue their journey, she and her sister had no hold here. The boy held no bargaining value to her, but she did however still retain an ounce of loyalty to Jane, and of course Carl, for saving her life. Just getting up and leaving with her sister would be cruel. Plus, of course, Gill would scorn her for just thinking this.

"What you up to Megan?" asked Carl, suddenly appearing in the doorway.

"Jeez Carl, you made me jump," she said holding her chest. "Don't you think I've had enough shocks tonight?"

"Sorry."

"I'm just snooping around, looking for some dry clothes," she said. "So, what's the plan?"

"I'll explain in a moment, just going to do some surveillance outside, I'm not taking any chances. I don't want to get complacent," he said.

Megan left the room with him, joining Jane in the booth.

Carl picked up his gun, slid up his hood and made for the exit.

"You ok, Jane?" asked Megan.

"Think so," she replied looking at Megan's hoodie, painted with the stains of the forest.

"How are you holding up?" asked Jane.

"Tired, confused, like it's all a bad dream."

"You're made of sterner stuff than me," said Jane.

"I'm no stronger than you, maybe I'm just better at putting on a front, I'm not as strong as you think." Megan turned to her sister asleep in the opposite booth. "She's the strong one, I'm like a duck, calm on the surface but underneath I'm paddling like hell."

Jane stared into her coffee. "I thought I was strong but honestly, I can't do this much more, I miss my family so much, my kids will be wondering where I am. I can't even call them."

Megan reached for her hand. "We'll get through this, I'll help you. I might just have to paddle a bit harder."

Jane blinked away her tears. "What about your family, I mean your father, I expect he will be worried?"

Megan's gaze rested on Gill again. "She's my family, she's always been my family. Our father is a stranger really, yes I want to see him again, but truth is, I don't need him, but I have a suspicion he needs us more, possibly clear his conscience before he leaves this world."

"You mean his conscience about your mother?

"Gill has no idea why dad wants to see us, but I do," Megan spoke softly, not wanting her sister to hear. "I think he's ill, I haven't been told that, but I know. Why else would you suddenly want to meet up with your daughters after twenty years? Even my auntie is oblivious, but then they were never that close. I don't think Gill could cope," she said.

"I'm sorry, but Gill is strong, right? I'm sure she will be fine."

"Yeah, she's strong, but everyone has a breaking point. I've lived with grief, anger and disappointment all my life, so to me, well it doesn't really make much difference, but Gill, well, I don't think she's been honest to herself about how she really feels. She won't admit it, but I've caught her crying on a few occasions. She's more excited about seeing dad than I am. He hasn't been in our lives for so long and honestly, I don't need him now."

"Your sister does though, right?"

"Yes, she does, so for her, I'm going to pretend to be excited."

"You need to take care of her," Jane replied. "I will do my best to take care of her medical needs, but the rest is up to you."

Hearing the doors sound, they both looked simultaneously, relieved at the sight of Carl, rainwater draining off his jacket and forming small puddles on the floor.

"I can't see shit out there, I doubt anyone would want to hang around out there tonight, it's all clear for now."

"So what do we do now, just sit here like it's coffee morning," said Jane, again conveying her sarcasm toward him.

"Nope, we're going to end this," he said.

They looked on curiously as he withdrew O'Connor's phone and dialled.

There was a cockiness in his demeanour, an assertive manner to which Jane and Megan could never hold in a situation like this. Sure, Jane could hold her cool and expedite clear controlled thinking in the operating theatre under medical life or death situations. But this was clearly Carl's bag.

The call connected and he spoke with precision and confidence.

"I have the boy, this needs to end tonight, no one else has to get hurt, but this exchange will only happen on my terms, I hope I make myself clear," he stated with a firm voice.

"I'm not sure you are in a position to negotiate with me. I imagined you, Mr security man, to be more intuitive to the situation at hand, so let me remind you," said the voice on the phone.

Carl listened to an exchange of words in the background, although Russian spoken, he deciphered that there are three people present. The next sound was not quite as easy-going on the ear. The discharge of a gun, its sound tiny in the phone's speaker, but Carl knew, in reality, it was a thunderous noise. This was briefly followed by a bellowing cry and Carl realised then, they had shot at McBride. Not to kill, but to wound. A classic tactic clearly in retaliation for his audacity to challenge their power.

The moans continued.

"Now, does that refresh your memory?" said the voice.

Carl sensed annoyance and decided to manipulate this to his advantage. "You think I give a shit about some detective I've never met? Tell you what we'll keep the boy, bury him somewhere and you do what you want with him."

Carl hung up.

Megan and Jane's expressions toward him were more menacing than the call.

Megan rose from the table and moved toward him with the conviction of a Great White about to nail its prey. Carl stuffed the phone in his pocket and braced for impact. But he didn't get the response he expected.

"That was either really fucking stupid or very clever, I can't quite decide," she said, gazing up to him with disdain.

He flashed a look to Jane at the table. She was not quite as understanding.

"You're unbelievable Carl. Not only are you playing games with a dead child, but you're also now playing executioner with someone else's life. How dare you," she spat.

Megan understood her anger, and to some extent, it would be the first thing anyone would respond with. But she also figured out what Carl was trying to do, even if it sat uncomfortably with her.

"Jane, you have to understand, if you show weakness, they have control," he said, approaching the table. "They will kill him anyway, they're not interested in an exchange, it's going to be an ambush. Trust me," he explained firmly.

Jane shook her head in disapproval. "How can you be so sure, Carl? they need the boy; they need the detective to trade."

Megan watched the pair of them thrash out their moral reasons for standing by their opinions. She understood what Carl was saying, O'Connor had already confirmed they would execute his boss. She was still quietly plagued by the disappearance of O'Connor. She wondered where he was. If he had in fact been caught or just deserted them for his own survival.

Carl retreated, grabbed the coffee pot from the counter and poured. There was no finesse in his action as he gulped the lukewarm coffee and wiping his face with the back of his hand. He didn't tell them about the shots he heard over the phone, he saw no point.

"They want us to think the exchange will go like a textbook delivery, you know, like in the films, where you stand fifty feet on opposite sides, nod politely and then each party walks to the middle, makes the exchange and then return to their respective sides only to disappear in the sunset, cue the credits blah blah blah."

"What about O'Connor?" asked Megan.

Carl shrugged. "Dunno, not my problem," he said, leaning back against the counter.

"What if they have him as well?" asked Jane.

"Now, hold on a sec. There's no point in speculating about things we don't know. What I do know, is if they did have him they'd have made a point of letting me know. Like I said earlier, I'm not going to be responsible for everyone. Right now, it's just you guys. Ok?"

Carl grabbed a solitary tuna sandwich from the display shelf on the counter and had devoured it by the time he returned to their table.

As he sat, the phone rang.

He answered, putting the phone on speaker.

"You have balls, as you English say," came the voice.

"Get to the point," he replied abruptly.

"You think the detective is the only one we can hurt? You need to think very clearly before you respond with anything other than something I would very much like to hear," he replied coldly.

Carl took a moment, trying to fathom who else they could hurt. He reflected on an earlier conversation with Fuller, regarding Jane's address. Could he really be sure they don't know where her family are and trust Fullers explanation about only having the pictures?

So, with that in mind, he turned to the question at hand. "Ok, where and when?" he asked.

"Jane will bring the boy at 6.15am. Taking the road North from Blackwater, past the Pines Cafe. She will take a left turn opposite a farm. Follow that road until she comes to a disused petrol station on the right. She will pull up on the forecourt and lift the bonnet of the car, leaving it open. She will wait in the car and we will remove the boy from the boot. She will look straight ahead; she will not turn around or try to look at us. If she does, we kill her. Once we are clear we will call you and inform you as to where you can find the detective. These terms are not negotiable, now do you understand, Mr security man?"

"I don't know where Jane is. I will bring the boy," he replied, registering the panic in Jane's expression.

"Do not try to insult my intelligence. And by the way, Mr security guard, it appears we are dancing around the elephant in the room. I believe this to be another popular English phrase."

"And what elephant might that be?"

"The elephant by the name of Felix."

"I'm guessing that bothers you, especially as I saw it coming."

"It educates me about your skillset, which in turn puts me at an advantage." He laughed. "She comes alone."

He hung up.

Carl chucked the phone on the table, exhaled a sigh big enough to inflate his cheeks and glanced at the clock on the wall. It was 03:44.

Jane shook her head repeatedly. "No way, I can't do this, please Carl, no."

Carl slid into the booth next to them, taking the top of Jane's arm. He could feel her trembling, resonating in his hand and every nerve ending that buzzed through her body.

"You're not going, don't worry, I have a plan," he said reassuringly.

"I don't understand," said Jane. "If I don't go, we heard what they said."

"We don't have a lot of time, but I need to disappear for about forty-five minutes."

Megan glared at him. "Just tell us the plan. Stop with this cloak and dagger stuff."

He leaned back against the soft leatherette cushion, spreading his arms across the top like an eagle. A sudden flash of light had them twitch like a startled rabbit. A stray car hurried by the cafe, it's lights playing long shadows across the room before disappearing into the distance.

"They're clever. The time. 6.15am is just dark enough to be hidden but light enough to make out what's going on around them. This is planned very well. They will approach from the front, not the rear like the conversation would suggest, but instead use the lifted bonnet as cover eliminating the chances of being seen in the rear-view mirror. They will execute the driver and then take the boy in their own time."

"That *is* quite clever actually," remarked Megan.

Jane tutted. "There's nothing clever about anything tonight."

"What about the detective?" asked Megan.

"He's probably dead already, they don't intend to hand him back, they never were. This is a snatch and grab."

"Bastards," blurted Megan. "Shame we can't give them a taste of their own medicine."

"Who said we can't?" smirked Carl.

"What the hell are you up to?" asked Jane.

"Remember the mannequin I had in the flat?"

"Yes, why?"

"Well, Betty, that's what I named her before I used her as target practice. She will be you again," he explained.

Megan frowned, so Jane explained the plan Carl had hatched at the flat as a decoy.

"So, here is how this is going to play out, Betty will be dressed as you Jane, they won't be there early as there is little or no cover, just grass moor. Likewise, they know there is nowhere anyone else can hide either. I know the disused garage. The only safe place to approach is from the front over a slight incline, hence the need for the bonnet to be raised," Carl then turned to Megan. "I need your help, I'm not going to lie to you, there is an element of danger and you need to trust me," he said.

Megan focused more on the adventure rather than thinking through what he was asking of her.

"What do I have to do?" she asked immediately.

"Really, Megan?"

Carl shook his head, "Thanks, Jane."

"It's ok. I want to do this; I need to do this. Let's just get this over with."

Jane pulled her weary body from the seat and headed for the counter. "I need to eat," she said, helping herself to one of the leftover stale sausage rolls, which had more than likely been on show since the morning before.

She sat on one of the tall red leather and chrome circular stools at the counter, and for a brief moment dissected the tangled mass of once blonde hair, picking out a mixture of pine tree needles and a mud paste, the only action which felt grounded at this moment.

Taking a bite, she stared vacantly into the glass-fronted fridge and its contents, allowing her mind to wander. Apart from her family, which she tried hard not to focus too much on at this moment, her thoughts turned to the boy. As she stared at the row of eggs, sat behind the glass door, a thought surfaced, an idea she'd associated with a previous body in the past. *Could this be why the boy is so important,* she thought.

She turned quickly in her seat, and yelled for Carl, swallowing the last mouthful of sausage roll.

"Yea?"

"I need to see the boy before you disappear, Carl, I need to indulge in an idea, it might be nothing, but it might be the answer," she said.

Carl frowned. "What idea?"

"I'm not sure yet but I need to see the body."

Megan sat up quickly, hanging on to her sentence. "Yea, if you know, tell us, this could change everything," she replied with equal excitement.

"Or complicate things. What exactly do you expect to find?" he asked.

"I may be wrong so don't get excited just yet, I just need to see him."

Carl looked at the large silver clock above the counter, made more facial movements and stroked his stubbled chin. "Ok, tell you what, we're pushed for time, I need to collect some equipment from my place, it's best the boy stays with me, just in case, when I get back we'll explore your idea then, ok?"

"Sure, but I need you to bring back a razor," she said.

Carl frowned, reached into his camouflaged backpack and removed a khaki green handheld walkie-talkie. He twisted the button on top, emitting a loud squawk before placing it on the table.

"Quicker and more reliable than a mobile phone, Channel seven, any problems call me."

"How long you going to be?" asked Megan.

"Forty-five tops, don't forget to lock the door behind me, keep the main lights off and the blinds down."

Carl shouldered his backpack, pulled up his large hood and made for the door.

"He doesn't like what you've done," said Megan picking up the radio.

"I haven't done anything; I just want to explore an idea."

"Exactly, he doesn't like to think someone else has an idea other than him."

Jane picked up the coffee pot. "Can I tempt you?"

"Please, it's the only thing keeping me going."

"Try adrenaline, it's natural and more potent."

"Had my fair share of that."

"So, what exactly are you looking for?" asked Megan, slurping her coffee.

"Honestly, I'm not sure yet, but I've got a feeling you'll be more receptive than him."

"You trust him?" asked Megan.

"Trust is all relative. You mean do I trust that he's acting in our best interests given the current circumstances? Well, the jury's still out on that one."

Carl's absence left an uneasy atmosphere, Megan dashed to the door and twisted the lock. She then checked on her sister before making her way to the small bathroom area beyond the kitchen, leaning on the sink and staring disapprovingly into the mirror. An unrecognisable reflection stared back, her face a canvas of dried mud, like badly applied fake tan. Only the trail from her tears had cleaned a path of natural skin and her hair resembled a bag of tangled wool.

She doused her face in water, relishing its cool soothing touch. She lifted her head and stared once more into the mirror and then at the murky coloured water below. "How the fuck did I get here," she mouthed to herself in the mirror.

Her moment of self-reflection was interrupted by a yell from Jane in the other room. She dashed from the bathroom, only to find a flash of light moving across the ceiling, proceeded by the crunching of gravel, cutting her dead in her tracks.

Jane was stood from the table, her face cupped in her trembling hands, her eyes wide and staring.

"Maybe it's Carl, maybe he forgot something," suggested Megan, feeling her mouth turn suddenly dry.

"No, I doubt it."

The lights slowed.

Jane dashed to the window, lifting one of the slats carefully. "Shit, it's turning in here."

The noise from the gravel carpark stopped, its beams bleeding through the bamboo slats, across the ceiling and reflecting off the aluminium counter.

Megan dashed to the table and grabbed the walkie-talkie, turning it to channel seven as Carl instructed.

"Carl, you there?" she yelled.

Only static sounded.

"Carl, pick up; for god's sake, we need you."

"Maybe it's just tourists, hoping for an early breakfast"

"Carl, you there?" continued Megan.

"They've pulled up at the back of the car park, I don't like this, why is he not answering?"

She turned to Megan, her face telling her everything she feared.

"I'm trying, he isn't answering; Carl, just pick up, we need help."

Again, the radio squawked.

Megan paced the black and white tiles, frantic for contact.

The headlights were killed.

"I'm here," he answered. "Sorry, what's wrong?"

"Carl, there's someone here, in the car park, just hurry up."

"I think they're getting out," yelled Jane, still eyeing the car through the blinds.

"Yea, I heard, listen, don't turn on any lights, can you see the vehicle?"

Megan peered between the slats. "It's difficult to see, it's too dark, I can't see anything through the rain."

"Listen, make sure the place is locked up, lay low, don't make a sound, hopefully, they might realise you're not there and move on, I'll be there as soon as."

"I just hope your right, just hurry will you."

"On my way, hold tight."

Jane scurried to the front door, checking the lock, even though she had seen Megan lock it. She peered from the cover of the large billboard by the front doors out toward the car park. The sound of a door clunk and the watery figure in view, standing by the car had her retrieving to the back, searching frantically for a place to hide, but nothing seemed ideal.

A few seconds later, a thunderous noise echoed through the cafe as the doors were tried in several quick successions.

A voice followed.

Not loud, but the single word spoken in Russian brought a sudden and crushing sense of dread.

A second voice followed, this time louder and irritated.

Megan turned the walkie-talkie off, stuffing it into her pocket, urgently trying to prise half a plan from a brain which is hardwired for fight or flight, but not thought.

Jane was glued to the floor under the window, her back to the concrete pillar, frozen with panic, mesmerised by the flashing lights on the fruit machine, blinking from the darkness.

Outside there was silence, beyond the rain-filled gutters spilling onto the ground and the hum of the fridges kicking in periodically, the voices had stopped. At least for now.

Megan's immediate thought was drawn to Gill, spotlighted above by the small circular emergency lighting.

The short moment of silence was short-lived, but it was not the voices that sent their hearts rocketing this time, but the pounding on the fire exit to the side.

"I'm not moving, they won't get in, they'll think no one is here and go," she snivelled.

"I'm scared too, but if they get in, well, I don't want to think about it, but I need your help; I need to move her, but I can't do it without you."

"Move her where?" asked Jane, confused about her intentions.

Megan looked to the large wooden booths, hidden in near darkness, only a shimmer of light cast from the dim emergency lighting picked out the red leather cushion. She moved to the nearest booth, studying the rectangular wooden base, its boxy construction gave her an idea. She pulled off the cushion and tapped the wooden board below. A hollow sound told her what she wanted to know.

Taking a cutlery knife, she prized up the wooden plywood base which was not fixed. As she suspected lay a hollow space, long enough and wide enough to crawl into, it was tight, but doable.

"Give me a hand to move Gill."

"You are kidding right, no way we going to fit in there."

Another thud bellowed through the room, shredding their nerves further.

Jane didn't argue, she took Gill's legs and they carefully lifted her into the hollow space, she murmured briefly, but didn't wake. Jane stuffed her red mud-stained coat under her head for support and replaced the base and cushion.

Jane had already pulled off the adjacent cushion and base and proceeded to climb in the tight space, barely the size of a coffin.

Another thud thundered out, this time it was followed by the sound of splintered wood.

Entry was imminent.

"Get in now," she said, watching Jane squeeze into the frame. "We stay here as long as it takes, until it's safe, don't make a sound, let's hope Carl turns up soon."

She nodded.

Megan secured the base and cushion on top, then climbed in the one behind, positioning the wooden base with the cushion above her like a hatch, and waited, poised to drop at any moment.

That moment was now.

The fire escape door was breached, it's metal handle colliding with the wall under force.

She dropped the board, squeezing into the recess.

It was dark. Not night-time dark, but darkness that only the deepest cavern could hold. The cold hard tiled floor felt gritty and coarse, years of accumulated dirt and misplaced food found its way beneath the cushions and lay amongst a network of cobwebs. It smelt musty too, but it was safe, at least for now.

The immediate darkness was short-lived as a small round hole appeared in front of her. Maybe it was a knot which had dried, shrunk and fallen out. Either way, it gave a small angle of sight a few feet wide. She watched and listened, her heart rocking her chest, her warm breath reverberating off the board, inches from her face, and the sound of her pulse beating in her ears.

She heard the footsteps first, then appearing in her line of sight, two men, one distinctly taller than the other, the tall stocky man wore a black leather coat with black and grey camo trousers and black military-style boots, a well-groomed beard, and slick raven hair, the other, thinner man dressed similar had a distinctive face, and was bald.

The two men circled the café, passing erratically back and forth, conversing in their native tongue.

Their movements were ungainly and hurried, accompanied by irritated voices and thumping of fists.

She spied the taller man lifting the coffee pot from the counter, his hand touching the side before conversing with his colleague, just out of sight.

"Shit," she thought.

She realised the hot coffee pot was a dead give-away to their recent presence, a detail she had never considered, but given the short time frame she had, she was still pleased she even managed to find a place to hide.

The thinner man stepped into view and looked directly down the line of the booths, his grey eyes fixed on hers, or at least that was what it seemed like.

She pulled her face away from the hole, sensing he was staring straight at her.

No way can he see me, she thought. *Can he?*

He stood statue-still, his hands resting in his pockets, looking, staring down the aisle.

The other man muttered something, but the reply was a *"Shush"*

He was listening, but the only noise was that of the rain trickling down the gutters and the low hum of the freezer.

Still, he didn't move.

But then came a sound, a whimper, not loud, not constant, but enough to confirm her worst fears.

Again, an exchange of words between the two men, this time quieter, and a nod toward her direction raised her fear.

The man stepped forward, slowly, quietly down the aisle, stopping occasionally to listen.

One thought circled. *Please don't make a noise, please don't make a noise.*

She could see his face clear as day, just a few feet away, his complexion was a weave of scars, his hands tortured by the same tragedy, a victim of fire maybe, and his fingers were short and stubby with the absence of any nails. But she felt no pity.

Another moan came from the next booth.

She closed her eyes and sighed.

More exchange of words followed by a brief flicker as the room was bathed in sudden light.

The man stood for a few seconds, but somehow the lack of conversation was more unnerving.

She followed his movement, closer and closer, his leg inches from sight and the intricate detail in his boots became crystal clear.

The voices continued.

Her gaze now rested on the booth opposite, the one holding Jane. She noticed the leatherette cushion was not seated straight, something she never considered in the panic.

She then witnessed the beginning of their end. As he lifted the cushion, she closed her eyes, like the worst game of hide and seek as a little girl, she would close them tight, just prior to discovery, her face tightly screwed, hoping and praying she wouldn't be found. But it would make no difference here and the consequences far more serious than a child's game.

With the cushion removed and several verbal exchanges made, he pulled up the wooden board.

Her heart sank, her stomach responded with a series of gargles and from now on she was just an observer, powerless to intervene.

Where the fuck are you, Carl? she thought.

Their voices were deeper and angrier, but this was overpowered by the screams from Jane as she was pulled from the booth with force.

Megan watched them drag her up the aisle toward the main cafe area. Despite her limbs flaying with as much ferocity as she could muster, it was no match for the two aggressive men that had her.

The screams continued from out of view, yelling at them to let her go.

All she could do now was listen to Jane's agonising cries from the next room, flinching at the distinctive sound of a face being struck in several successions, followed by a whaling cry.

The struggling subsided.

"Where's the boy?" came the aggressive voice, this time in English.

"You're not here on your own, are you," she heard. "There are three coffee cups, Alexi, search the other seats."

She watched in nervous anticipation as he worked his way up the booths, ruthlessly abandoning the cushions and tearing up the bases. Then just a few passing seconds later a blinding white light was upon her, only a blurred outline of a man could be seen bearing down on her. This was followed by a sharp pain in her arm as she too was hurled from the booth like a rag doll. A combination of cramp and a vice-like grip made her whimper out loud as he marched her into the other room, his pace faster than her cramp ridden legs would carry her, and she collapsed to the floor just feet away from Jane, tied to a chair in the middle of the room.

She glanced up to see her beaten face, a narrow horizontal cut was drawn under her eye socket. A stream of mucus hung like a silver thread from her nose, and a mixture of snot and blood were patterned across her cream coat.

She sat hunched over a single seat; her hands cable-tied behind her, now at the mercy of these barbaric men.

"Leave me the fuck alone," hailed Megan as his hand clenched the back of her t-shirt.

She felt a sharp pain searing across her cheek before she realised he had even raised a hand.

She fell, clutching her face.

She was then pulled from the floor and hurled onto a chair next to Jane, her arms pinned tightly behind her as the larger man bound her wrists. She saw no point in struggling.

Another strike followed and she could taste the blood in her mouth.

"We can do this the hard way or the even harder way," he said with a fake smile.

"Now, where is the boy?"

She prayed for Carl to return. She wasn't strong enough to resist their physical interrogation, it all looks so cool in the films, the hero laughing back at the interrogator, seamlessly oblivious to the pain and never for one moment considering giving up the information. But in real-life, the pain was much more searing, and her resolve was low, she valued her life and that of her sister more. Let them have the boy. She wouldn't have blamed Jane for giving him up.

"I'm going to ask you one last time, where is the boy?"

Jane turned her beaten face to her and muttered as clearly as her distorted lips would allow.

"Carl has him."

"I'm not talking to you. I'm asking this bitch next to you."

Still towering over Jane, he turned back to Megan, reached out and stroked her face with the back of his hand. "Such soft skin so easily blemished," he said laughing.

Alexi was busy pouring coffee.

"It's true, a guy called Carl has him, he's coming back," she said quickly, staring up at his menacing eyes, as dark and void as his jacket.

A flash of light flickered through the blinds in front. For a moment she had high hopes it was Carl, but a rumble a few moments later only threw up another disappointment.

"Carl, Carl has the boy, in his car, please believe us, he's meeting us later for the exchange," she pleaded, hoping she wouldn't feel his hand on her face again.

Alexi called to Sergei, clearly the one running this freakshow, but spoke only in native tongue.

Alexi was leant against the counter swilling the last dregs of coffee around his cup like it was a casual gathering.

"So maybe the third cup belongs to this Carl," said Alexi.

"You'd better not be lying to me," said Sergei, grabbing her face with his hand and compressing her cheeks hard against her jawbone.

Megan was thankful they had not found Gill, if they'd lifted one more cushion, she'd be sharing her pain right now, but there was little consolation at this moment.

"Where are you meeting this Carl? And don't play games, I'm not a patient man."

Megan's eyes were sticky with tears, her face was a throbbing mess, and her arms, pulled tight behind her, were now beginning to feel like they were detached from their sockets, but she whimpered a reply.

"Here, he's coming back here," she replied, coughing up the mucus which poured into the back of her throat.

He grabbed her hair, yanking her head back to look up at him. "When?" he ordered.

Megan didn't know when, she thought he would have been here by now, maybe he wasn't coming back, but that thought scared her even more. She was oblivious to the time, and so she replied with something to stop him from hitting her again.

"Thirty minutes, he'll be here in thirty minutes" she muttered, praying she was buying enough time.

Sergei pulled a weapon from inside his jacket and pressed it hard against her temple. "You have thirty minutes, if he's not here by then. Bang, your dead, and her," he said looking at Jane. "She will be coming with us."

Chapter 23

Saturday 28th 04.25

Cal's return journey to the cafe was slowed by the unpredictable climate. The rain ricocheted off the bonnet like tiny ball bearings, in sound and sight, the wipers barely coping with the deluge.

He was anxious about their safety; he could only imagine the fear they were experiencing. He looked to the walkie-talkie, clipped to the dash, but hesitated to press the talk button, conscious his transmission could give them away.

He cursed himself, thumping the wheel.

A few minutes into the journey he was side-tracked by the sudden vibrating in his jacket, and pulled over to the side of the road. He removed the phone and stared inquisitively at the number.

For a second he imagined a conversation with his perpetrators, wanting to alter the exchange. This he feared the most because he would need a new plan.

"Hello?" he said tentatively.

The voice was not what he was expecting.

"Carl, is that you?"

He recognised the voice but didn't place it straight away.

"Carl?"

He pressed the phone hard against his ear. The rain may as well be gravel for all the sound it made.

"Jesus, O'Connor is that you? Where the hell have you been?"

"I will, well, I can explain, where are you?" he stuttered.

Carl sensed fear in his words.

"On my way to the café, why?" he asked curiously.

"Do you have the boy?"

"Yes, but why the interest O'Connor, I don't understand."

O'Connor's voice was hesitant.

Carl felt a twinge in his gut, like something wasn't quite right.

"You ok, O'Connor, what's going on, where are you?"

"I'll see you at the café then yea?"

Carl could hear his erratic breathing, his words strained and awkward, like everything he said was forced. He couldn't decide if O'Connor was alone or if someone had got to him, coercing him to make the call. He had now made it known he has the boy. At least if they thought this then hopefully no harm would come to the others. He assumed someone was listening in on the other end and decided to use this to his advantage.

"Yes, I'm bringing the boy, meet you in thirty minutes, If for any reason Jane and the others get hurt, I'm going to bury the boy in a deep grave."

The call was ended abruptly.

He had a suspicion someone else was listening to the conversation, adding the last comment was the only thing he could think of to help protect the others until he got there.

Carl twisted the key and tore off up the road, pushing the Land Rover as hard as he dared on skinny tyres and surface water.

With one hand juggling the wheel, he pulled out his Beretta with the other, chambering a round at the ready.

He thumped the wheel. "Shit," he yelled to himself. The call had thrown him a curveball, he didn't like it, the added pressure, not only did he have the lives of Jane and the others, it seemed O'Connor's life hung in the balance as well.

The miles past along with the minutes and slowly the disfigured lights of the cafe appeared in view. There was no way he was just going to drive anywhere near the café.

He pulled up a few hundred yards short, nosing the Land Rover into a roadside bush and turned off the engine. He reached behind the seat and pulled up a small square plastic box and popped the lid. Inside was a set of military-grade night-vision goggles. He then pulled forward another long box from behind the seat and flicked the catch. With pin-sharp accuracy, he assembled an LA115A3 sniper rifle, complete with a suppressor, each piece snapping into place with micro precision, complete with sights, capable of picking out a smile from a thousand yards. All dressed in clothing of tangled camouflage.

Securing the rifle across his back, he cut through the hedge line, avoiding the road and limiting the distance by walking diagonally towards the cafe. Each step was carved with confidence and with the aid of high-powered night vision. Each tree, bush and uncharted path was painted in varying shades of luminous green, translated into a clear and distinguishable route. He arrived at the line of pine trees, a good three hundred yards from the café. From there, he had an elevated view of the entrance and car park.

He bedded down in the soggy undergrowth, belly down, legs splayed and chambered a round as he gazed down the sights, surveying the area. He focused on a black BMW saloon, parked away from the entrance that appeared to have someone in the back seat.

He switched his sights across to the café, the three large windows were obscured by the bamboo blinds, only a couple of broken slats gave way to a limited line of sight inside.

He didn't like this, the pressure was mounting, he felt helpless in the moment, no clear plan and the control slipping steadily through his fingers. Mission failure. A crack of thunder announced its presence, followed by distant flashes. An image appeared to him, accompanied by the sound of destruction. The diplomat's wife, standing in a ruined street, surrounded by fire and smoke, her eyes full of sadness, beckoning him to come closer. The baby, wrapped in a blanket, soiled by the stains of the very buildings which fell around her, toppling into the street. Tears of disappointment filled her eyes as she held the baby, arms stretched out, pleading, shouting above the riot of shale and brick which threatened to engulf her. He reached out but it was no use. A plume of smoke and flames whisked her away in a flash and she was gone.

He flinched.

A sharp pain stabbed him in the face, a pain more real than the flames around him. A small branch whipped around in the wind, catching him across the cheek and bringing him back to reality. But was this reality any better than his flashback?

He caught his breath and focussed his sight toward the car, the night scope picking out the multitude of nocturnal eyes like luminous marbles in the shrub beyond. He zoomed in on the rear window of the black BMW. Small movements in the back confirmed his worse fears as the rear door opened and O'Connor was manhandled from the car, hands bound and forced to walk to the café by a single figure, dressed in black and holding a semi-automatic machine gun to his back.

He had a clear shot and only a few seconds to execute it before he would disappear into the café, and once inside there would be one more hostage.

He twisted the dial on the sights, click by click, his finger poised on the trigger, a few seconds later the dull sound of his weapon exhaled, followed by a distant thud and the figure fell, face down onto the gravel.

O'Connor stood in a moment of confusion before scurrying off into the darkness, toward the treeline beyond. With his hands still tightly bound, his balance was compromised, coupled with the long-wet grass which wound around his ankles like a sea of hands, bringing him down with every few hurried steps.

Carl ran to his aid as he stumbled across the wasteland. He pulled out his knife and cut the cable tie.

O'Connor fell to the ground, gasping for breath and massaging his bruised wrists.

"Stay here, be back in a sec."

O'Connor nodded, his breathing still playing catch up.

Carl sprinted off toward the car park, pulling his Beretta and cocking it at the ready, with the white noise of the rain covering his footsteps on the shingled ground, he quickly searched the body and removed the weapons and phone before dragging it to the back of the BMW, popping the boot and dumping the body in.

He returned to O'Connor who was sat up, nestled under a bush, his hands shaking and hyperventilating as he withdrew a crushed, water-soaked packet of cigarettes.

"Fuck sake," he cursed, discarding the packet to the ground.

"Yea, like they're gonna help right now."

"Hey, O'Connor, look at me, breathe. Slowly," he said crouching in front of him. "Well that explains your absence, how'd they catch you?"

"In the cabin, I didn't leave straight away, not with Megan. She was lucky, about ten minutes after she left, they stormed in, can't tell you how scared I was, they just wanted to know where the boy is, I thought I was quite a courageous person, but Jesus, these men are ruthless. I don't ever want to go through that again, and thanks, Carl, I know I've made some judgmental comments, but you have no idea how thankful I was for that shot. Look Carl, I...um, back there..."

Carl cut in. "It's ok, I get it, you had a gun to your head, you had no choice but to spill your guts, I guessed something was wrong, your voice was as nervous as a teenager asking for a dirty magazine." He smiled.

O'Connor wiped the cold rain from his face and pulled his thick padded jacket collar from his throat like it was choking him. "I've never been so scared, really thought my life would end tonight, I now know how McBride feels, or did feel," he grunted. "Poor bastard, can't help thinking how stupid we both were, I really should be calling this in, I mean look at me, what the fuck am I doing in here, shit, I almost forgot, Jane and the two sisters, they're in there Carl," he said, burying his head in his hands.

"That's why we're going to get them out, but I need your help, they're expecting me to turn up with the boy, that's the only reason they're still alive, and it's not going to be long before they discover they're one man down, and you've vanished, so we need to act fast."

"What, you just going to go in and shoot them?"

"Nah, not possible, if I go in blind they could be anywhere, the minute they put a gun to their heads or mine I've lost my advantage, I can't even see into the café, ideally I need a blind up, I need to see in. This is where you come in," he said placing a comforting hand on O'Connor's shoulder.

He frowned, hard enough to expose the deep lines on his forehead. "Ok," he replied gingerly. "What do you want me to do?"

"I need you to get in that car," said Carl pointing to the black BMW. "On my queue, I need you to beep the horn couple times and flash the headlights, lighting up the café like a Christmas tree, the rest is down to blind luck, but it's all I have right now, O'Connor."

"And what if they come out to the car?"

"That's a bonus, look, I know your scared, and yes, it could all go tits up, but any minute now they're going call the dead guy in the boot, if that happens their going to get suspicious when he doesn't answer, and that's when things start to get unpredictable. Right now, they're calm and Jane and the others alive, so I need you to just dig deep and do what I tell you. Ok?"

O'Connor raised to his feet and grabbed Carl's coat, twisting it in his fist. His face close enough for Carl to smell the tobacco on his breath.

"This may be a walk in the park for you, but you don't have any concept of what it's like for mortals like me to go through what I've just gone through, or even them in there," he pointed. "I'm not used to this world *you* obviously thrive in, I may have been in organised crime, but doesn't mean I was out in the field, we worked with data, information gathering and such like, I'm not ashamed to say I've never even fired a gun."

O'Connor released his grip and Carl straightened his collar.

"So, do I have your help or not O'Connor?"

He eyed the high calibre rifle nestling on Carl's back. Despite saving his life, he had no time for Carl, his inflated ego and his assumption that he can go around wielding firearms like its downtown Miami with no respect for the law. That aside, he remained objective, and given the exceptional circumstances, put his personal views to one side for now at least. His agenda was the welfare of the three women, currently caught up in this mess, and personal feelings aside, he knew that Carl, on a practical level, was an asset at this time and his only ally.

Carl held out his berretta. "Here, take this, just in case."

O'Connor stepped back, withdrawing his hands. "No way, did you not hear me, I've never even fired a gun."

"Point and shoot, I'll even take the safety off for you, just don't shoot your foot off, or any other extremities," he chuckled, still waving the weapon in front of him.

Reluctantly, he took the weapon, holding it like it was a fragile crystal glass, before strapping it to his padded vest.

"Good man, now, you know the plan, wait for my call."

"Ok."

Carl headed for the trees.

O'Connor slipped out from the shelter of the bushes, heading along the edge of the car park to the rear of the car. A nervous tension gripped him in the pit of his stomach, hesitating several times before making the dash to the driver's door, his heartbeat feeling harder against his tight-fitting police vest.

He reached to the gun but felt no more secure for its presence.

Visibility through the windscreen was glazed by the entrance light as the rainwater cascaded down the screen, fierce and noisy.

Another crack of thunder sounded.

He waited, his fingers tapping the steering wheel.

The phone vibrated on his lap.

"You all set, O'Connor?"

"Yep, think so"

"Count to ten after this call, then beep the horn and flash the lights a few times."

"Then what?"

"You'll know, O'Connor."

"That's it?"

"Just do what I ask."

Carl hung up.

O'Connor counted under his breath, then sounded the horn three times, followed by flashing the lights which reflected off the small square panes of glass. He pushed his face against the screen, eager to catch movement.

It wasn't long before the corner of the blinds was raised, and the dark outline of a face appeared through cupped hands.

There was no noise above the sound of the rain, only the sight of a figure, appearing momentarily before falling backwards, spewing blood on the inside of the window which ran like heavily applied paint.

O'Connor exhaled a deep breath before exiting the car and making a dash to the entrance. He felt the phone vibrate in his pocket but ignored it, it would only be Carl ordering new instructions to him, but this time he wasn't going to be his puppet, he already knew what he had to do, freeing the women was the only thing on his mind.

As he stepped inside, his heart leapt in an instant as the end of a pistol was thrust so close to his face he could see the metal swirls inside the barrel. He had no words, just flashes of jumbled thoughts.

The menacing stare from the man in the shadows was overstated by his blistered skin, a latticework of scar tissue.

O'Connor's gaze lay beyond the perpetrator and on to the two women, slumped forward in their chairs. He was powerless to intervene. Jane opened just one eye, the other a raised scarlet and beetroot purple lump. Streaks of dried blood stained her chin, and below the chair, dried spats of bloody saliva.

Her expression was begging in its delivery toward him.

Megan was conscious to a point, there didn't need to be any words exchanged for him to understand her, even if her gaze toward him was only momentary.

He raised his hands.

The man searched him, removed his phone and the revolver Carl had given him. He looked toward the windows, and to the body lying on the floor, a few feet away, his face destroyed by Carl's speeding bullet.

He felt powerless. How had he been so stupid, he was so intent on saving them he never for one minute considered another threat still inside. He now realised the call he failed to answer was the one call he should have taken, the one call which could have saved his life.

How dumb

The man ushered him to his knees, pressing the barrel against his forehead.

"You have balls coming here, as you English say, but that is ok, because now you get to watch me set the balance right," he said, his accent strong, but his words were distorted by the unforgiving scar tissue around his mouth. He glanced at his comrades' body, swinging his arm slowly from him to Megan, as if the smooth movement made more of a point than a quick snatch.

"So where is the boy?"

O'Connor's brain was strangled by fear.

He cocked the hammer of the pistol against her head. Another scare tactic.

"Listen, I know where, I mean someone's bringing him, look—"

"No good enough, you have five seconds to give me a straight answer, otherwise she is terminated."

It was crystal clear he was dealing with a psychopath and no amount of talking was going to alter anything.

Just tell the truth, was all he could say to himself.

A rash thought popped into his head. What if he made a grab for the gun? But his fight, flight or freeze response was firmly stuck in freeze for now.

The man's focus was momentarily stolen, and for a moment fixed on the fire exit. A muffled sound brought him to postpone his interrogation.

He swung the gun back to face O'Connor. "Move and I kill you."

O'Connor spied the gun, still attached in the hand of the body just a few feet away. He switched his gaze to the man, now preoccupied with the sound emitting from the other end of the room, his gun still trained on him, but his head in the opposite position toward the fire escape.

He felt his pulse throbbing in his neck, his nerves tingling with the surge of adrenalin, coursing through his veins.

His eyes returned to the gun, less than a few feet away.

In a moment of blind courage, he grabbed the gun and raised it toward the man, standing with his back to him. The gun felt heavy and awkward in his trembling hands as he raised to his feet.

"Drop the gun," he said, his voice holding no simmer of confidence.

The man swung around but was not fazed by the weapon aimed at him.

He studied O'Connor, standing awkwardly, handling the weapon like a man with little experience. And he knew it.

The man gave a short laugh, but his messed-up face did not form any expression, just his eyes narrowing was the only tell-tale sign.

"You're not going shoot me." He looked to the body of his comrade on the floor and back to O'Connor. The penny dropped. "You didn't shoot Alexi, did you? No, I think maybe you have a partner." He nodded toward the window. "He's out there, isn't he?"

O'Connor lacked a smart reply. He may be the one aiming the gun, but he was the one feeling the most intimidated.

The man stepped closer.

Megan raised her head.

"Shoot him," she shouted from the chair. "Just shoot him," her voice raspy, rocking as fiercely as she could in desperation to break free, but each movement only served to cut into her narrow wrists even more.

He caught her imploring gaze.

O'Connor momentarily lost focus, glancing at her and then Jane who was sat on the edge of her chair, vacant, barely vocal and pasted with congealed blood which oozed from the small half-moon cut under her swollen eye socket.

O'Connor's gaze returned to the man, except now he had advanced enough to make a grab for the weapon, knocking it from his hand. The gun bounced across the floor, coming to rest under a nearby table.

Hope was lost.

Then came a knock at the front door.

The man sidestepped toward the front doors, switching his aim from O'Connor to the doors, now in front. The muted lighting inside formed only his own reflection in the glass.

He stepped forward, now a tall, dark, shadowy figure appeared at the door, face pressed up to the watery glass. Another step forward revealed the familiar face of his comrade, black and grey camo trousers, black hooded coat, and the unmistakable wide nose of Ivan, his cousin.

He lowered his weapon.

Except Ivan wasn't wearing his usual half-moon grin, the one he always wore in his presence.

Under the surface of twisted skin was a bemused expression, verbalised with an "Ugh?"

The lifeless body of Ivan crumpled to the floor suddenly like an inflatable doll that had just burst.

Now standing behind the body was Carl.

He was wearing a smile.

The sound was silent, except for the smallest crack as the bullet penetrated the glass door and came to rest somewhere inside the man's skull. He fell backwards onto the black and white tiles, a lake of blood swelled from the back of his head in an almost symmetrical spread.

From where he was standing, O'Connor had no view of the main doors, just the stone pillars framed by two large terracotta plant pots. He witnessed the demise of his threat, as the man fell backwards, catching sight of just his upper body and the puddle of blood which grew quickly.

A wave of relief washed over him, and now his hands and legs trembled, more than if he'd been stripped naked and locked in a freezer. He felt the taste of post adrenaline in his throat and his heart returning to a slower beat.

Carl stood in the doorway. "Everyone ok?"

Chapter 24

After Carl had removed the second body and placed it in the boot of their vehicle, along with the other one he'd used as bait earlier, he returned to the others, untied, comforted and now sitting vacantly, processing a cocktail of emotions. The café was starting to feel like a cosmic black hole, where nothing could escape its gravity, death, misery, and a darker world, infesting their lives like a virus.

A demoralising silence was all that remained as they sat pondering the aftermath of their ordeal. Even Carl failed to utter any words about what had just taken place. Partly because he felt some responsibility which was now weighing heavy on even his broad shoulders.

Megan was the first to break the silence, sitting up from her slumped position at the table, eyes rimmed with bloodshot red, and sensation returning to her arms which felt like they had been torn from their sockets, from being bound tightly behind her in the chair.

It wasn't to talk about the horrific ordeal or any words of comfort and as if she was in complete denial about the last hour, she centred only on something Jane had said earlier. Much to the surprise of the others.

"Jane, didn't you say earlier you wanted to explore an idea, about the boy?" she asked, watching her press the swallow lump under her left eye with an ice-filled tea-towel.

Carl raised his head. "I don't think it matters now, do you? It's time we walked away from this, return the body to the hospital, preferably before it turns to trifle, and let the police conduct a post-Morton. I mean shit, there's going to be an awful lot of questions, but if we don't do this the right way you won't be able to piss in public without looking over your shoulder. I'm just saying, that's all."

Megan stood from her chair, her swollen lips looking like she had just eaten a jam doughnut. "You serious Carl? After everything we been through, you're just going to give in now." She gestured a hand to Jane. "She said herself she may have the answer, you not even the slightest bit curious?"

Megan began to feel her internal drive for excitement was pushing her further than was necessary, maybe even at the expense of endangering the lives of others. But her curiosity was overpowering, like a small child waiting impatiently to open a present.

"It's not about being curious, it's about knowing when you're beaten, we don't know how many others are going to come barging through those doors, and next time, we may not be so lucky. I may not always be on hand to keep saving your ass. Whatever secret that body has, they're just going to keep killing to get it."

Megan's voice crept up a couple of optics, strawberry lips delivering her wrath and her tiny hands orchestrating against the fake marble tabletops. "You didn't exactly save my ass in the woods, because when you found me in the backseat of the car I wasn't exactly in any direct danger, but somehow you managed to turn that into a heroic act." She folded her arms tightly across her chest. A pearl of tears tricked down her face and she cleared them with the back of her hand, smudging more of the mud across her cheeks.

"Look, you've been through hell and back, you all have, I get you want to know whats in pandoras box, I'm just as curious as you, but where is that going to lead us, even if we find the answer, then what, this isnt a few people we're dealing with, this is a large criminal organisation and we are not an army. Be thankful we all have our lives still."

Carl raised from the table, removed his heavy jacket and stood by the counter. He splashed another serving of coffee into a large white mug and devoured it, so hurried was his actions that most of it ran from his stubbled chin and dissolved into his already faded black t-shirt.

Megan shook her head, not just at Carls patronising attitude, but because if her sister was here, she'd be horrified by his less than social etiquette.

O'Connor raised his hand from the corner booth. "Just for the record I actually agree with Carl. It's time to do this through the correct channels, tonight has probably cost my superior his life. Maybe, just maybe I might still have a job at the end of this. I can live with the truth better than burying a head full of stories and lies."

Megan stared at the clean circle made by the bullet in the glass. A small deep blue tear in the early morning sky signalled the start of dawn on the horizon and the first chorus started to play outside. Gone was the dark imageless scenery from earlier, now the outside world was taking shape. Morning had broken, but a new day carried still more uncertainty.

"Did you even bring back a razor Carl, like I asked?" mumbled Jane, still nursing her makeshift icepack.

All eyes turned to her. Her pale fragile form adorned with the scars and blemishes which resembled a victim from a survival horror movie.

"Megan's right though Carl, stop trying to make amends for what happened in a previous life. It's not about whether you saved us or not, it's about not making us feel guilty afterwards. You forget, this is not our world, it's yours."

Carl's eyes fell to the floor, again for the second time she was right.

"So, what now then Jane?" he asked.

"I need to see the boy; I need to know what's so important that they took the time to blackmail me, hurt me and Megan, why send this Fuller to take pictures of my family, why all this bloodshed, why maintain this for a boy who's now dead?"

"You not heard the phrase; curiosity killed the cat?" said Carl still leaning against the counter.

"It's a bit late for that now don't you think?"

"I'm not sure what you hope to achieve, I mean even if you somehow discover why they want him, how is that going to benefit you now, you think you're just going to blackmail them even more?"

Jane just looked at Carl and pointed to her face. "I didn't get this just to give up now, now please, go and fetch me the body before it really is too late."

"Ok, but I just hope this is not driven by revenge, because if it is, then I don't want any part of it."

"Don't look at me," said O'Connor, catching a glance from Jane.

"Ok, I will humour you, I will get the body for you, then what?"

"Just let Jane have her moment Carl for God sake, she deserves that after all this. Then we'll return him to the hospital and just accept the consequences, tell the police. I want to get my sister to a hospital as soon as I can. She's been shot and dragged around, buried in a wooden box and I'm tired now Carl.

Carl disappeared in a pace which suggested he was sulking. Several moments later he returned with the black body bag suspended in his arms. He carefully laid down the corpse on the floor.

They all watched as Jane pulled herself from the chair and knelt at the side of the body. She placed one hand on the smooth black plastic cover, as if she were making a spiritual connection. She then tucked her mangled hair inside her coat before leaning across the body bag.

Carl joined her, kneeling beside her, he placed a comforting hand on her shoulder. "I should never have led you into this, I should have made you take a step back, instead I encouraged you, the mannequin at my place, the exchange, which by the way is supposed to take place in an hour and twenty, but who knows what they expect now."

"Did you bring the razor or not." Her request was short.

Carl grabbed the orange Bic razor from his rucksack and handed it to her. "What's the razor for again?"

"You may want to put something over your face," she said, rolling up two balls of paper napkin from the table and wedging them up each nostril.

"That bad?"

"Yep, that bad."

Carl followed her lead, Megan's curiosity brought her closer, forgetting her tantrum with Carl.

O'Connor pulled a crushed packet of cigarettes from his padded vest, stuffed one between his lips and lit, drawing heavily and exhaling a hazy blue cloud.

Megan looked at him disapprovingly.

"What? So, it's ok to kill someone in here but the minute I light up a fag I get a death look? Jesus."

Jane slid the zip on the body bag down slowly, as far as the top of the chest. She exposed the boys head, his waxy pale complexion, contorted and blotted from the decomposition process already taking hold. His eyes, a milky silver, stared skyward. Red foam erupted from his nasal passages, along with a putrid odour which filled the air, instantly bringing the others to place hand to mouth.

Carl winced, even with the tissue, Megan turned away at the sight of the contorted corpse, with memories of her mother's face. O'Connor pulled his chair closer, still drawing on his cigarette, hoping his nerves would level, curious as to what Jane's revelation might be.

"You didn't say what the razor is for." Asked Carl.

Jane ran her fingers through the boy's thick curly hair, a few inches above the ear, feeling for the wound on the side of the head.

"Remember I told you, back at the hospital what this Max expected of me? Don't tell the police, lose the paperwork. It wasn't until I explained the surgical procedure to remove the bullet that he then told me not to shave the head. I found that very odd, to the point they were prepared to let him die. It's the one thing that's been eating away at me. Don't you find that odd?"

"Yes, yes I do, very odd, but how would that compromise them? Doesn't make sense."

"I don't understand, why shave the head now?" Quizzed O'Connor stamping out his spent fag butt.

"Yea, what do you hope to achieve?" followed Megan, eager for a chance to continue what she still saw as an adventure. Quietly and ashamedly she didn't want this to end, despite a brush with death, beaten, chased and consistently living in fear, she was avoiding a return to a stale mundane life of boredom and little excitement. A world she didn't want to return to. But as she knelt alongside the others, a calm and clear thought entered her head. Maybe this was the kick she needed, a stepping stone to a richer life, she'd almost forgotten that in the last twelve hours or so she hadn't once felt the pain of grief, and now, as she thought about her mum, for the first time she felt no grief, no pain, no anger, all dissipated from her conscience.

"Earlier, when I was at the counter drinking my coffee, I was staring at the row of eggs through the glass fridge door, it dawned on me, the sell-by date printed on the eggs."

Megan frowned, curious about the connection. "What about it?"

"During my nursing career, it's not unusual for some people to have their blood type or important medical information tattooed somewhere on their body."

"Ok, but how is that information useful to us?" asked O'Connor.

"Think about it, if you wanted to hide a message or information on a body, where would you put it? I mean information other than for a medical purpose. Information you didn't want to be exposed?"

"Oh my god, that's genius," said Megan.

Carl and O'Connor looked at each other, shaking their head.

"You know you might actually have something," said Carl.

"Well, let's find out," she said excitedly.

Jane first cut the lengths of hair using scissors from a utensil drawer, trimming back as much as she could, its thick black locks falling with each snip. Once she had cut as close to the scalp as she could, she then exchanged the scissors for the razor. Cradling the boys head to one side, she carefully shaved, concentrating on the area around the head wound. Layer by layer, she shaved the hair, careful not to tear the delicate decomposing skin which peeled away like soggy paper.

"I need your torch please, Carl," she asked, concentrating as best she could, trying not to be distracted by the throbbing pain under her left eye.

The nauseating smell was all but ignored now and conversation stopped for a moment as they watched Jane carefully reveal the scalp.

It wasn't long before a distinguishable mark became visible. A raised, congealed bloody shape, distorted but legible.

"That doesn't look like a tattoo," said Carl.

"It's not, it's a cut."

"And what kind of cut is shaped like a number 4."

Gradually more of the boy's porcelain white scalp was visible, along with more similar cuts, all in the shape of numbers and letters.

A bemused Megan pushed her nose in closer, despite the stench. "Why would someone deliberately cut numbers into a boy's head, I mean, they don't even make sense, and why are there letters as well?"

Carl hovered the torch over the sequence. "I know what that is, it makes sense now."

"Well, enlighten us," asked Jane eagerly.

"Coordinates. Longitude and Latitude, hence the letters, it accurately pinpoints a precise location.

O'Connor blew a sigh. "I guess we've found the end of the rainbow," he said pulling himself up.

"More likely a rabbit hole of dark and dangerous things," replied Carl.

"Well, at least we know what they want, I mean it's a good thing right?" asked Megan.

"Let's not get ahead of ourselves just yet, we don't know where that is or what's there," said Carl moving back to his seat, his face morphing different expressions.

O'Connor rubbed his tired face. "None of this makes sense, I mean, why take him to hospital, if they knew about the marks, then why not just retrieve the information and dump the body? Why risk being exposed at the hospital?"

"There's a lot we don't know."

With the exchange deadline fast approaching, Carl wrestled with his conscience. The same curiosity which resided in all of them told him to hold fire on the exchange and see where the coordinates lead.

Carl left the others to talk., stepping outside where the air felt less stale. He watched as the distant sky drew ever lighter with each passing minute and the rain easing to a fine drizzle.

O'Connor joined him a few moments later and pulled another cigarette, relishing its rush.

"By the way, I found this on the guy I shot, the one who had you." Carl pulled out a business card with the title *"Figure of Eight flying school"* and handed it to O'Connor. "Thoughts?"

O'Connor grunted and tapped the card on his fingers. "Well I doubt it's to learn to fly, but now we have those coordinates I bet they were looking for a lift, and I doubt they were asking either."

"To blackmail."

"Threaten, blackmail, doesn't really matter how you put it, they're looking for something, something at the end of those numbers that's worth killing for. I think we need to know where those numbers lead," said Carl.

"I guess this changes things now, right?" asked O'Connor stubbing out the cigarette under his large boots and staring toward the ink-blue sky bleeding through early dusk of graphite cloud.

"Possibly, no point risking an exchange if we already know why they want him. Gives us the upper hand but we have to be careful how we play it. They don't know we know and they're still expecting the boy's corpse. Of course, the burning question is where does it all lead."

"That's the million-dollar question."

"That statement may well be more accurate than you jest."

Carl dropped his thoughtful expression and pulled the confiscated phones from his pocket. "I'm going to fetch my GPS unit from the Landy, have a look at their phones I took, see if you can find anything useful in there, but I imagine they will be encrypted."

Carl wandered off through the semi-darkness to the Land Rover; O'Connor returned inside and set about searching for any information.

"Where's Carl gone" asked Megan, returning to her feet.

"Getting the GPS, finding out where the coordinates lead."

"So, we going to this place, wherever it is?"

"You not hear what Carl said?"

"Come on, aren't you just as curious as I am about what's there?"

"And what if we're just walking into the belly of a monster, haven't you been through enough already, does it matter now? Like Carl said, take the body back to the hospital and hand over all the information we have to the police, let them wrap this all up and we can all go back to our lives."

Megan watched Jane zipping up the body bag, she then made her way to the small bathroom area behind the counter. Megan followed, standing at the doorway as Jane washed the dead skin and congealed blood from her hands, scrubbing them as hard as she could.

"Penny for your thoughts," said Megan, watching her stare into the bloody water.

"Thinking about my family, where the hell do I start, what do I tell them, the terrible things I've done."

"It's called survival, we all did what we had to in order to survive."

Carl stole the moment rushing in with the GPS unit. "Sky's breaking and the rains easing, I think whatever we decide we need to think about moving out of here, O'Connor, any luck with the phones?" he asked placing the unit on the table and punching in the coordinates.

"Nah, like you said, both encrypted, no chance without the right tech."

O'Connor's attention was side-tracked by a vibration and bright light out the corner of his eye. One of the phones danced on the table. Carl dashed to pick it up but hesitated long enough for it to stop ringing.

"Why didn't you answer it?" asked O'Connor curiously.

"Think about it, they'd be expecting one of these three corpses to answer, they'd know instantly it was us and exactly where we are, and they were compromised. They may already know; I mean they might have been expecting them to check in. I don't like this," he replied hurrying back to the GPS unit.

Carl finished entering all the Latitude and longitude coordinates. He furrowed his brows. "That's interesting."

"What's wrong?" asked O'Connor.

Megan edged forward, a mixture of curiosity and nerves made her edgy.

O'Connor grabbed a look for himself. "Where the hell is that, square miles of trees and wilderness, you sure you got all the numbers?"

"Yep, that's it, explains their presence up here, that's only about forty clicks from here."

"In English please." Asked O'Connor.

"Sorry habit, it's about twenty-five miles, give or take."

"So, there's nothing there then?" asked Megan, watching them exchange curious looks.

"No, it just means there's nothing on the map, nothing in the landscape like a building or an obvious location but clearly something of value to them is there."

Jane stood holding the ice pack, eyes glazed. "So, what are we suggesting then," her voice raised, and hands upturned. "Twenty minutes ago, you were calling this all off, now it sounds like your contemplating going there, I'm sorry, you can all go, I just want to get back to my family, I'm done risking my life."

The conversation was side-tracked by a groan in the distance and heartbeats raised in a blink. Carl raised his hand to signal everyone to stay still as he made his way to the window overlooking the road. Distant lights surfaced on the horizon, drawing ever closer, his body language spurring the others to rise from the booth.

"Hide the boy, now," shouted Carl.

O'Connor dragged the body to the booth and secured it.

Carl dropped the GPS under his seat.

Their fear was confirmed when two dark SUV's came speeding into the car park.

Panic rose. Megan climbed over O'Connor desperate to escape and stood in the middle of the café, hands cupped over her mouth in disbelief as the piercing headlights fanned through the blinds, falling on their terrified faces.

She looked to her sister, curled up in the corner booth, oblivious and yet vulnerable, powerless to help her.

"What do we do Carl?" shrieked Jane.

O'Connor screwed his face tight and buried his head in his hands, realising this could be the end.

Doors slamming and the sound of hurried footsteps across the gravel signalled a chilling realisation.

Jane sat motionlessly, her mouth dropped and eyes filling with yet more tears, each one falling onto her tightly clenched hands. She looked across at Carl, wondering how he was going to get them out of this. Even O'Connor an experienced police officer had that look of unalterable lost hope, like he had given up. Then she rested her eyes on Megan, the woman who's resolve was unexpectedly strong throughout this whole nightmare. Now even she had all the signs of surrender as she just fell to her knees, her head lowered, so far it looked as though she might even be sacrificing herself for them.

Screams echoed around the café as the sound of multiple gunshots rang out. The front doors shattering into a million pieces, bullets filling the air and lumps of plaster exploding around them as shots impacted the wall behind.

Jane threw herself onto the floor into a tight ball, head buried into her hands, feeling the debris settling on her back.

Carl closed his eyes for a second, a flash entered his head, there in front of him stood the woman, clothed in a beige robe and white headscarf. He shook his head and opened his eyes. The vision was shorter this time.

The café was breached by six men, emerging from the smoke and falling dust, all carrying light machine guns. They stood, grouped around the five of them, weapons pointed, and waited like worker bees waiting for the queen.

Moments later as the noise of the shots faded away and the dust from the plaster walls settled onto the floor, a figure of a man appeared at the doorway. Black full-length woollen coat, red silk shirt highlighting a heavy gold linked chain and immaculate shoes, stood in silence, gesturing his men to stand down.

The instant the cars pulled into the car park, escape was not an option to Carl, but his trained mind remained focused, a plan already forming.

The man crouched in front of Jane, carefully lifting her chin to meet his eyes.

"We meet again nurse Stevens; I was wondering when we would make another acquaintance," he said in a clear articulate accent. "Ah, and you must be Mr security guard," he continued. "Please sit, how rude of me, the floor is no place for two fine young women like yourselves," he said, gesturing them to sit. "It appears we have a special guest," he said, his eyes falling toward Gill laid out on the leatherette cushion.

"You leave her alone," said Megan.

"Another spirited young lady, a friend of yours Jane?"

She didn't answer.

"Allow me to introduce myself, my name is Mikhailov, but you can call me Max. Jane and I have already had the pleasure, oh and Mr security man, I will take the rifle if you don't mind and any other special toys you might have." He smiled.

Max signalled one of his men to retrieve Carl's mini arsenal. He then spoke to another man in Russian who brought forward a large, square, polished wooden box the size of a microwave oven and placed it on the coffee-stained table in the middle. Max then drew up a chair to the end of the booth, resting his clean-shaven face on his hands. His ruby sheen cuffs displayed a single gold letter 'M' cufflink. A silk handkerchief peered from his dark jacket and the aroma of aftershave, its smell pleasing but somehow unfitting for the moment drifted over them.

"So, who here has played the game, guess who?"

His Calm, polite manner was more disturbing than the vulgar rants they experienced earlier. The café was calm, no voices other than Max's, even Carl was sat quietly, in anticipation of what is yet to come. Actions would not get them out of here now, six men, all with weapons, told him that.

Megan and Jane both avoided eye contact, instead choosing to find small patterns in the intricate fake grain of the table, both ragging like a storm on the inside, occasionally eying the smooth polished oak box in front of them, the neatly chiselled dovetail joints and the fine polished chrome hinges, curious and in equal measure frightened at its presence.

"Ok, well, since the cats got your tongues, then I will pick someone." He smiled, revealing his milk-white teeth.

Max looked directly at Megan, his gaze cold and without expression.

"Go on, open the box, it's time to play guess who," he said calmly.

Megan placed her trembling hands on side of the chrome hinged lid.

"Is this necessary, why don't you just tell her instead of playing sick games," ranted Carl.

At that moment, she had opened the lid and was already staring at a severed head.

She leapt from her seat and vomited on the floor. O'Connor peered over the box, his eyes suddenly widening and his heart reacting like it had a thousand times today as he stared in horror at the head of his boss, McBride.

Jane felt repulsion at the way he showcased an act of inhumane proportions.

"I'm guessing my three employees I sent earlier are no longer on my payroll, judging by the trail of blood everywhere."

Carl stared at Max, his gaze as cold as the one he received. "You know, if you had just accepted that Jane was trying to do the right thing and hand over the boy, without trying to kill her in the process, then maybe we wouldn't be in this stalemate situation."

"Forgive my English," he laughed. "But surely stalemate suggests a position counting as a draw, in which a player is not in check but cannot move except into check, and as I see it you have no move Mr security man."

Carl leaned forward, his large muscular arms flexing with the tension in his voice. "I have the boy, that's my move, you want the boy, you let the others go. Like I said, Stalemate."

Max's six men, all dressed in various shades of black and looking like characters from the Matrix, stood in a half-circle, surrounding the table, machine guns poised, could not be any more intimidating if they tried.

Max clapped his hands. "Bravo, Mr security man, it would appear I underestimated your diligence, and if I may be so coarse as to say your blind stupidity."

Max once again clicked his fingers and instantly two of his men grabbed O'Connor, hurling him to the floor, his eyes filled with horror as he was made to kneel, and a pistol pressed firmly against the back of his head.

Max nodded to his comrade who then cocked the gun and fired.

O'Connor fell to the ground, blood spilling from his head, the shot still ringing in their ears.

Their reality suddenly looked dire.

Megan and Jane were lost in conscious thought, vacant and numb, their minds in lockdown. Carl looked across at Max, wearing a sickly grin, like a five-year-old on Christmas morning.

"What the fuck. Why?"

Max stood from his chair and buttoned his long, black coat, brushing the lapels of minor contaminates. He nodded again to his men who dragged O'Connor's body to the side, almost as if they were emphasising the execution.

The blood-stained chessboard floor now resembled the massacre it was. Dozens of holes littered the back walls, white plaster strewn from the explosion of bullets and the countertops and tables covered in a fine white settling of dust and grit.

Max withdrew his phone, dialled and had a short conversation in his native tongue, then flicked a glance to Carl. "You alone have precisely one hour to bring me the boy, failure to do so will result in the rest of you joining the detective. Oh, and Jane," he said turning to her with a sickly smile. "Your children's school is lovely, such a nice environment in which to be educated in," he ended, this time with the lack of any smile.

Jane remained seated, in disbelief, her anxious mind vacant to the conversation which had just taken place.

Carl stood, dazed from the experience and the callous act he didn't see coming. He grabbed his coat and looked to the others, no words from him would give them any hope, but this was going to end tonight.

Chapter 25

Saturday 28th 06.35

Time now was very much the enemy, and he felt the full weight of this hour as he ran to his vehicle, leaving the others in the wake of these barbaric people. His mind drew up a plan, but he would need more gear if his plan was to work. He could of course just tell them they were sitting only a few feet from the body, but then the option of walking out of there would be as slim as Elvis being declared alive and hiding.

Carl took off toward his place, the horizon now a burnt orange scar on an otherwise ink blue sky and dawn was now only a short time away.

Carl took no chances, having already had one of Max's men, Felix, visit the house earlier.

The dawn light was still weak enough to give cover and he approached from the side, crawling through the overgrowth that engulfed the back of his house. He gained entry from the rear, retrieving a key he had hidden, taped to the back of a drainpipe.

Entering from the back, he edged the weathered door ajar and made his way in stealthily.

But something didn't look right. The window to his right was a couple of inches shy of closing. Only he knew the knack to close the decade-old rotten frame, a silly detail which alerted his suspicions.

Reluctant to put the light on, he carefully rolled up the large rug in the back room in which he had entered and quietly removed a long unsecured floorboard, retrieving a Glock 17 pistol, complete with a suppressor. He then placed his hand on the loose brass doorknob, its worn mechanism sounding louder in the silence, but not to open it just yet. Then he stepped away and stood silently. A few seconds later, his suspicions were confirmed as the unmistakable creek of a floorboard told him exactly where an intruder was standing, six foot in front and two to the right.

He acted quickly, pulling open the door, pointing his weapon into the semi-darkness and fired off two rounds.

The sound of a body falling followed soon after.

He flicked on the light. There, lying in front of the fireplace was a large portly man, round potholed face, jeans, black leather jacket and stubble length black hair, holding his stomach and looking up at Carl with fading grey eyes.

He kicked the gun away and sat in the chair opposite him.

"I should have known Max would send someone here," he said, watching the blood spill on to his carpet.

The man coughed blood, his face as pale as the white marble mantelpiece above him.

"He doesn't trust you," he said with a strained accent, "He's covering his bases, he guessed you might hide the boy here," he choked. "But the boys not here *is* he?"

"No, he's not, but I guess you've already searched my house."

The man cocked a half-smile. "Something like that."

Carl fetched a towel from the kitchen and pressed it against his wound. "It won't save your life, but it will slow the bleeding."

"So why did you come here, if the boy's not here?" he asked, the sound of blood curdling in the back of his throat distorted his voice.

He held the towel tightly over his stomach. Beads of sweat surfaced on his face.

"I'm not returning the boy, I know why Max wants him anyway, I know about the coordinates carved into the boy's head. That's right, I've seen them," he said, responding to the man's surprised expression.

"You didn't answer my question, why come here?" he asked.

Carl knelt in front of him. "If I tell you that, you tell me about the pot of gold at the end of the rainbow."

He mustered a smile. "Max is not a man you want to cross; I paid the price for that when I refused to carry out a hit he ordered." He repositioned himself against the large red chair behind him.

"You mean even stone-cold killers like you have a line? Give me a break."

"When it involves shooting a thirteen-year-old girl, then yes I do." He took a shallow breath. "So why are you helping me? I'm going to die here anyway."

"Good question, because I'm hoping you can give me some answers to what's going on tonight, and maybe your life will end on a good deed."

"We are similar you know, except you don't kill for money; your actions are for a morally higher agenda," said the man.

"Doesn't mean I sleep any better than you; you mentioned paying a price?" asked Carl.

"I'm not going to defend what I do, I will pay my penance, God will see to that, but I draw the line at women and children, so when I was presented with a hit on a thirteen-year-old witness to a murder, I turned it down, two days later my brother was killed in a hit and run. I knew who was behind it."

"Max," exclaimed Carl

"Mikhailov Cherskov is his real name, ex Russian mob." He raised his finger, emphasising a point. "Very dangerous man."

"Yea, I've discovered that. So why the loyalty still," asked Carl.

"Loyalty? It's not loyalty comrade, it's survival, keep your enemy closer, isn't that how it goes?" He groaned in a series of successions, repositioning himself against the chair, he gazed down to the light blue towel, now coloured with his blood. "You mind if I have a last smoke?" he asked pulling out a packet from his leather jacket.

"Go ahead."

He lit the cigarette with trembling hands and savoured its taste for a second. Outside, the morning light crept through the large bay window and orange highlights played across the stippled ceiling.

The man drew on his cigarette, saying nothing for a few seconds, but to savour the rich taste. A final pleasure before death came knocking.

"Diamonds," said the man, drawing once again on the blood-stained cigarette. "At the end of the rainbow."

Carl leant forward. "Did you say diamonds?"

"Fifteen million Euros in diamonds to be precise."

Carl's eyes widened. "Jesus, it's all starting to make sense now."

"Three days ago, a small plane carrying a case full of precious stones, not far from here, crashed. On board was the pilot, Mikhailov's brother Uri and his son Stefan, along with two other comrades. All but the two comrades escaped, moments before it burst into flames. The only clue to their position was the coordinates, noted by the pilot seconds before the crash. Once Uri obtained this information he shot the pilot, but he didn't trust his memory, and so Uri laid out his unconscious son and proceeded to gouge the coordinates into the side of his son's head with a piece of metal, with the intentions of returning the next day, that's when he noticed the hole in the side of his son's head, made by a fragment when the plane exploded."

"So the boy wasn't shot then?"

The man shook his head. "He was given no choice but to call Mikhailov, but not before he wandered miles from the plane, still intent on disguising its location. There is an old Russian proverb which goes, *When you are in a pack of hounds, you either bark or wag your tail.* He wanted to be the one barking, like his brother, he was always living in his brother's shadow, and now he had a chance to forge his own future, but he had a dilemma, in order to save his son, he had to take him to hospital but knew the numbers carved into his sons head would be questioned on examination by the hospital and involve the police, so he was left with a choice, tell Mikhailov, realising his brother had the resources and connections to cover it all up and retrieve the diamonds, or let his son die and come back for the briefcase full of diamonds for himself."

Carl sighed loudly. "Well it seems he's lost both now, so how do you know all this?"

"A vodka fuelled night with Uri and a shared dislike for Mikhailov." He smiled.

"How do you know the plane hasn't already been found?"

He shrugged his shoulders. "I don't, but they removed the transponder unit and flew under the radar at night, leaving from a secluded farm, east of Amsterdam. It's in the middle of nowhere."

"So where was the plane heading for?" quizzed Carl.

"A fishing boat, off the west coast of Scotland, fly low and drop the case into the water, it was fitted with a transponder, but now the case is destroyed in the plane, so can't be tracked."

The man coughed and blood surfaced from his lips, trickling out of the corner of his mouth and his breathing rattily.

"Where are the diamonds from?"

"You don't want to know."

"Stolen blood diamonds I'm guessing."

"Originally, maybe, but Mikhailov deceived the devil himself, Bratva, which means brotherhood."

"You mean Russian Mafia?"

"Exactly, *Death is not found behind mountains but right behind our shoulders*," he quoted. "It's only a matter of time before he gets burnt."

Carl sat in thought, processing the information. As he did, the man's eyes faded, and the last rattle of breath left his lungs.

"The ticking clock on the mantelpiece showed twenty minutes remaining. Carl hurried to the backroom, ripping up more floorboards. He pulled out a large sandy-coloured canvas bag, which was heavy and cumbersome, then dragged the mannequin out from the dark heavily carved antique wardrobe in the corner and placed it into his army sleeping bag and made his way back to his vehicle. The light was more prevalent now, dull orange clouds lined the horizon and day had very much arrived.

He slung the heavy bag behind the seats, along with the sleeping bag.

This was an ambitious plan and one he ran over multiple time in his head. He didn't dwell too much on the consequences and was aware it was still subject to some luck, which was all he had in the short time remaining.

Carl gripped the wheel like it was a lifeline and his mind battled the anger, an emotion he despised. It served no purpose but to interfere with rational decision making, especially in the field. But the image of O'Connor needlessly being executed brought about that very emotion. If his plan was to work, then there would be no room for this.

He pulled into the far end of the car park, behind the other two black vehicles, providing the cover he needed, and a blind spot, fifty or so yards from the entrance.

The morning light was now bright enough to expose the colour of nature and no longer hid any surprises, and the rain was for now no more than a fine mist.

Carl switched to task in hand and began to set the trap. He placed the mannequin inside the khaki green sleeping bag, zipped it up and lay it behind the seat. Then carefully removed a large round heavy steel disc from his canvas bag. He pulled up the square, black foam seat cover on the passenger side and placed the disc underneath carefully.

Moments later, the sound of crunching gravel underfoot drew closer. As he climbed back into the driver's seat Max appeared, and predictably he was facing down the barrel of a Makarov.

"The boy?" asked Max abruptly.

"In the back, behind me, can we talk?"

Max tried the doors, but they were locked.

"It would not be prudent to make me ask again."

Carl looked into his soulless eyes. "Get in, I have something to tell you," he replied, hands above his head and nodding to the passenger seat.

"Either you hand me the boy in the next thirty seconds, or I return to the café, and if I do that, well, the outcome will be less favourable for you."

"Please, just give me the courtesy of a short conversation, you can see I have the boy through the window."

Max peered through the rear window; the military green sleeping bag perfectly shaped for a body. Carl had made sure he emphasised the shape by tucking the bag into the curves of the mannequin.

He ran the same sentence over and over in his head. *Please get in the passenger seat. Do it, go on, there you go*. His eyes following Max as he walked slowly around the front of his vehicle.

He kept his hands deliberately high, persuading Max he had nothing to worry about.

Max unbuttoned his long coat, pulled open the door and placed himself on the passenger seat, with the Makarov still directed toward him.

As he did so, a hard-shaped object felt suddenly uncomfortable.

Max looked down to the seat, and then to Carl.

"At this moment, you are sitting on an IED, that would explain the uncomfortable seat, and in doing so activated the trigger, but you're fine as long as you don't get up. I will give you a few seconds to process that," he replied, in the same calm tone as used by Max.

The realisation and sudden loss of power Max was experiencing began to creep in, Until this point, Max had not experienced the helplessness felt by so many of his victims, but here he was, powerless in a second, his usual calm demeanour delivered in cold chilling moments preceding an execution, provoked a demonstration of just that. His face beaded to a cold sweat; his cheeks drained of any colour, and his eyes now full of anger.

Carl watched him, desperately trying to think his way out, shifting about on the hard shape beneath him.

"I will personally make it my goal to ensure your death is not only uncomfortable but prolonged, there is nowhere you can hide, you can't even perceive to imagine the connections I have and resources at my disposal. There is not a corner of the planet you can escape to," he raged, with fire in his eyes.

Carl removed max's weapon and phone before climbing out.

He turned to him, hand still on the door.

"I know what you're thinking, and I'll give you the heads up. Its primed for a two-second delay, so the question you need to consider is, can I get out of this vehicle and far enough away in two seconds, then you have to consider how big is the explosion, will I survive, possibly, will I still have all my moving parts," he laughed. "More than likely not, but at least you have a chance, which is more than you gave O'Connor, you worthless piece of shit."

Carl pulled the sleeping bag from behind the seat, then slammed the driver's door.

"Oh, one more thing Mikhailov," he replied turning back. "That's your real name, isn't it? Just before I go and kill your brother Uri, I know about the diamonds."

The ragging outcries from his vehicle faded the closer he came to the café. Morning Larks sang in the nearby woodland and the mirrored puddles reflected an orange sky above.

He approached the entrance, holding the body shaped bag in both arms, dark shadows moving behind the blinds.

Two men gathered either side of the broken doors, weapons poised, standing like nightclub bounces. The front entrance now looked like a war zone, hollowed chunks of wall adorned the facing pillars, besieged with bullet holes. Hard to believe this was a quiet roadside café only hours ago, where the only drama was a dropped glass or broken duke box. Beyond the twisted frames, the fragile faces of Jane and Megan acknowledged his return.

"Where is Max?" asked one of them, weapon raised.

"Making a phone call, he told me to bring the boy inside," he replied confidently.

The two men ushered him in, the other three inside sat in a booth by the window, playing cards and drawing heavily on smelly Russian cigarettes, oblivious to Carl standing there.

"Hey, comrade, put boy on floor," asked one, while another took liberties with Jane, reaching out and squeezing her ass, joking to the others with a belly laugh, their feet crossed on the tabletop. "How about you and me have fun, yes? I always wanted a blonde," he laughed. "Be shame to waste you with bullet," he joked.

She backed away, looking to Carl to react. Megan was behind the counter preparing more coffee and cooking bacon from the fridge, casting a pleading glance to Carl.

"Where the fuck you going, I not finished with you yet," he laughed to his other comrades.

"You want coffee?" she asked nervously, looking for any excuse to evade their groping hands.

"Yes, yes, you learn pretty women, bring coffee, tell other bitch to hurry up breakfast, then you can sit on lap." He laughed again, blowing out a cloud of obnoxious smoke.

The men continued to laugh, engaged in Russian conversation, the air filled with stale cigarette.

Carl turned to the counter where Jane was now stood with Megan, pulling a glass coffee jug from its stand, her hand trembling.

Jane whispered. "Carl, what are we going to do, when Max—"

Carl placed a reassuring hand on her shoulder. "Relax, he's out the picture for now."

"I don't understand, the sleeping bag," whispered Megan.

"It's Betty the mannequin inside and, well, a few other surprises."

As the five men joked around the table with the sleeping bag, preoccupied with Russian banter, Carl took a small black cylindrical device from his pocket, the size of a large torch battery and held it in his clenched fist. "If I press this it's going to get very ugly and very loud, so when I pick your sister up and bring her behind here, I want you both to lie down behind the counter here, no hesitating because they are going to get very suspicious very quickly, understand?"

They both nodded.

Uri disengaged from the banter and laid his eyes on Carl, lifting Gill from the cushion.

"What are you doing, you leave her alone and tell the other bitch to bring our coffee and breakfast," he yelled.

Carl dashed behind the counter and dropped to the floor with Gill under his coat, holding her tight, followed by Jane and Megan, hands over their ears.

He pressed the trigger.

A second later the room was filled with smoke and noise.

Like a small earthquake, they felt the shockwaves, dust and debris fell like a winter blizzard, covering them in a fine a layer white and grey grit.

Carl rose from the counter, surveying the extent of the damage. None of the glass windows remained, tables and chairs were blown to the corners of the room and a large hole appeared above in the ceiling, revealing coloured cables and trunking. A thick film of dark smoke hung in the air and the five bodies, torn apart in varying degrees, were strewn across the floor. Carl took a fire extinguisher and quenched the small fires still feeding off the wooden booths.

"It's over now, you can get up," he said helping them to their feet.

They stood from the counter with him, hardly believing the scene in front of them, the devastation and destruction caused in a single moment.

He lifted Gill from the floor, carrying her in his arms across the rubble. Her eyes opened momentarily, and he told her she was safe. She mumbled an inaudible response before closing her eyes again.

They followed him through the remains of the café and out to the morning sun embracing their faces.

He led them to the grass bank and gently lay Gill amongst the tall soft grass. Jane and Megan collapsed, exhausted next to her, sitting up, watching the funnel of smoke rising from the café.

Carl made a phone call and then sat with them, explaining the conversation he'd had with the man in his house and of course his ruse to get Max into the position he is still in.

"So, what happens now Carl?" asked Jane.

Carl pulled off his jacket, staring up at the new sky, spoilt only by the vapour trails.

"We just wait, I've just called the police, O'Connor would have done that, he said it's better than living with a head full of stories and lies. He's right, I'm ready to face whatever is decided, besides, whatever we might have done, we are still victims in this, in fact in my eyes you are all heroes." He smiled.

"And Max? Won't they get hurt getting him out, surely they—"

"It's a dud," interrupted Carl, still wearing his winning grin.

"Hold on, so, you mean he can just get out?" asked Jane.

"The power of suggestion, he's got no reason to question it, especially after the explosion in the café, even more so."

"But the diamonds, you really just going to give all this info to the police. Are you not just a little bit tempted, I mean that's a lot of money," Megan asked.

"No, it's evidence, we do this the right way, the boy's body is unharmed, he was covered in the frame from the blast, it all points to the diamonds. Having your life back is worth more than the value of the diamonds surely."

Megan hugged Carl, her slender arms barely reaching around his sculptured torso. "Thank you, Carl, thank you for saving my sister, but more than that, thank you for saving me, saving me from myself. I now have to tell my sister, I have to watch her go through what I went through, but this time I'm going to be the strong one, it's my turn now." She smiled.

Carl left them for a second in the comfort of each other to process the overwhelming tornado of emotions and the realisation of their long-awaited freedom. He stood by his Land Rover and looked at Max, hunched over the dashboard, buried in his arms, contemplating his future. Powerless, quiet and hopefully wallowing in the same gut-wrenching pain from witnessing the death of his brother Uri in front of him, just as he did to others.

Looking at the carnage strewn across the car park and black smoke pouring from the obliterated window frames, he realised something significant. Amid the explosion and mini warzone, he had not once suffered a flashback, not one throwback to that guilty day. One thought entered his head as he turned the other way, watching them pour out to each other. Megan was right, this was about saving them, and he *had* saved them, and in doing so he'd saved his conscience.

He smiled.

The End

Milton Keynes UK
Ingram Content Group UK Ltd.
UKHW040650120923
428521UK00004B/192